3—

The
Ordinary
White
Boy

The Ordinary White Boy

Brock Clarke

Harcourt, Inc.
New York   San Diego   London

www.harcourt.com

Library of Congress Cataloging-in-Publication Data
Clarke, Brock.
The ordinary white boy/Brock Clarke.—1st ed.
p.   cm.
ISBN 0-15-100810-8
1. Young men—Fiction. 2. Fathers and sons—Fiction. 3. Missing persons—Fiction.
4. New York (N.Y.)—Fiction. 5. Racism—Fiction.   I. Title.
PS3603.L37 O7 2001
813'.6—dc21   2001024184

Text set in Palatino
Designed by Cathy Riggs

First edition
A C E G I K J H F D B

Printed in the United States of America

For Lane, and for my parents,
Peter and Elaine Clarke

Thanks to the Lightseys, Clemson University, and the Sewanee Writers Conference for their generous financial assistance while writing this book.

The
Ordinary
White
Boy

ONE

CHAPTER 1

I AM READING the newspaper when my father calls, asking me
to cover an Oppenheim Central School Board meeting. I know what
this means. This means I will say, "no," and my father will have to
talk me into it. He will remind me about the impressive twenty-
minute drive north to Oppenheim: toward the looming Adirondacks and past all the noble, dying elms and the wind-whipped
white pines. Or, he'll take a slightly different approach and talk
about Oppenheim's many double-wide trailers with their expensive
satellite dishes, their neglected patches of cow corn, and their rot-
ting Dodge Dusters. My father, who is fond of detail, will tell me
that I should pay real close attention to the Dodge Dusters, which
will have chickens roosting in them.

"Right in the front seat," he'll tell me. "Chickens."

I know why my father, Lamar Kerry, Sr., will tell me about these
things: he believes my life has no substance. This is true: I am completely insubstantial. So my father wants me to go out into our desperately beautiful, desperately poor countryside so I can see how

. awe-inspiring and tragic, and maybe learn some-
.t about myself in the bargain. But to be true, I'd
, in my apartment and keep doing what I'm doing,
.ding an article about a double homicide over in Utica, a
y miles to our west. The article is on page one of the Little
Falls . .ey News, the daily newspaper my father edits. The piece, which my old man wrote, says the murders were "gang-related." This information comes from "anonymous sources." I know what all this means, too. This means that the gang-related dead and their killers are black. It also means that my father copied the information from the Utica morning paper. He doesn't credit the Utica paper as his source, which makes it anonymous.

So this is me. I, Lamar Kerry, Jr., am the disappointing son of a newspaperman who steals from other writers and does not care about any honor codes or rules of professional conduct, and so I will not debate him or you about the differences between the high and low roads, between those who lead the parade and those who sit on the curb and watch it go by.

"I mean it, Lamar," my father says to me over the phone after I have declined, he cajoled, and I declined again. "I need for you to get up to Oppenheim. Seven tonight. It's an *emergency* meeting."

"What kind of emergency?"

My father promises big things. He tells me there will be bad blood. He tells me there will be fireworks and hurt feelings. He tells me the proceedings will be emotionally charged.

My father tells me that he'll pay me forty bucks for my two hours of work, plus mileage.

I take his offer as a good piece of news, sitting around shirtless at four in the afternoon in my hot, one-bedroom apartment, reading the paper my father edits and for which I work part-time. I normally only get paid $5.50 an hour for my work at the newspaper. My father offering me forty dollars means that he can't get anyone else to cover the meeting and he's in a bind. And I could use the forty dollars. To be true, I could use a lot more than forty dollars. But outside on Albany Street the city construction crew is shouting, laying blacktop, and some bird is chirping, and Andrew Marchetti is waiting behind the bar at the Renaissance for the twenty-three bucks I've owed him since Memorial Day. My father's forty dollars is just enough to bust the door to happiness wide open. And in my experience, if the door is not heavy, then you don't have to wear jackboots to break it down. No, you do not.

About fifteen years ago my cousin, Bradley Kerry, drove his Dodge Ram pickup truck onto Caroga Lake and did donuts on the snow-covered ice. He did this until the truck broke right through the ice. Bradley did not drown. Bradley died of a heart attack from the freezing cold water. The truck was ruined. A sober person would not have done such a thing, of course. But Bradley had been drunk, extremely drunk according to the girl he was trying to impress, and who demanded that he let her out of the truck before he made a doomed eighteen-year-old asshole of himself out there on the not-so-frozen lake.

Anyway, after the county paramedics pulled Bradley out of the lake, I found myself standing outside the Little Falls Memorial Hospital with my uncle Lee, Bradley's father. Uncle Lee was my father's older brother. It was the middle of January. The wind felt like thumbtacks against my face and it was coming down like snow's revenge. My uncle was in the middle of some fierce grieving, the kind of grieving where you assume that everyone is at the bottom of the same deep pit of sadness. But to be true, my sadness over Bradley's death was pretty shallow. I was only twelve, but I already knew all I needed to know about the kind of people who drove their trucks onto frozen lakes. I also knew all about Bradley, who was inclined toward temporary tattoos and the torture of domestic animals.

"Bradley is dead," my uncle said to me.

"Yessir."

"It's a sad thing," he said. "You're pretty sad, aren't you?"

I was sad about my *uncle's* sorry state. I liked my uncle Lee. He was a kind man, a dairy farmer who had held almost every form of public office at the city and county level. My uncle was so torn up about Bradley that he could only manage to speak in between and around these big, wet gasps. I felt sad for him.

"You're going to have to be brave now," he told me, sucking in a long, heaving sob. "It's all right to be sad. I'm sad, too. Of course I am. But you also have to be brave. *I* need you to be brave. Can you do that?"

I told him that I could, no problem. Was that it? Did he want me to do anything else?

"Do you want me to do anything else?" I ask my father over the telephone.

He sighs and says, *no,* that all he wants me to do is cover the emergency school-board meeting.

So I put on a collared shirt, hunt around for my spiral-bound notebook and my number-two pencil, and generally get ready to go on up to Oppenheim to cover the emergency school-board meeting.

MY PARENTS did not expect me to be what I am. What parents do? I wonder. What I am, basically, is a twenty-seven-year-old ordinary white boy who wears khaki pants, work boots, and flannel shirts. I dance like Mick Jagger when I dance at all, which is rare, unless I am drunk, which is not so rare. My parents do not understand this dull thing I am, even though ten years ago I was a seventeen-year-old ordinary white boy who wore khaki pants, work boots, and flannel shirts. It is true, I did not dance at all ten years ago. What I did do were push-ups, and I did them religiously, honestly. Everything else, I faked. I faked academic disinterest. I faked epileptic seizures at the dinner table. For the benefit of my friends, I pulled up my shirt and faked the jutting profile of a pregnant belly, which was hilarious. I drank beer with the idea that I would have to someday stop and would be able to, no problem. In other words, I was normal, is what I was.

Parents do not want normal. This is not part of the big picture of parenting. So my parents sent me away to college—to St. Lawrence, the Laidback Larrys, dude, and my father's alma mater—to become extraordinary. This did not happen. I took on a Russian Studies major, maintained a gentleman's C average, and acquired a barely working knowledge of the differences between the Bolsheviks and Mensheviks. I also joined a fraternity, where I learned the consequences of losing your pledge pin while in the company of men named Lugnut, Candy Ass, and Herb Jew. I learned to drink beer through a funnel stolen from Lugnut's uncle's service station. I learned to forget the difference in taste between cheap beer and low-grade fossil fuel. I learned how to debate the difference between friendship and brotherhood. I learned to refer to good-looking women as Betties. There were women who did not want to be called Betties, and with them I learned to avoid debate of any kind.

I also wanted to avoid debate with my parents when I moved home after graduation. This was five years ago. Home is one mile north of my apartment, on Yellow Church Road. The house where I grew up is a three-bedroom Greek Revival with white vinyl siding and chipping black shutters. Picture two hilly acres and a babbling brook and forsythia bushes. Picture a Ford Taurus in the driveway, another one in the garage. Picture yours truly, sprawled out on an overstuffed love seat, wondering what a boy like me could actually do in this world.

Picture my parents, wondering the same thing.

So I told them that I was going to do nothing for a good while. That was my plan.

"Guess again," my father said. "You can't do nothing here."

"That's true," my mother said. "Don't even think about it."

"Don't even think about it," my father repeated, gently placing his hand on my mother's shoulder.

You should know here that my mother, Judy Kerry, has multiple sclerosis and has been in a wheelchair for a year. Since my mother's been sick—about five years now—my father tends to regard her in the manner of someone looking at a hutch of white bunnies, not in the manner of someone looking at their lifelong love and domestic partner.

On her own illness, my mother is a stoic: "Someone threw me a curveball."

As we all know, my parents were right. You cannot go home and do nothing. So I moved one mile south, into this very apartment on Albany Street, where I did nothing for four months. At the end of those four months I was broke, and so my father suggested I work for him part-time until I "got on my feet." I've been his part-time employee for four plus years now. My parents cannot understand any of this. When I moved, I moved one mile away. This is not a move at all. I made this nonmove so I could do nothing, which I did not do. Instead, I have a part-time job plagiarizing the Utica paper and covering emergency school-board meetings, a job that my father gave me. I don't exactly understand why my father has given me this job. This is one of the great unknowns of parenthood. It is so unknown that my mother doesn't understand it either. When my father is out of earshot, my mother tells me that a monkey could do my job. What is the difference between you and a monkey? my mother wants to know. This is a provocative debate, but I will not engage her in it.

UNLIKE MYSELF and the monkey, there are plenty of differences between Utica and Little Falls. Little Falls is only twenty some miles east of Utica. But Little Falls is not at all a suburb of Utica. Utica does not inspire suburbs. Utica did not inspire the forty thousand citizens who have left town over the last ten years, nor the eighty thousand folks who have stuck around to watch all its textile and paper mills also pack up and leave. The mills have mostly jumped ship for Alabama, Mississippi, or any place that appealed to the mill owners' taste for warmer weather, lower pay scales, and state-of-the-art physical plants. Before they left, the mill owners got together and told Utica's desperate chamber of commerce that city's outdated brick industrial buildings and demanding workers' unions did not inspire them one bit.

"We're getting the fuck out of Dodge," one of the mill owners told the chamber of commerce. And they did.

When the mills first got to Dodge, some one hundred years ago, Utica was full of what we white liberal folk like to call "ethnic neighborhoods," which we are in favor of. Now that the mills are gone, there are only black and white neighborhoods, which we are not so enthusiastic about. The name John F. Kennedy is everywhere—on housing projects, welfare administration buildings, middle schools. But unlike JFK in Berlin, Utica does not inspire.

One thing Utica *does* inspire is letters to the editor. I read two of them this morning on the subject of the two gang-related dead black men. One, anonymous, suggested that what goes around comes around, and good riddance to bad rubbish. The other, written by a sociology professor at Utica College, argued that the city had fallen victim to a long history of racist urban planning. The professor's letter said the dead black men were meaningful symbols; the professor also wrote that he was organizing a rally to protest the racism of the city police and the city in general. To prove that no letter writer is free from cliché, the professor finished his letter by saying that Utica had made its bed, and so on.

The other thing that Utica inspires is historical revision. I was once asked by my seventh-grade social studies teacher—the subject was local history—if I knew what Utica meant.

"I don't know," I said. "It means something?"

"It does mean something," he said. "Utica is Indian for *toilet*. Write it down."

I wrote it down. Then I went home and told my mother what I

had written. At that time, my mother taught social studies in Herkimer, the next town over.

"Utica means toilet," I told her.

"Utica does not mean toilet," my mother said back. "Utica is a Greek place-name. It doesn't mean anything."

My mother was correct. Utica doesn't mean anything—not to most of us twenty miles to the east it doesn't. This is why the sociology professor's march, if it happens, will not make much sense around here: if something does not have any meaning in the first place, then there is no use in protesting its significance.

And without a doubt, people in Utica think the same thing about us in Little Falls, if they even think of us at all. Little Falls has never had any more than three paper mills, one of which—Corrigan's Paper Co.—it still has. Little Falls doesn't even have any black residents at the moment, let alone black neighborhoods. It basically has one main drag, which is lined with red brick buildings and white canopied sidewalks. We call this main drag "downstreet." Downstreet is my street; my apartment is right above Ponzo's Pizzeria. The smells and the heat from Ponzo's can get overwhelming, so I always leave my window open, even in the winter. In fact, the winter is the prime season in my apartment. The snow flies through my open window, while the heat of the pizza ovens blasts up from Ponzo's. It is very pleasant, like a hot tub.

There is nothing much else to Little Falls but farms, miles of them. Plus there are a few local stores—Aiello's News, Hadley's Yarn and Fabric Store, Ron's Sports Shop—that haven't gone out of business yet but probably will and soon, and a series of bars—the Happen Inn, the Full Moon Saloon, the Renaissance, which is the bar I go to—that will probably never go out of business. Then there's an army depot north of here, way past Oppenheim, which has recently closed and which the state is turning into a maximum-security prison. There are so few jobs in Little Falls that people are applying for work at the prison, even though it's at least an hour's drive from here.

The only other thing notable about Little Falls is its middling family dynasties. I am a member of one of them. My mother, who met my father while she was at Potsdam State and my father at St. Lawrence, is from Watertown, up near Canada. She is also an only child whose parents are dead, and so she has become a part of the Kerry dynasty by virtue of marriage and attrition. The Kerrys themselves moved to Little Falls from Ireland during the potato famine. My family has lived here since. We are, or were, farmers. My great-grandfather and grandfather were dairy farmers, and, as you know, so was my uncle.

My uncle Lee was our last farmer. He is dead from lung cancer, as of about three years ago. He spent a year dying that slow death, in and out of the hospital. Nearly every afternoon I would go by the hospital and take my uncle outside in his wheelchair. I'd stand and he'd sit and we'd watch the ambulances cart all the other goners to the hospital where they, too, would soon die.

One day, not too long before he died, my uncle asked me if I remembered the day that his son, Bradley, crashed through Caroga Lake with his pickup.

I told him that I did.

"We were standing right here," he said.

"I remember."

"I am dying," my uncle told me.

"It's true," I said.

"Explain something to me," my uncle said. "Why is it that men stand outdoors when something bad happens? We stood outdoors, right here, while Bradley was dying. Why is that?"

I told my uncle that I did not know.

"I don't know either," my uncle said. "It's a mystery."

Of course, it is no mystery why men stand outdoors during

tragedy. They stand outdoors because tragedy, no matter where it begins, always winds up indoors and men are afraid of it. My uncle got lung cancer because he smoked cigarettes, a pack a day for forty plus years. That is no mystery either.

But I didn't tell my uncle any of this. I wheeled him back in the hospital. He died a few weeks later.

Now there is only my father and his younger brother, Eli, who is in prison for reasons I cannot avoid and will soon address. That is it for our branch of the Kerry family.

This is the reason my father is disappointed that I have moved home. At one time, sons were expected to stay in Little Falls and work the family farm and be ordinary. They were disappointments if they did not. Now, there is no family farm for a son to return home to. So the father wants his son to go away and be extraordinary. When the son does not go away and become extraordinary, when he stays at home in the tired, nearly comatose small-town world of his father, then he opens himself up to a whole new world of disappointment.

So why do I stay here? you ask.

The answer is simple, really: I stay because it is difficult, so very difficult for me to imagine living elsewhere, whereas living here in Little Falls is easy. One does not have to imagine living in such a place: one just does it.

And will I live here forever? you want to know. Will I always find it so easy to do so? Will I always be unwilling to imagine life elsewhere? Will I ever leave home?

In all honesty, I do not know.

In order to understand why I live where I live, however, it might be helpful to know this fact: Little Falls is officially a "city," just like Utica, even though there have never been more than eight thousand people living here. There are less than six thousand now. There is only one reasonable explanation for this: Someone fucked up.

I was in a high school study hall once, about ten years ago, watching the launch of the space shuttle *Challenger*. As you know, the shuttle exploded. While it set off its accidental fireworks and rained down its unrecognizable human remains, the boy sitting next to me leaned over and whispered, "Guess someone fucked up."

There it is. Someone fucked up. The space program lost several million dollars, seven astronauts, one schoolteacher, and the public confidence, and Little Falls is a city just as Utica is. This is on the same train of thought. My father steals his stories from the Utica newspaper despite a series of moral and professional rules that says he should not. I only get paid $5.50 an hour to work part-time for the story stealer and father, even though I went to college and presumably am capable of great financial and creative accomplishments. The only way anyone can figure out how I got to this place in life is that someone fucked up.

I HAVE been known to spend some time with a woman named Glori Burns. Like my mother, Glori is not from Little Falls. She is from Heath, Ohio. Glori came to Herkimer County Community College to study travel and tourism. After Glori earned her associate's degree, she stayed around with the hopes of getting on at the local AAA. In fact, we met at a travel and tourism conference at the community college. I was covering the conference for the newspaper. It was during my second year out of college, and I was just coming to realize that despite my satisfying ordinariness and despite having a place of my own and a running tab at the Renaissance, I was lonely. So on the car ride over to the conference, I convinced myself that I would fall in love with someone at the conference. And since it was a travel and tourism conference, I logically decided that I would fall in love with an airline stewardess.

I did not fall in love with a stewardess—there weren't any there—but there were plenty of travel agents and travel agent instructors and travel agent executives and travel agents-in-training. So I found the most disgruntled one, Glori—who was stationed by the drink table, looking very pretty in a black pantsuit number, with her curly black hair pulled back and her white, freckled Irish face all pinched up as she stood there, drinking, smoking, passionately bitching about how she would never get a job in her field, asking if I knew what it felt like to waste two whole years of your life (I told her I did)—and fell in love with her.

But my falling in love with Glori did not help her get a job as a travel agent. So now Glori works as a secretary for the Monroe Street Elementary School, where she has developed the quirks that secretaries sometimes do. Her most enduring professional quirk is that she listens to the emergency scanner while she types up faculty memos. Some of Glori's coworkers have complained about that scanner of hers. I don't blame them. It is difficult *not* to develop a depressing worldview after listening to all those cryptic accounts of combine accidents, spousal abuse, and the general clang and holler of our wrecked lives. But should Glori have to type up fliers that say, "Don't Forget the Home-School Luncheon!" and "Q: Are You Ready for Native American Week? A: And How!" all day long in complete silence? This, Glori tells me, is not an option.

I am telling you all this because when Glori turns off the scanner, she turns on the radio and listens to *The Rest of the Story*, by Paul Harvey. She mostly listens to the program at home, and when I come by she makes me listen, too. On *The Rest of the Story*, Paul Harvey always tells you about a boy in some ruined condition. Maybe he's lost an eye or a parent. Maybe he's grown up in the Depression or contracted rubella. Paul Harvey is fond of young children with infectious diseases. When he tells their stories, Paul Harvey's voice gets brittle with empathy. My Glori believes Paul Harvey didn't drink enough milk when he was a child. She claims she can hear his bones crack and crumble right over the radio.

But the reason Glori listens to old creaking Paul Harvey is what comes after the tragedy: the Rest of the Story. The rest of the story is that the boy with rubella became Jesse Owens, that fast-moving anti-Nazi; or the boy who ate only white bread for a year straight became Chief Justice Warren Burger with his appreciation for the righteous underdog; or the boy who developed rickets at age two became my swivel-hipped idol, Mick Jagger. The rest of the story is that these boys became outstanding men, despite their pretty depressing childhoods. They became something special. They became important. Their stories *mean* something. You can hear the meaning in Paul Harvey's voice. He is not creaking at the end of his five minutes. By the end of his five minutes, Paul Harvey sounds completely lubricated.

"Listen and learn, boyo," Glori tells me after every program. When Glori says this she is both happy and distracted: she twists her long, wiry black hair around her index finger, and her skeptical blue-black eyes relax and get almost dreamy. "Listen and learn," Glori says again. Sometimes when she says this, she pokes me in the chest with her other index finger. When Glori does so, I grab the tip of her finger and kiss it very, very lightly.

"I will listen and learn," I tell her. "Trust me."

But does Glori really expect me to listen and learn? And will I? Can she trust me? These are important questions, which is why, maybe, we don't ask or answer them. It is possible that Glori and I are together *because* we don't ask or answer these questions. If these questions were raised, then who knows what might happen? If the questions were raised, for instance, then it might be impossible for us to do what we always do after Paul Harvey has had his say and the radio is turned off, which is this:

"I love you," I say.

"That's sweet," Glori says. "I love you, too."

Then we go see a movie at the Cannonball Twin Cinema. Afterward, we eat the spaghetti dinner at Ponzo's, where we drink red wine out of chipped juice glasses until our unasked and unanswered questions are forgotten and we take comfort in all our true, fine feelings for each other and we do our best to ignore the world

outside of Ponzo's, a world that might just show our true, fine feelings to be something other than true and fine.

But that is not the point.

The point is that my parents—and maybe Glori, too—want to
know the rest of the story. They want to know how and when I'm
going to be something special. They want to know when I'm going
to stop messing around and start leading a meaningful life.

But the truth is that there might not be any rest of the story. The
truth is that I don't want to be special. Who would want such a
thing? When you become special, that means you've also become
meaningful dead black men in Utica, New York, or a stricken-but-
courageous fifty-two-year-old woman in a state-of-the-art wheelchair. Being special can make you believe that you are something
you're not: it can make you believe, say, that you live in a city when
in reality you live in a shrinking little mill town. Being special can
also make you believe that you're too important to go out and cover
emergency school-board meetings for forty dollars a pop, plus
mileage.

CHAPTER 2

I ARRIVE late to the school-board meeting. I park my car behind the Oppenheim Central School District's administrative office—a gray, single-story cinder-block building sunk in the middle of a vast gravel parking lot—and by the time I slip inside, settle into a folding chair, and whip out my notebook, Red Craig, owner of Red's Body Shop, is already addressing the school board.

"I'm here tonight not as a businessman," he says. "I'm here as an individual and a taxpayer."

Red Craig is also here, he says, because he is a music lover and because the Oppenheim Hilltopper marching band is a disgrace. This is my father's emergency.

"The way you practice is the way you play," Red says. "If you don't practice right you don't play well. The band leadership is not there. This lady isn't a leader."

This *lady* is the marching band director. She is sitting in the second row of folding chairs, one row in back of Red, four seats to the left. I don't catch her name. The band director glares at Red Craig while he tells the school board that he sits on his front porch—day in, day out—and watches the marching band throw stones at each other instead of practicing their instruments.

As for the band director herself, she looks like she wants to do more than throw stones at Red Craig. She looks like she wants to take Red's pompadour—which is jet black and greasy and impressively complicated in its curves, swoops, and dips—and weave it through his small intestines.

I glance around. There are about twenty men and women—probably parents of children in the marching band—sitting in the folding chairs, sweating profusely in this hotbox of a conference room; their faces are eager, eyes shining, as if they believe that the band leader just *might* take hold of Red's pompadour and thread it through one or two of his inner organs.

Their eagerness fills me with terrible dismay, a feeling not unlike heartbreak itself.

I groan and prepare myself for a half hour or so of great, throbbing tedium.

The reason for my dismay is this: it is surprisingly difficult to sit through an entire emergency school-board meeting once you've hitched yourself to the ordinary life. For one, the emergency, whatever it is, will be downgraded, the time bomb defused. You *know* this, but still you must sit there and wait out the duration of the defusing. You sit there, regarding your fellow ordinary citizens and their shit kickers, plaid shirts, and chapped, red hands. Unlike yourself, they are *full-time* workers, which means they've left their fields, their wood shops, and their grinding minimum-wage jobs early so they can sit on the edge of their uncomfortable folding chairs and wait for the bomb to go off. Is it possible, you wonder, that you are the only one who knows there will be no explosion? It cannot be possible if you ascribe to a certain theory of ordinariness. So you swallow your doubts and sit there—not on the edge of your seat—for a good long time, until you find yourself on the verge of saying, Enough already. You find yourself on the verge of standing up and shouting, I am better than this! This feeling of superiority is unseemly in an ordinary white boy. Very.

For this is one of my dirty little secrets, one of the dark smudges on the otherwise clear surface of my existence: I am ordinary and yet estranged somehow from other ordinary people.

I know I am estranged because, unlike my fellow citizens, I already know what the band director's reaction will be to Red's harangue. And sure enough, Ellen Varner—Red Craig mentions her name during his testimony—doesn't do anything, not even when Red suggests that she should be removed from her position, banned from having contact with any boy or girl of school age, and maybe even tossed out of town ass-over-bandbox. The band director shifts around in her seat, smoothes out the pleats of her blue pantsuit. She is calm. Red has planted the bomb and set the timer. Still, the band director is calm. She is calm because the bomb squad is already on the scene and she knows it.

The bomb squad turns out to be a teenage boy in a crew cut and a blue plaid shirt. The band director smiles at him as he stands up to address the school board.

"My name is Vernon. I play trumpet," the boy tells the board. "You never seen me throw a rock in my life," Vernon says to Red Craig.

"I've seen you," Red says, sitting down. "I see." But he doesn't look too sure. Red squints in the boy's general direction, obviously not seeing. There are two possibilities here: either Red is losing his eyesight, or he's realizing that it is difficult to tell one teenage rock thrower from another when that rock thrower is out of band uniform.

Red's squint becomes a scowl as Vernon explains how much Ellen Varner has meant to his development as a social creature and complete human being.

"I like to play," Vernon tells the school board. "I have volume." The boy also has confidence, in spades. Vernon's self-assurance makes sense. You obviously cannot be the bomb squad without some kind of ego.

Vernon has so much confidence that he concludes by telling the school board what a pussy he was before the band director got her hooks into his musical potential. It is obvious that the school-board members disapprove of the vocabulary, but they like the sentiment. The school board is composed entirely of defensive linemen and linebackers from the 1978–80 Oppenheim Hilltoppers football squad. They are now insurance salesmen and phys ed coaches; their knees crack and pop when they walk and they like the pain. I'm guessing that some of them have boys at home who are also pussies. They know exactly what Vernon is talking about.

The school board goes into emergency session. This means that they disappear into some back room and smoke cigarettes. When the board members come out a half hour later, they smell like tobacco and the band director still has her job.

The school-board president bangs his gavel and wobbles away in his best linebacker style.

All of this makes Red Craig none too happy.

"That's tough luck, Red," I tell him. I know Red from the many times he has fixed my 1977 Chevy Monte Carlo, which has a recidivist low idle. Red is a loyal, cheap, but not very competent mechanic, which may account for the recidivism.

"Luck nothing," Red says. "I've been screwed. The whole town's been screwed."

"Can I quote you on that?" I ask him. "For the paper?" I hold up my notepad and wave it at him like a third hand.

"No. Tell them I said this: That the good name of this community is being dragged through the mud by this marching-band lady. Tell them that those kids don't know the difference between a tuba and a tambourine. Tell them that the chickens always come home to roost."

"Got it," I say. I don't even bother writing any of this down. I make dramatic cursive motions with my pencil and tell Red that my car is stalling at stop signs again. He tells me that he's done all he can do with what God has given him and that my car is cursed.

"You need a witch doctor, not a mechanic," Red says.

"I'll bring it in on Thursday," I say.

"Don't even bother," he says.

After Red leaves, I go over to Vernon. I at least want to get his last name down for the article. Vernon is busy talking to Ellen Varner.

"I am proud of you," she tells him. "You are a fine boy and speaker." What I get from their conversation is that Ellen Varner is not only the marching band director; she also teaches senior civics and social studies. This is not that surprising. Teachers often pull double duty out here in the boondocks.

"You should go into politics," she tells Vernon. "If you don't go into music, of course."

Vernon looks at her seriously. "Thank you," he says, shaking her hand. "I've been thinking about it some already. I really have."

I know where this is headed. This is headed for a long discussion about membership in the Young Republicans and the public responsibilities of private citizens. So I interrupt the conversation. I say excuse me, twice. I wave my notepad again.

"Yes?" she asks.

"What's your reaction to the school board's decision?" I ask her.

Ellen Varner says that she is happy. She also tells me that justice has been served, and that she's thankful for the chance to do what she does best, which is teach. I gratefully scribble all this down. This kind of stuff is the lifeblood of the local interest story.

I thank Ellen Varner for her help and turn to Vernon. He does not appear to be impressed by me or my reporter's pad.

"What?"

"One question," I say. "Maybe two."

Vernon gives me the superior smile of a professional baseball

player being asked for an autograph, not the smile of a hillbilly ado-
lescent grateful to be getting a little local publicity.

"First question. Were you surprised that Ms. Varner kept
her job?"

"Surprised?" he asks.

"Yes," I say. "Surprised."

Vernon acts like he's never heard the word "surprised" before,
let alone felt the emotion. His big country face shrinks and puckers.
The bomb did not go off, his face tells me, and that's because *I* defused it, and you're asking me if *I'm* surprised. Weren't you paying
attention? Vernon's face wants to know.

"Surprised?" he asks again. "No way. I was not surprised. Why
should I have been surprised?"

I already have had enough of this kid and so I thank him without asking the second question. The second question was: What is
your last name and how do you spell it? I go home and write up the
article in twenty minutes. I title the piece, "Marching Band Contro-
versy Reaches a Crescendo." I say the boy who stood up in the band
director's defense was "unidentified." I quote him as saying he was
"not surprised" by the board's decision. I make the kid look as bad
as possible. I say that he is eleven years old, even though he is at
least sixteen.

This is another reason why it is difficult to be a local reporter
after you've hitched yourself to the ordinary life. You interview
your fellow citizens for your article and they tell you what they
think you need to know. They expect you to write it down and take
it seriously. And you do. This makes you feel inferior. So you exact
your revenge in print by demoting a teenage boy to prepubescence.
This makes you feel even more inferior. I tell you, it is difficult to be
ordinary.

IT IS difficult to be ordinary. This is what the emergency school-
board meeting teaches me. The other thing it teaches me is that

mystery needs change. Vernon, myself, the school board, even Red Craig, all of us knew that Ellen Varner would not be fired, that there would be no shake-up in the band leadership, that nothing would change. Since there was no possibility of change, there was no mystery attached to the emergency meeting in the first place.

But if the bomb went off, just once, then we might have the possibility of change. Then, maybe, we might actually get a new, go-getter band leader, a more activist school board, and a more polite hillbilly boy. Then, maybe, I might be able to sit on the edge of my seat through the next school-board meeting, just like my fellow ordinary citizens. If the bomb goes off once, then there is the chance it might go off again. If the bomb goes off once, then that will be all the mystery we need.

I CALL Glori after I'm done writing the article.

"Mystery definitely needs change," I say over the phone.

Between Glori and me, there is a fair amount of mystery. Sometimes there is also passion, sometimes boredom, sometimes magic. But our real mystery is how long we will last, and whether we will marry. We have been together for over two years and have never spoken about marriage. That is mystery enough.

"Is that your theory?" she asks me after I'm done telling her about the board meeting and my ideas thereof. I can hear her draw on one of her badly hand-rolled cigarettes and then exhale. Her apartment is in one of the old paper mills on the Mohawk River, but I cannot hear the water rush and roar by, like it does, for all her in- and exhaling.

"That's *one* theory. I have others."

"I'm real tired, Lamar. Let's just hear about the others tomorrow, OK?"

"OK."

She hangs up. Glori has heard all my many other theories before. She thinks she knows all she needs to know about my ideas regarding mystery and the ordinary life. Glori believes that I should stop quoting myself and start liking life a little more.

What Glori does not know, maybe, is that I do not dislike life all that much. What she also does not know is that I have a theory about her smoking and breathing loudly while we are talking on the telephone. The theory is this: I would rather listen to Glori struggle with her loose tobacco and her soggy rolling papers all night long than listen to the river roar on and on over the shale and sharp rocks, over the mills' paralyzed water wheels, past the brick industrial shells, past Glori's apartment on the second floor of the former Millington Brothers' Paper Company. There is a reading light glowing in the window of that second-floor apartment. Inside, Glori is lying in bed with her hair pulled back, not reading. She is smoking and wondering about the worth of the man she has just hung up on. The river I could do without; the woman smoking and wondering I could not. That is one theory Glori does not know.

CHAPTER 3

THE BOMB goes off this morning, Wednesday, July 18. I am in the editorial room of the Little Falls *Valley News,* drinking coffee and plagiarizing the Utica *Observer-Dispatch.* This morning's *Observer-Dispatch* has run an article on the Fairfield town supervisor's monthly meeting. I have copied the article verbatim except for some minor revisions. Specifically, I've written that the debate over legalized trash burning was "charged," whereas the *Observer-Dispatch* says it was "heated."

I am just about to send the story down to the layout room when my father walks into the office.

"Good morning," I tell him.

"Not so good," my father says. He sighs, throws down his briefcase, pours himself a cup of coffee, and then sighs again. My father looks to be consumed by something: exhaustion, guilt, anxiety, *something,* I cannot tell what.

"What is it?" I ask him. "Is there something wrong with mom?"

"Your mother is fine," he says, and then tells me all about the disappearance of Mark Ramirez, owner of Mark's Precious Metals, and Puerto Rican patriarch of Little Falls's lone minority household.

Like all ordinary white boys, I am also a self-taught racial theorist. So allow me to propose this theory of race and geography. There are three varieties of white student in the small-town high school: those who embrace the lone minority kid, those who hate the minority kid, or those who ignore him. When Mark Ramirez moved to Little Falls in the middle of our sophomore year, I ignored him. I ignored him because it was easier to ignore him than to love or hate him. When there is only one nonwhite student in the small-town white high school (there is rarely more than one), and when that student is continually mobbed by white imitators or white antagonists, then that student is not likely to notice a cold shoulder from someone like me. I never asked Mark Ramirez over to my house. I never asked how he wound up in white-bread upstate New York. I never asked, period. I ignored Mark Ramirez, and he ignored me. We carried this relationship out of the school yard and into adulthood. I know that Mark Ramirez has a coin and jewelry shop on Albany Street. That is all I know.

Or almost all I know. I know one more thing. My father told me, when I was away in college, that Mark Ramirez had married a white woman. Apparently for my father, Mrs. Ramirez's whiteness was enough. He never even told me her name.

It was enough for me, too, apparently, because I never asked.

"He hasn't been seen for seven days," my father tells me. "Seven. His wife finally called the police last night. They looked in his shop. Nothing, no signs of a break-in or a struggle, nothing unusual. The only strange thing is that his car is still parked out in front of the shop. It's been there for all seven days. So he's been declared missing. It's been all over the scanner, Lamar." My father points to the scanner right next to me, which I have not turned on and never do, even when Glori is around. It hurts my ears.

"How do you know he's *missing*?" As I ask this, the coffee in my mouth starts to taste like so many metal objects: pennies, refrigerator magnets, car keys. Why did I complain that the bomb never goes off? Why was it that I wanted mystery? Oh, Oppenheim. Oh, Vernon and Red. Oh, minor school-board brouhahas. Oh, ordinary life. "Why isn't he just a husband on a bender?" I ask hopefully. "Why not just a husband who gets up, hitches a ride somewhere, and leaves his wife and family? Why not just a man with a bad sense of direction?"

"He's been gone a whole week, Lamar. No word from him at all. His wife says he's never been away for even a night. They've never been apart in seven years of marriage. Not a once. She said only something truly, terribly bad would keep him away for this long."

"This is what the scanner told you?" I ask my father. "Their marital history and stuff."

"This is what the police told me. I called them after I heard something about it on the scanner at home."

We are both silent as my father turns on his computer. The computer blinks and hums as my father, without turning to face me again, tells me the thing that I hope—please, please, please—he does not actually expect me to do.

"I'd like you to go by Mark's house, Lamar." My father gives me the address: 116 Gansvoort, up the hill from my place, down the hill from my parents' house. My father tells me to ask Mark's wife a few questions. Find out the what, the where, and maybe the why.

I tell my father that I would if I weren't so swamped. I hold up the Utica paper and tell him the ins and outs of the story I'm preparing to rewrite. I share with him all the details concerning the possible prosecution of the Ilion Golden Bombers' football coach for pedophilia. I am enthusiastic as I explain my ideas about changing "suspected" to "accused" and "anger" to "outrage."

"If the police are there, ask them some questions," my father says, ignoring me. "If they are not, go to the station after you're done at the house. Talk to Uncle Bart, if you can."

Uncle Bart is my father's first cousin, Bart Kerry, the chief of police. I am not one of his favorite people, nor he mine. I am prepared to further protest my assignment. But now that he has issued his orders like an editor and father should, old dad begins typing something into his computer, acting as if I've already left the office. Which leaves me to wonder if I am right in the middle of something important, maybe, in the middle of a mystery, possibly; in the middle of somewhere truly ugly, somewhere I know from experience that I definitely do not want to be.

I READ a magazine recently that gave states grades on racial relations. They called this grading system their "Report Card on Race." Minnesota, for instance, got a B; Wisconsin, a B+. Both received kudos for their hiring practices, Scandinavian-style worldviews, and progressive, color-blind urban planning. The magazine did not list all the fifty states, and New York was not given a grade at all. But if we were to receive a grade up here in Little Falls, then we would not be getting high marks for our worldviews. We might not even get Ds on our report cards, which would be delivered to our sorry homes in brown paper wrappers. In fact, after taking and failing the proper tests, we would likely be placed in the remedial section of racial-relations class.

And we could use the remediation. If we had received the extra help, maybe Mark Ramirez would not be missing. Maybe my uncle Eli wouldn't have burned down the house of the only black family in Little Falls, two years ago this past May, either.

Like this time with Mark Ramirez, my father dispatched me to cover his brother's fire. He didn't know, at the time, that it was his brother who had set the fire. He didn't have to listen to the scanner to know the fire had been set, either. All my father had to do was look out the window of the newsroom and see the smoke rising high above us, a few blocks to our north.

The house my uncle burned to the ground was a three-story wooden frame home on Furnace Street with crumbling gray asphalt siding, a triangular stained-glass attic window, and an unattached garage. The black family (father, mother, two young girls) were the only blacks up here in Little Falls at that time. When I got there, they were standing off a little bit from the fire. They looked scared, obviously. They also looked black. There is no other way to describe them. The fire chief, for instance, once he got there, was the fire chief. I was and am a part-time newspaper reporter for the Little Falls *Valley News,* son of the editor-in-chief and his handicapped wife. These are known facts. But I didn't know if these folks worked for their fathers or had sick mothers or anything. I didn't know their names. I didn't know where they were from or how they got here. I didn't know how they made their money. The only thing I did know about these four people was that they were black. They lived in the middle of five thousand plus white folks like myself (plus one Puerto Rican), and their house was burning, and I was standing in front of the house taking notes about how the flames were *leaping* and how the furnace exploding sounded like the Fourth of July.

I remember looking over at the family and smiling. They looked back at me as if I had started the fire. I was not the one who set the fire. I didn't tell my uncle to set the fire, either. But who can blame them? Their house was burning right to the ground, and the only person who was doing anything active at all was not throwing water on the fire or comforting them. That person was taking notes. I sympathized with them, fully.

I was also glad it was not my house.

There were plenty of other people on hand who were also glad it was not their house. Those people were on their lawns, watching the fire. Most of them were women. Since it was the early morning, around seven, they were wearing housecoats and drinking coffee. Sixty years ago, you would have called these women Italian or Irish. They would have been yelling at each other out of open upstairs windows. Their husbands would have always come home from their mill jobs drunk, talking about the union, and arguing about that cunt the Virgin Mary. Sixty years later, these women looked like normal white Americans, a little stunned and ugly in the bright early morning light, but obviously happy that they were not black and that their houses were not on fire.

I wasn't exactly sure what I was supposed to do. The fire department wasn't even there yet, even though the station was only five blocks away. If they had been there, I would've asked the fire chief questions like, "Do you know what caused the fire?" and "When will you have an official report?" Then, since I used to drink with the fire chief, I would have said, "Let's have a beer later this week."

But the fire department was not there. So after standing around for a while, looking at my notebook, tapping my good number-two pencil against my bad cavity-filled teeth, I went over and talked to the black family whose house was burning out of control.

"I am sorry about your house," I said.

"I know you're sorry," the man said. He had a big voice and hard, unblinking eyes.

"Where do you think the fire department is?" the woman asked me. She was wearing a pink sweater, black jeans, and had a nice, quiet voice. About her husband, I had the definite impression that he was trying to scare me. If this was the case, then he was succeeding. But I liked his wife, even though she had asked me a question for which I had no adequate response.

"You should relax," I said. "I am sure they'll be here soon."

The man stiffened, and his two girls—both of them had braids with pink butterfly-shaped things clipped to them—melted into

him. The father glared at me murderously. Again, this was under-
standable. Here his house was burning right to the ground, and the
fire department was late in putting it out, and I was telling his wife
to *relax*. So I didn't give any more advice. I asked them where they
were from. The family's name was Rohal. They were from North
Carolina. He, Maurice Rohal, had been stationed at the old army
depot out toward Oppenheim. When he was through with the
army, Maurice Rohal apparently got on at Corrigan's paper mill
working the overnight shift. His wife told me that she stayed at
home. She also mentioned that her daughters were in third and
fourth grade at Monroe Street Elementary School. I told her that my
girlfriend worked at the same school, but Mrs. Rohal didn't seem
interested in who my girlfriend was or what she did. I didn't get the
sense that those two kids would be going back to that school or anywhere except back to North Carolina, which is exactly what happened a week later.

In the face of all this information, all I could think to do was
smile and write furiously.

So I smiled and wrote furiously, for three long minutes, until
the fire department finally showed up.

When the fire trucks got there I excused myself and walked
over to where the chief, Bob Shumaker, was watching his men survey the fire, drag out the hoses, and wet down the flames. The
water flew in great ineffectual arcs as Bob Shumaker watched,
smoking a Kool. As I said, Bob Shumaker and I were friends. But
when I was working and he was working we did a kind of professional minuet. He was the barely patient, usually condescending
public official; I was the annoying, ultimately shortsighted private
citizen impeding the interests of the population at large. This relationship made for not much drama, and for even less truth, but it
was the best we could manage.

So you won't be surprised when I tell you that when Bob Shumaker saw me walking toward him, he smiled thinly at me in the

manner of a highly evolved, highly superior cat, not in the manner of a helpful civil servant.

"Hello, Lamar," he said, smoking.

"I suppose you got lost."

He asked if this were my attempt at humor, which it was, kind of.

"Any comments about the fire?" I asked, a stock question.

"It looks pretty bad," he said, putting out his cigarette.

"Arson?"

"We just got here, friend."

"You could guess," I said.

"I could," he said.

Our banter was interrupted by one of his men. I didn't recognize the man, because he had his helmet on and his face was blackened by all the fire and smoke. The man whispered something and Bob nodded, his face changing in small ways and degrees as he listened closely.

I know now that the man had found something that pointed toward arson. But I didn't know that then.

After a minute of this whispering, the man walked away. Bob told me to call down to the station tomorrow. He said he would have something for me tomorrow.

"Tomorrow," I said, "is a long time from now."

Bob Shumaker stared at me as if we were not friends at all, as if I didn't even mean enough to him to be his enemy.

"Don't call me until tomorrow, Lamar," he said.

I did what I was told. I did not call Bob Shumaker until the next day, when he didn't tell me anything more than he already had. I did not challenge this lack of information. I took it quietly, just like a muckraking journalist should not. And I didn't want to know anything, either. For instance, I didn't want to know that it was my uncle who set the fire because he had been laid off at Corrigan's and Maurice Rohal had not. My uncle had heard that Maurice Rohal was talking about bringing his brothers and cousins to town so maybe they could work at Corrigan's, too. My uncle reportedly re-acted to this piece of news by saying: "When it gets pitch-black dark, someone had better light a fucking candle." I didn't want to know about that remark, either. I didn't want to know that our fire chief—who is still our fire chief, but who is not my friend after I fi-nally ran an article on his questionable handling of the fire—did not even investigate the blaze that my uncle had set and that had run the Rohals back to North Carolina. And I didn't want to know that the only reason that my uncle was caught, two weeks later, was because his own wife turned him in. His wife, my aunt Fay, would get at least a B in racial relations, if only for effort; the rest of us would get Fs and be in remediation in a hot second.

As for my aunt, I never heard the specific details of her turning in Uncle Eli. Aunt Fay left town as soon as the deed was done. No one knows where she went. Maybe she's in Minnesota. After all, most of the smart kids don't really care if the racial retards actually learn anything; they just want to stay out of the special class them-selves. So this is what they do: they tutor the dumb kids, eavesdrop on their conversations, rat them out to the principal, and then they slam the door to the school behind them.

And truth be told, I want to be one of the smart kids. This is my ambition, another dirty fingerprint on the glass of my ordinary days. I do not want to be like my uncle, nor do I want to be the me I was, the boy who ignored Mark Ramirez back in high school. How one actually gains admittance into the smart class, I have no idea. All I do know is that I don't want to be held back, stuck on the wrong side of the wall that divides the advanced class from the re-medial class. My uncle and his kind are on one side of the wall, and I want to be on the other side. Where I belong. Or where I think I belong.

My father wants to be in the smart class, too. In fact, for some reason, he thinks he already is. My father had enough foresight to go to college and then get a middle-class job, and not to remain a farmer or to become a manual laborer like his two brothers. Perhaps he believes this gives him the right to offer unsolicited advice to his less successful jailbird brother Eli. So when my old man went up to visit my uncle in the prison in Plattsburgh, where Eli is serving seven to nine years for arson, he told him, "Eli, I hope to hell you've learned something from all this."

My uncle reportedly scratched his head and rubbed his chin at this question. "Learned something?" he finally asked. "What am I supposed to have learned?" Then he laughed.

My father told me this story after he got back from the prison, admitted how much his brother's laughter pained him. But what else did my father expect his brother to do? Uncle Eli would have laughed at the course requirements and grading curve of Racial Remediation 101, too. In order not to laugh, you would first have to actually be enrolled in the remedial section of racial relations. If you were enrolled, then maybe you would not burn down the Rohals' house, nor would you abduct or kill Mark Ramirez. But if you needed the remediation, then odds are you would not enroll yourself, nor would you allow yourself to be enrolled. If you needed such an education, then you would not get it.

CHAPTER 4

THERE IS a crowd, of sorts, gathered around the Ramirez house when I arrive. It is a crowd of neighbors who have their own scanners, and who have therefore heard the news about Mark Ramirez. It is not, however, like the mob out in front of Maurice Rohal's house two years ago. No, this is a more circumspect bunch—whispering to each other on the sidewalks, peeking out their windows, etc. It is not a three-alarm-fire crowd; it is a missing-persons crowd.

It makes sense, then, that the people inside the house are missing-persons *victims*. They don't exactly know whether they are really victims, and if so what they are victims of. This makes Mrs. Ramirez, Jodi, none too happy. She wants to know, now.

"Tell me what you know," she demands, spooning the yellow ooze of baby food into the mouth of her six-month-old daughter. Jodi Ramirez is the kind of woman who is probably always pretty except when she is tired. Right now she is very tired: she has black half-moons under her eyes, and her short blond hair is as greasy and limp as short blond hair can be. She is wearing cutoff jeans shorts and a soiled, peach-colored tank top. Her daughter splatters the shirt with her baby food and Jodi doesn't even bother to wipe it off. She just sighs and keeps on feeding her youngest daughter. Jodi also tells me that her other daughter is five years old. I can hear the older daughter watching television somewhere else in the house.

"Haven't the police been here?"

"They've been here. They didn't tell me anything."

"The police should be able to tell you something."

"Tell me what you know about my *husband*," Jodi Ramirez repeats after it is clear that I'm trying to avoid her first request.

"Your husband," I repeat. "*Mark.*" Then I tell her all the things I know, which is basically that he owns a jewelry and precious metals shop.

When I am done with this very short narrative, Jodi Ramirez stops feeding her daughter and glares at me. Her eyes are perfectly round, miniature blue versions of the searching beam of a lighthouse. Even her daughter, whose face is covered with the mush she's been eating and which looks undefined like mush anyway, stares at me with those same clear, beaconlike eyes.

"Don't be dumb," Jodi Ramirez says. "Tell me about what's *happened* to my husband."

I am not dumb. I already know that this is what Mrs. Ramirez wants me to tell her. But I, of course, don't know what has happened to her husband. Now that I have to tell her this, Jodi Ramirez becomes a more confident victim. She starts wailing. Her mush-eating, mush-faced daughter starts wailing, too. In some other room, over the sounds of the television, I can hear the *older* daughter wailing.

I have a long enough career in self-pity to know that when someone is crying, you should never tell her to stop. So I just stand there and let the Ramirez women cry themselves out. After an agonizing minute of false stops and heaving restarts, Jodi finally stops weeping. Then, she tells me everything that she told the police: that her husband has been missing for a week, that everything has been just fine at home, that Mark's business was doing well enough, that track season has just finished—Mark, she tells me, is the junior-varsity coach—and it had been a perfectly fine season. And Jodi insists, when I ask her, that her husband has no known enemies at all.

"You told the police all this?"

"Yes," Jodi says. "They told me not to worry. Not to worry about a thing."

"Not to worry."

"They told me to just take it easy," Jodi says.

"Do you have any family?"

"Family," she says, waving her hand dismissively. It is likely that her family is less than pleased with her choice in husband in the first place.

"How about Mark? Does he have any family?"

"His mother went back to Puerto Rico after Mark graduated high school. He hasn't seen her since then."

"Back to Puerto Rico?"

"Yes," Jodi says and explains that Mark's parents were migrant workers who came up north one summer and then stayed. If you drive north from here, an hour or more, you see the workers every fall, spring, and summer. They live in rusting trailers way up in the mountains. They pick our apples and grapes, work the larger produce and dairy farms, enter their kids in local Adirondack schools, and then they leave before the first report cards come out, before it gets too cold, before they actually have to be thought of as a *part* of something. Mark and his family are the only migrant workers I've ever heard of who actually stuck around after the fruit had been picked.

"What about his father?" I ask. "Does he have a father? Siblings?"

"He has a father, but Mark doesn't know where he is. He left home before Mark's mother did."

"Bad relationship?"

"No relationship."

Jodi Ramirez's mush-faced daughter begins to wail again.

Jodi herself does not renew her weeping, but I feel like I might start crying myself. So I stuff my notebook in my back pocket, shake Jodi's hand, and tell her that I'm confident, extremely confident, that her husband will turn up, safe and sound. I assure her that I'll be in touch. Then I leave.

I know I'm not the one who should feel like crying, but this is the problem with being a reporter: you ask all the right questions and you get your answers, and the answers don't tell you anything you actually need to know. Then you end up feeling disappointed in *yourself*. I am disappointed in myself because I still have no idea what happened to Mark Ramirez.

WHAT I do know, now, is what happened to Jodi Van Horne, a girl from my high school class who wore her racy cheerleading uniform to school every Friday. I haven't even thought of her in near a decade.

How could I stand there, you might want to know, and talk with Jodi Ramirez about her missing husband and pretend that we did not graduate high school together? And how could Jodi stand there and pretend that she didn't recognize me, either?

The answer is this: we could do such a thing because it is easy. On the other hand, it would have been difficult, so very difficult, if I had said, "Jodi, it's me, Lamar. Lamar Kerry." Then, she and I would have had to do a certain amount of breast-beating about losing touch, about the arc of our post–high school lives, and about old times. And then our reunion would have become even more difficult, because the false, happy facade of our surprise get-together would have inevitably crumbled under the weight of Mark's disappearance. We would have become very grave, knowing what we do about each other and the world in which we live. Finally, before parting, Jodi would have had to say, "It doesn't look good, does it?" and I would have had to admit, "No, it doesn't."

But since I did not admit to knowing her, nor she me, it is easy to pretend that I have no shared history with a victim like Jodi Ramirez; it is equally easy for Jodi to pretend that she has no shared history with a fuckup like myself. And since we have no shared history, then I can pretend that I will be able to find her missing husband, and Jodi can pretend that she has faith in my ability to do so. All of this pretending is most likely futile, of course. But we must at least try.

I GO DOWN to the station after I am done with Jodi Ramirez. I have some questions for Uncle Bart about the official police investigation. My uncle is sitting behind his big wooden desk. He is sweating through his white uniform shirt. It is July, after all, and near ninety outside. The police station does not have air-conditioning. But my uncle has been known to sweat through his shirt even in the cold heart of winter. In a family of rail-thin men with low blood pressure, my uncle is the one fat, hypertensive Kerry.

"I'm busy," he says.

"I can appreciate your situation, Uncle Bart."

"Superbusy," he says.

"I need to know something about Mark Ramirez."

"Mark Ramirez is missing," my uncle says.

"That's one thing I do know," I say. "Tell me something else."

"His wife," he tells me, "is white."

"I know. I went to high school with her," I say. "She was white then, too."

"Whiter than a ghost."

"I already agreed with you."

"Well, Jesus, Junior. Do the math then, why don't you?"

Part of the mathematical equation here, and the reason my uncle and no one else on this earth calls me *Junior,* is that he believes

I slept with his daughter, Loreen. One Saturday morning, when Loreen and I were both seventeen, Uncle Bart found us intertwined like two pubescent snakes on the couch in his basement rec room. We'd been drinking Boone's Farm wine out in the woods all night long and somehow wound up, body parts all tangled, on that fuzzy green couch in that dark, cold basement the next morning. To my uncle, it was as if he'd barged into a scene ripped straight from the pages of Genesis.

"Adam and Eve, get up off that couch."

"Oh, Daddy," Loreen told her father as she peeled herself off of me. "We weren't really *doing* anything. We were just drunk and passed out."

This news didn't make Daddy too happy. And he shouldn't have been. What Daddy probably knew was that if it had been up to me, we *would* have been doing something. I didn't care if Loreen was my first cousin, once removed. I didn't care that in ten years, Loreen would go on to teach first grade at St. Mary's Elementary School. I didn't care that in ten years she would wear asexual corduroy jumpers and a large wooden crucifix affixed to a thick necklace chain. I didn't care that in ten years, Loreen would still live with her parents, whose evangelical Catholicism she would adopt, and whose low opinion of me she would also adopt. When we were seventeen, Loreen had ass-length platinum blond hair and an easy, sexy way with young turks like myself. She also went barefoot whenever she could. From time to time, she would run her bare toes up the inside of my leg and chant, "Elevator, elevator, we got the *shaft*!"

When you are a seventeen-year-old boy and you have a hot girl running her bare foot up your inner thigh and *chanting*, then you do not care about incest. When you are in this situation, incest sounds like the best thing imaginable.

Of course, this is exactly what my uncle did and still *does* imagine. This is the math. The math is that my uncle dislikes and distrusts me and always will.

But this piece of Kerry family intrigue aside, the arithmetic of the moment is that a Puerto Rican man cannot marry a white woman and get away with it. This is my uncle's theory about Mark Ramirez's disappearance.

"That's your theory?" I ask him. "That's your *only* theory?"

My uncle says that it is.

I mention the other possibilities: that Mark Ramirez simply ran away from home like adult males are known to do; or that he is hurt and lying in the woods, in the mountains, *somewhere*. As I list these theories, I am struck by how feeble and unlikely they sound. But I persist.

"Don't you think maybe you should have an alternate theory?" I ask Uncle Bart.

My uncle says that he does not. He doesn't appear to mind my asking these questions. Uncle Bart smiles in the manner of fire chief Bob Shumaker, who two years ago smiled at me in the manner of a highly evolved cat, and so on.

So I give up and simply ask Uncle Bart for the official version of the investigation. My uncle's official version is not that he believes Mark Ramirez's abduction is racially motivated. He tells me he has several possible leads and that the department is pursuing all of them. Uncle Bart says he has reasonably high hopes that the investigation will be successful, and that Mark Ramirez will be found and returned to his family.

I take down this information, go back to the office, and type it up in article form. Then I hand it to my father. My father has already dug up a picture of Mark to run with the article. In the picture, Mark is wearing a button-down striped oxford shirt and a painful, forced smile. It is a posed, studio photograph, and it's clear from Mark's awful little smile that he was tired of the photographer telling him to put which arm where, and to smile like he had just seen which naked movie actress. My father reads over my article and then publishes it in the afternoon paper, along-side Mark's picture, accompanied by the sober title: "Local Man Reported Missing."

AS YOU know, Glori has a problem with my theories. But she also dislikes theory in general. Her problem with theory is not that it is never right, that it is always shown to be false in the cold, hard con-ditions of the real world, but that theory is always right. Theory is *too* right. Of course change is impossible in provincial upstate New York. Of course mystery is impossible without the chance of change. Of course it is true that when a Puerto Rican man marries a white woman up here on the hillbilly fringes of the world, then that Puerto Rican man gets abducted or worse. Of course.

But, when I call Glori at work to tell her about Mark's disap-pearance and my uncle's theory, she claims that just because some-thing is probable doesn't mean it is true.

"You're not listening," I say. Then, for the second time, I explain the details of Mark's disappearance and of my uncle's theory.

"What he says makes sense," I say. "Doesn't it?"

"Of course it does, Lamar," Glori says. "Your uncle's theory makes perfect sense. But it is so ugly. Obvious, too."

Then Glori says she has to go back to work and hangs up.

And I want to believe what Glori believes. I want to believe that the world is not as predictable as my uncle says it is. Can it be that this is what I have to do to get into the advanced racial-relations class? Do I simply have to allow myself to be surprised by how the world works? Perhaps, then, all I have to believe is this: that, true enough, twenty-seven-year-old overgrown white boys like myself may need racial remediation; that we may be related to racially mo-tivated and unrepentant arsonists; that we may be grateful not to be black, Puerto Rican, or anything not white; and that we may be scared of nonwhite people in general. But that does not necessarily mean one of us scared white boys abducted or killed Mark Ramirez, or that one of us did so for obvious reasons.

Perhaps this, then, is what I must believe. And I want to believe it. I truly do. I do not believe it, but I want to.

CHAPTER 5

FAMILY DINNER night at the Kerry house. Every Wednesday, I go up to my parents' place, where I eat and listen and talk a little. This Wednesday, the menu: flank steak, corn on the cob, and rosemary fried potatoes. The chef: my father, who isn't bad. The setting: my parents' newly stained outdoor deck. The conversational theme: family, and in particular, our upcoming annual Kerry family reunion. The participants: family.

Glori, on the prospect of accompanying me to my parents' house to eat flank steak and talk family reunion: "Thanks, but no thanks."

"I'm thinking big this year, Lamar," my mother says. The black flies buzz around her bleached-blond hair, but she doesn't seem to notice. For years, our family reunion has been your ordinary beer-and-potato-salad affair. But this year, my mother acts as if she's organizing the Olympics. She mentions three-legged races, name tags, and mailing lists. She mentions rented tents, karaoke machines, and a round-robin softball tournament.

"Take it easy, Judy," my father says.

"You don't need to tell me to take it easy."

"Fine," my father says. "Just take it easy."

This is my father's favorite postdiagnosis phrase. It makes my mother furious, and so I never tell her to take it easy myself. But I know what my father means. For instance, wheelchair or no wheelchair, my mother is absolutely gone over the prospect of hosting our family reunion. I envision her at the reunion softball game, rounding the bases in her wheelchair. She is rounding second base, telling the slow-moving Kerry base runner in front of her (maybe Uncle Bart) to get the *lead* out.

It is not an unamusing daydream. I suspect it will be an unamusing reality.

"Don't worry," I tell my mother. I figure I will gently ridicule her into taking it easy. "I'll bring the softball. Maybe a mitt." I pretend to think about my offer for a second as I chew on a piece of flank steak. "Definitely a mitt," I say.

"That's right," my father says. He does not miss the small sarcasm, I don't think, but he does not officially recognize it, either. "Lamar will do his fair share."

"My fair share," I repeat.

"Absolutely. I knew he would," my mother says. She begins to list all who will come to our family wingding—the various and sundry distant cousins and widowed great uncles who live in Herkimer, in Buffalo, in Albany—and the few who will not. As she talks, my father and I eat and eat. My mother has barely eaten anything at all. Since her MS has gotten worse, my mother doesn't eat much of anything and drinks not at all. I am not sure about the reasons for her lack of appetite, but I don't think it has anything to do with the disease. At least, I've asked my father and *he* doesn't think so. What I know for sure is that my father and I seem to eat and drink more and *louder* now that my mother doesn't do either. We're not so much father and son at the dinner table as we are lip-smacking barbarians at the postpillage feast, or newly released prisoners of war.

My mother doesn't seem to notice the lousy table manners of her two men. We finish up our trip to the trough as she tells us that the only people who won't be at the reunion will be my uncle Eli, of course, and a group of Utah Kerrys who never come to these things. Most of us New York Kerrys have never even met them. This, in the eyes of our local Catholic clan, makes them Mormons, guilty by region and in absentia.

Now that the roll call is completed, my mother peters out. That is, she abruptly stops talking about the reunion. Her left eye begins to flutter and then droops noticeably. My mother, suddenly, is the personification of quiet. I know why. It has been brutally hot for the past week. Sometimes, on hot nights especially, my mother simply cannot sleep. My parents have recently installed air-conditioning, but it doesn't always help. On those hot nights, my mother's hearing goes in one ear or both, or her eyesight blurs, or her synapses misfire, making her speak just as a dyslexic reads. My mother's sudden, dramatic transformation can only mean that another of her long, terrifying nights is just beginning.

It also means that my father, unnerved as always by my mother's bad turns, tries to fill up the sudden silence by talking shop. He does this by congratulating me on my article on Mark Ramirez.

My father doesn't get far. He tells me that I did a good job interviewing Jodi Ramirez. He compliments me on how *politic* my questions were. My father asks me how my conversation went with his cousin. I tell him that it went fine. I also tell him that his cousin is a perfect jackass. My father says it sounds like I really stuck it to my uncle Bart.

"Did you stick it to him?" he wants to know.

Before I can answer, yes, I did stick it to him, my mother lets out her most peeved sigh. Then she begins to back away from the dinner table. My mother has always hated shop talk at the dinner table. She calls such talk "ugly," by which she means "boring." I agree with her, either way. But that's not really the case here. The case here is that she's tired and sick and doesn't want to admit it. My mother does not want to admit that she's defined by her illness, and so she wheels away in overwhelming, twitching fatigue disguised as table manners.

"You'll be driving me to church tomorrow?" she asks me. I drive my mother to church when she wants to go and my father can't take her.

"I will."

"All right, then. Good night, Lamar," my mother says, by which she means me.

"Good night."

Then my mother is gone, up one of the ramps my father has built in and around their home, into the downstairs bedroom that she keeps so air-conditioned that it feels much like a remodeled cave.

Good night.

My old man and I sit in silence as my mother wheels away from us. *Old man* is not really an expression in this case. Suddenly, my father looks old. Suddenly, I know that my father does not really want to talk shop at all. He does not want to talk about Mark Ramirez or hear what I think about him. Suddenly, I know that my father would have Mark Ramirez stay missing or worse—and that he would have me stay as ordinary and unsuccessful as I am—if he could only get his old, beautiful, fully functional wife back. If he could get her back, then he could get himself—confident, successful, sufficiently virile husband—back as well.

All this, suddenly, I know.

So I leave. Who wouldn't want to leave? Who wouldn't want to leave a home that no longer seems like a home but, with its ramps, handrails, and special bathrooms, like a well-equipped minor-league baseball park? Who wouldn't want to leave parents who no longer seem like real parents but like miscast, reluctant Florida dinner-theater actors? Who wouldn't want to leave a place that makes you no longer seem like a loving son, but the ungrateful sole survivor of a car wreck? The car is crashed. Now, before the paramedics come and the character of the survivor is revealed, the survivor wants to flee the scene.

"Dad, I better be going," I say. The black flies swarm the flood-light and a night mist settles wet and heavy over the valley below us. I tell my father that I promised Glori I'd pick her up at her apartment, and that I'm late already.

"Of course," he says.

"I'm sorry to cut and run."

"Don't even worry about it," he says. "Go on ahead. Cut and run."

My father walks me to my car. He does not hug me or even shake my hand, for which I am grateful. Instead, he simply tells me to have a good night. He also tells me to give his best to Glori. My parents have met Glori before, of course—at Ponzo's, at my apartment, downstreet. They've had us over for dinner twice. My father likes Glori, as he's told me repeatedly. Why is this? I have always assumed that he likes her because of her unusual name, or because she's a type: the tough, cigarette-smoking secretary who doesn't take any shit. But maybe this is not the case. Maybe my father likes Glori because she makes me happy. As I think this, it seems like not just a possibility, but the truth.

Suddenly, I do not feel like abandoning the kind of father who knows when not to touch his son, and who appreciates the son's girlfriend for the right reasons.

Suddenly, the car is wrecked but the sole survivor is not yet sole nor soulless.

But it is too late. I am already in the car, and like my mother into her cave, gone.

"Bring Glori with you next time!" my father yells as I pull out of the driveway.

"I will!"

"Tell her we won't take no for an answer!"

"I promise!"

CHAPTER 6

I PICK up Glori at nine o'clock at her place.

"How was dinner?"

I tell Glori that my mother doesn't want to admit that she's defined by her own illness.

"Join the crowd," Glori says.

I ask Glori what illness she is defined by.

"Menial labor," she says. "Plus, you."

This is close enough to the truth to make response unnecessary. Dangerous, too. So I don't say anything.

"What's your defining illness, Lamar?" Glori says, her hand softly gripping the back of my neck.

"We're here," I say, pulling up outside the Renaissance. I don't answer Glori's question. Instead, I grab her by the hand and walk inside. Andrew Marchetti is standing behind the bar, waiting for us.

Andrew's defining illness is the Renaissance itself. The Renaissance is his family-owned bar. It has cheap beer and good-looking stained-glass windows. But beyond this there is not too much to recommend it, nor the Marchettis themselves. Some of them are alcoholics, some of them are criminals. Some, like Andrew—who is a balding, puffy-faced drunk, and who takes bets on local high school football games—are both.

Glori and I take our seats at the bar. I reach over and give Andrew Marchetti the twenty-three dollars I've owed him since Memorial Day.

"Treat us like family, Andrew."

"Whose family?"

I shrug. My request was meant to resemble a simple mathematical equation: your family owns the bar, so if you treat us like family, then we obviously receive what we want. What we want are two beers. But now my original mathematical and filial meaning is long gone, even to me.

So I shrug again.

Andrew pockets my long-overdue twenty-three dollars. He turns to Glori.

"Whose family should I treat you like?"

Glori also shrugs. Fortunately, hers is a graceful, suggestive gesture, whereas mine was an ungainly intellectual surrender. Andrew reads the limitless possibilities in Glori's shrug and he gives us two bottles of Utica Club. He refuses my two dollars when I offer it to him, and everyone is happy.

Glori is especially happy because this is euchre night. On euchre night, we meet her friend Sheila (who is also a secretary at the Monroe Street Elementary School) and Andrew (who is Sheila's husband, plus my friend since junior high school) at the bar and play cards until we are too drunk or poor to continue. But when Sheila gets here, it is obvious that we are not going to be playing cards at all. Sheila is already fantastically drunk: her face is blazing red and her strawish blond hair is coming out of its ponytail and her tank-top T-shirt has come partially untucked from her too tight designer-knockoff jeans. Moreover, Sheila is yelling at Andrew the

moment she enters the Renaissance. Andrew comes out from behind the bar and he's yelling, too. Like most drunken yelling, it
makes limited sense. As far as I can tell, the upshot of it all is that
Andrew is tired of being a fucking alcoholic cock-sucking bartender
for his family, who are also fucking alcoholics, etc. So he's decided
to become a guard at the new maximum-security prison. And
Sheila, it would seem, has some reservations about his decision.

Sheila's and Andrew's yelling ceases only because Andrew's
brother Till hasn't shown up yet for his shift. Until Till arrives,
Andrew has to work behind the bar. Andrew's father died two
years ago, and Andrew runs the bar, even though his mother still
officially owns it. So while Andrew pours beers and shots for the
sad-sack regulars who have been around since Andrew's parents
were young alcoholics, Glori and I move to a table and listen to
Sheila explain why her Andrew is simply not cut out to be a prison
guard.

"He's just too smart to be doing that kind of work," Sheila says.
She's already started slipping down the drunk ladder from anger to
melancholy. "Isn't he too smart?"

"He is," Glori says as she quickly and carelessly rolls a cigarette.
"Way too smart."

"Way too smart," I repeat.

"That's exactly right," Sheila says, scrambling back up the ladder a little. "That's what I keep telling him."

What I don't say is that I'm not so sure Andrew is too smart to
be a prison guard or *anything*. He definitely wasn't too smart in
high school, where he took mostly home-ec courses. In home ec, he
was surrounded by girls in training for young Christian mother-
hood. These girls were sufficiently scared by prematurely alcoholic
Andrew, and so they left him alone and didn't dare tell him how
unbelievably *dumb* he seemed to be.

And to be true, Andrew doesn't look too smart now, either.

When Till finally arrives, Andrew gets all over his younger brother's case for being late two days in a row. As Andrew reads Till the riot act, he looks like a punchy hound dog who has been run over by cars so many times that the only piece of wisdom he can share with his only slightly less punchy younger brother hound dog is to watch out for the *cars*.

"Listen to your friends," Sheila tells Andrew as he sits down at the table. "They also think you're too smart to work in a prison. Just listen to them."

"It's absolutely true," Glori says. She leans forward to emphasize her point. She has been holding my left hand with her right; now, she moves that hand on top of the table. Glori is no longer a woman who wants to play her regular game of euchre; instead, she is Khrushchev staring down JFK over the Bay of Pigs. All she lacks is the banging on the table and the translator's headsets. "Besides," she says, "just look at the life of your everyday prison guard. Just look at it."

Andrew adopts the bored, superior smirk of a twelve-year-old boy. "It's a done deal," he says. He tells us he's already applied and been accepted. But Glori does not give up. She goes on and tells Andrew all she knows about the average working day for a prison guard. She mentions male rape. She mentions knife fights. She mentions high rates of alcoholism, divorce, heart failure, violent deaths in the wood shop, and extremely low levels of job satisfaction.

"I've got all of that now," Andrew says, gesturing all around him. He has a point. Till, who's behind the bar, looks less like your average Italian-American than he does your average Italian American who has been dunked in a vat of wax. This is true of all of the Marchettis, who look like they regularly bathe in a mixture of alcohol and cigarette smoke. Which is precisely the case, of course. Next to the occupational hazards of our local Madame Tussaud's, rape and knife fights must not look so terribly bad.

But Glori isn't done yet. She takes a strong, last drag on her cigarette, and mentions that she's recently read that prisoners have taken to throwing their own feces at their guards.

"You will be the target of human *shit*," Glori says. "Do you have that in here, too?"

Now it's Andrew's turn to fall down the drunk ladder. The problem, as Andrew explains it, is not that he might have shit thrown at him; the problem is that he's absolutely terrified of having shit thrown at him. But that fear, he says, isn't enough for him to choose *not* to be the target. What's worse, Andrew wants to know: working as a bartender in your family's bar for the rest of your life, or working in a prison and having feces thrown at you?

Andrew answers his own question. "At least shit washes off. The way I see it, you can go to work and have shit thrown at you. Then you go home and get clean."

Glori doesn't have any good answer to this. Sheila, who looks like she's been asked to eat shit and *like* it, doesn't have a good answer to this, either. There is no good answer to this.

"Besides," Andrew says, finishing his beer, "the pay is out of this fucking world."

There is no good answer to this, either, which is why none of us speaks for what seems like hours as the ceiling fan whirs and the television set flickers. The jukebox says something to the effect that life is a highway, which is true, sort of. The pay is out of this fucking world. That's true, too.

Finally, because I am my father's son, I start talking shop to break the silence. I tell the story of Mark Ramirez's disappearance and my interview with his wife. I mention how Jodi Ramirez and her two young daughters wailed like air-raid sirens.

"That's very sad," Sheila says.

"I just let them cry themselves out," I tell her. "I didn't even try to stop them."

"Very sad," she says again.

"It's all in this afternoon's paper."

"Who do they think did it?" Sheila asks.

"*They* don't know who did it. That's in the paper, too. In so many words."

"Whoever did it," Andrew says, "we'll get him."

I don't think any of us miss the *we* here. Apparently, Andrew has already left our civilian world for the omnipotent, fraternal universe of law enforcement.

"We'll definitely get him," Andrew says.

"No doubt about it," Glori says.

"I'm not kidding," Andrew says. "This is a promise. We'll get him."

I tell Andrew that no one thinks he's kidding. I ask him if he has any theories about Mark Ramirez's disappearance. Since he's soon to be in law enforcement. But Andrew doesn't have any theories. I know this because he doesn't even answer me. Andrew sits there dully, thinking about prison, maybe. I don't blame him. There is a lot to think about.

In an ideal world, of course, Andrew would not have to think at all: he would immediately be able to tell me all about Mark Ramirez's disappearance. In the ideal world of our fathers, a bar owner's son would be hooked into local politics, local commerce, local everything. The bar owner's son would know all about the fate of a missing Puerto Rican precious-metals dealer. Of course, in the ideal world of our fathers, a man unhappy with the family business would also have the opportunity to go work in the mills. In the mills, he would develop a nagging, eventually fatal cough, but he at least would not be the target of human excrement.

But we are not in the ideal world of our fathers, and the bar owner's son could not possibly get on at the mill because the mill is not hiring. So the bar owner's son goes to work in a prison an hour away from home, and doesn't know a single thing about what has happened to Mark Ramirez.

"We'll get him," Andrew says.

"Andrew," Glori says, "do you even know what in the hell you're talking about?" She is Khrushchev again. Khrushchev is finally realizing that Kennedy is just not worth the headache. I have come to a similar conclusion.

"Good night, Sheila," I say. I grab Glori's hand and make a big deal out of a fake yawn as I tell Andrew and Sheila I have to get up early in the morning. "Good night, Andrew!"

"Lamar," Andrew shouts, the way drunks do when their friends walk out on them. "Once the prison opens, I bet your uncle Eli will be transferred."

"You're right!"

"You'll be closer to your uncle!"

"That's true!"

CHAPTER 7

"GOOD-BYE, Andrew."

I say this to Glori as we go to bed at my place. Outside, a group of young turks are coming out of the bars. They are shouting at each other, then peeling out underneath my window in their El Caminos. Inside my four brick walls it is unbearably still, breathtakingly hot, and when I turn my fan on it does nothing but push that hot air around. Glori is wearing a silk shorts and tank-top pajama outfit, and, inexplicably, rag-wool socks.

"Good-bye, Andrew," she says. "Good-bye, euchre. Hello, state penitentiary. Good-bye, Mark Ramirez."

"You think?" I ask.

"I think he's dead," Glori says. "I don't know why I think that. I have no definite theories. But I do have a feeling. I have a feeling that he's dead. I definitely do."

"You sound like Uncle Bart," I tell her. "I thought you said you didn't agree with his theory."

"I said that I didn't have a theory and that I didn't feel the need to have one. That's the difference between me and your uncle."

"Fine."

"What do you think?" she asks.

"I don't think," I say.

This is true. Mark Ramirez is either a missing Puerto Rican man who happens to be married to a white woman, or a Puerto Rican man who is missing because he's married to a white woman. Any way you cut it, I have asked my questions and written my article. I have fulfilled my responsibilities as a reporter, if not as a human being. Besides, it's late and I don't want to think anything for right now. Glori doesn't ask me to. She doesn't ask me to do anything but lie there in bed with her. Even that she doesn't ask; she just does.

This is another thing about a few of the nice kids in the smart class: they know when to push the kids in the remedial section, and when to just let them lie there and be dumb.

"Andrew Marchetti is not too smart for *anything*," I tell her.

I immediately regret this thing I've said. Even if I am fed up with Andrew at the moment, he is still my oldest friend, and he is still going to work in a prison. I should be at least scared for him.

Glori doesn't say anything once again. The only thing she does is hold me tighter as we kiss and listen to the roar of the El Caminos on the street below us.

This, by the way, is why men idealize women. You say something that's not true enough or too true. Then, if you are lucky, you have someone who can just hold you and not point out that you yourself are either not smart enough or too smart. When you are in the grip of this ideal woman, you don't even want to think. All you want to do is lie there and idealize. Which is what I do.

Of course, sometimes all this idealizing can come back and hurt you. Sometimes your idealized woman is a mother, wife, and social studies teacher who gets sick and is no longer ideal. This transformation can truly wound you if you are a certain kind of lazy idealizer. But then again, if you are that kind of man, then you are too lazy to think about future heartache or about perfect women eventually turning into real people. The only thing you are not too lazy to do is to lie there in bed with the perfect woman and listen to the hot rods on the street below and think about how lucky you are.

CHAPTER 8

I GET up, send Glori off to work, and then take my mother to church. By the time I get to my parents' house it is ten of eight. My father has already left for the office. It is a strong day: clear blue sky, big wind, and not much wet or heat yet in the air. My mother tells me she feels strong enough to use her walker this morning. So I do not fold and then load her wheelchair into the trunk of my car. But my mother is her own wheelchair, and I am her folder and loader. I fold and load her into the front seat of my car, then I throw the walker into the trunk. When I handle her, my mother feels like hard, knotted, useless muscle and will. Which, of course, is what she is. Or part of what she is.

"We're off."

"God is with us today," she says. "Can you feel it?"

I tell her that I can feel something.

"I can feel it," she says.

You should know here that my mother is not the kind of hypocrite who gets ill, finds fear, and in the process finds God. On the contrary, my mother is the kind of true believer who finds God early on in life and sticks with him. I, on the other hand, *am* a hypocrite, the kind who accompanies his mother to church even though he does not believe in God. I accompany my mother to church because I think it makes her happy.

We park in a handicapped spot in front of St. Mary's. It is about twenty feet from curb to door and we cover the distance slowly, very slowly, my mother struggling behind her walker. I keep pace with her, taking tiny, empathetic steps. We do not make a scene of any kind, tragic mother and helpful son, because most of the people who go to Mass on a Thursday morning are themselves much older than my mother. These old women have their own walkers and their own empathetic children. They're setting their own staggering turtle's pace.

By eight o'clock, all of us parishioners are sitting in our hard, dark brown wooden pews. There are twelve of us total. St. Mary's is a large, high-ceilinged church, and it is so empty this morning that it feels as if we are in an extraordinarily ornate airplane hangar.

The twelve of us sit quietly, waiting for the priest, Father Begnini. But Father Begnini is running a little behind. We are left to sit and stare at the elaborate stained-glass windows, at the marble stations of the cross, at the high, dramatic ceilings, and the antique pipe organ.

Looking at these beautiful objects, I feel compelled to risk a religious generalization. I have heard numerous Catholics explain that the real difference between Catholicism and Protestantism is that Catholics value beauty. And since God himself is beautiful, this Catholic twist of logic goes, then God is Catholic.

But this is wrong: we twelve Catholics are not waiting for a beautiful God. No, we are waiting to hear the prayers, receive the body and blood, and then to just get on with the rest of the day. Even if the rest of the day promises to be only a more domestic version of church, with our little daily rites and routines, we want to get on with it. In this we are rarely disappointed, as Father Begnini's Masses are efficient in-and-out jobs.

What I'm saying is that the twelve of us don't care whether God is beautiful or not. All we want is to not be disappointed. This is God: God is not disappointing.

Today we are disappointed. It is Father Begnini who does the disappointing. He starts Mass five minutes late. When he finally steps up to the pulpit, his robes are flowing and his normally jaundiced, sixty-year-old, pockmarked face is flushed, every little crater full of fire. He is obviously *feeling it* this morning. We know he is feeling it because he gives us the complete Mass, including a sermon, even though the sermon is short. This wouldn't normally be a problem. Father Begnini's sermons are usually straight scriptural interpretations. Sometimes he reads us a message from the bishop. But today, the subject of the sermon is *us*.

"I saw you come into church today," Father Begnini says from the pulpit. "I saw you come in, up off the sidewalk, into church with your walkers, and with your children. And I thought to myself, Charlie, if Jesus needed saving, your parish would not even make it up the hill to Calvary. The hill would erode and wash away before they even made it to the top. And then I thought to myself, Charlie, you know what else? Your parish is not at all beautiful. Your parish is not at all easy to look at."

An audible, echoing rustle from the cavernous spaces of the church. Someone coughs. My mother's walker clangs against the kneeler. I sneak a sideways look at her sitting next to me. Her lips are pressed tight. She stares straight ahead at the priest.

"So this is the truth I'm here to tell you," Father Begnini says. "You are not an easy group to look at. I am not easy to look at either. I have learned to accept this truth. I became a priest, in part, because I am not easy to look at. I have learned to accept this truth, too. Scripture tells us that we will not find peace in our hearts until we have accepted our ugliness. This was what Jesus told the poor; this was what Jesus told the lepers; this is what Jesus is telling you. Jesus will not accept that you, his children will not admit to your own ugliness. You come to this church because you are ugly, and you want some solace in your ugliness. You will not have peace in your heart until you have accepted this truth."

More coughing and clanging. Father Begnini must hear it from the pulpit but it doesn't seem to affect him. Instead, he goes on with the rest of the Mass. This is the nuttiest thing he's done so far. After saying what he has said, I expect the priest to at least stomp on out of church in a holy rage. But Father Begnini doesn't do anything so dramatic. He sends around the collection baskets and walks down the aisle, giving his twelve ugly invalids their communion. We give our money and we take the body and blood as if nothing unusual has happened. This is the second nuttiest thing that occurs in church this morning. No one shuffles out the door. No one sits in head-shaking, mute refusal of the wine or the communion or the collection basket. We just sit there and give and take. A week from now, we might find out that Father Begnini has had an affair with an altar boy, or that he is being investigated by the diocese for long-standing financial turpitude. Then, his sermon will make sense: it is obviously the sermon of someone who has cracked. But for now, the sermon makes sense because we ignore it into making sense.

This is another side of the Catholic God: when God is disappointing, we simply ignore the disappointment.

My mother, unfortunately, does not entirely ignore it. Me, I am prepared to ignore everything. I shuffle alongside her after the Mass is over. Then I load my mother and her walker into the car and drive them home. The day is still relatively strong, but the heat and the wet are creeping into the air a little and the day is weakening some, definitely weakening.

"That was a sermon, wasn't it?" my mother asks as I pull into their driveway. Like the day itself, my mother is weakening. Her voice is rough and dry. It sounds like her throat has developed deep, painful cracks.

"It was something, all right," I say. "It was interesting."

"Do you think it's true?"

"I don't think Father Begnini meant what he said."

"That's not what I asked you. I asked you if you think what he said was true. That we are ugly and need to admit it. Do you think it's *true*?"

I look at my mother sitting there, folded into the front passenger seat of my car, and I think that what Father Begnini said isn't true because it is either too true or it isn't true enough. My mother's crippled body and occasionally crippled spirit are ugly enough. This is obviously true. But it is also not true because she is still my mother. Mothers who have done nothing bad enough to deserve ugliness are never ugly to their sons. The sons themselves would be very ugly for even thinking that their mothers are anything but beautiful.

"Do you really want to know what I think?"

"I already told you I did. Twice."

"I think that you're beautiful," I say. "I think that Father Begnini didn't know what he was saying. He was just *feeling* it."

I mean for this flip comment to make my mother happy. But I should know better. Do we ever make our mothers happy when we tell them what we think they want to hear? My mother is not at all pleased with the way I have answered her question. I help her out of the car, up into the house. She isn't happy about my helping her, either. Or rather, she *is* happy, but only because I cannot actually help her struggle up the stairs, through the front door, into the house she has made beautiful over the years, and pretend she is not ugly.

"I'm going," I tell my mother after I've let her down on the couch.

"Fine," she says, "go. Thanks for the ride."

When she says this, my mother inexplicably reminds me of one of history's sexpots—Lana Turner, maybe—stretched out on the couch, saying Thanks for the ride, to the man who has just told her that she is beautiful. I desperately want her to be Lana Turner and me Lana Turner's son. I want to walk out the door and be able to ignore the fact that my mother is not Lana Turner and I am not Lana Turner's son, that she is ugly and I am uglier for thinking so. And so, since there is apparently no limit to my self-deception, I walk out the door and get in my car, all the while pretending that my mother is Lana Turner and I am Lana Turner's son. After all, if my mother were not Lana Turner, then it would be very disappointing.

TWO

CHAPTER 1

MY UNCLE identifies a suspect. I find this out when I go down to the *Valley News,* after I have dropped off my mother at home. It is not yet nine o'clock and my father is by himself in the office, typing something into the computer.

"Uncle Bart has a suspect *already*?" I ask my father after he has told me the news.

"It happened early this morning. Bart called me at home and told me he had a suspect."

"Mom didn't mention it."

"She didn't wake up when the phone rang. And she was still sleeping by the time I left to come down here."

"What did happen this morning, exactly?"

"Bart brought in Eric Chisholm for questioning."

This is promising news. I know Eric Chisholm. Everyone in town knows Eric Chisholm. Or rather, we are all familiar with Eric Chisholm through his criminal record: DWI, check fraud, spousal abuse, public drunkenness, petty larceny. I know from a recent police docket that he lives not too far from me, on the very west end of Albany Street, above a consignment shop.

"Why did Uncle Bart bring him in?"

"Someone overheard him at a track meet in early June, complaining about Mark's coaching decisions. Apparently, Mark refused to allow Eric Chisholm's son to run the hundred-yard hurdles like the son wanted to. Mark put Chisholm's kid in the eight hundred instead. Chisholm's kid finished last, and Chisholm was complaining about it in the stands, saying loudly that 'the fucking Rican' would be sorry, very sorry that he didn't listen to his son."

"'The fucking Rican'?"

"That's supposed to be a direct quote."

As my father tells this story he sounds strangely upbeat. And in a way he should be: Eric Chisholm's involvement in Mark's disappearance makes good, final sense. Chisholm, who is a scrawny, forty-year-old estranged husband, deadbeat father, and on-and-off farm laborer with dirty blond hair and a perpetually wispy, half-grown-in beard, certainly seems like someone capable of committing a hate crime, especially since he has proved capable of committing nearly every other crime. Like my father, I feel upbeat after hearing about Eric Chisholm's implication in the case. These kinds of stories come in over the AP wire nearly once a week, and so my father and I both know how they usually run their course: either the crime is solved immediately, or it is solved several painful, dragging years later. Sometimes it is never solved.

"Have you talked to Uncle Bart since he called you?"

"He said he'd call us."

"When?"

"When he's done checking Eric Chisholm's alibis."

"Eric Chisholm has alibis?"

"That's what Bart is checking on."

"So what do we do for now?"

"We wait."

"We wait for what?"

"We wait for Bart to call."

"No problem."

I get up, pour myself and my father some coffee, and then I sit back down again and wait. Justice is suddenly a patience-is-a-virtue proposition.

CHAPTER 2

MY FATHER lacks the proper patience. Unlike yours truly, he is not willing to just sit around all day and wait for the news to come to him.

So, after waiting around for an hour for Uncle Bart to call, my father tells me to go down to the police department.

"What for?"

"I want you to find out what's going on with Eric Chisholm."

"I thought Uncle Bart was going to call us when he found something."

"He was. But I still want you to go down there."

I give him a persecuted look. I know what my father's motivation is here. He is afraid that my uncle has fouled up the investigation somehow, and so he wants me to go down to the station and find out what Uncle Bart has done with Eric Chisholm, our racist ace in the hole. I understand this. But I am so content in my waiting.

"Jesus, Lamar," my father says. "Just do this one thing for me today. *Please.*"

"Then I can go home?"

"You come back here and tell me what you found out. Then maybe you can go home."

"Fine."

So I walk down to the police department, which is only four blocks away from the newspaper building. The lobby to the police department is empty when I get there, except for two men: Geoffrey Lasalle—who is the desk clerk—and Ian Chisholm, Eric Chisholm's older brother. Ian Chisholm, who has an arrest record only slightly less impressive than his brother's, is doing my work for me.

"I want," Ian Chisholm says, "to see Kerry." He's speaking, of course, of my uncle.

"Chief Kerry isn't in right now," Officer Lasalle says, standing at his desk. He sees me standing behind Ian Chisholm and nods hello in my direction.

"The fuck he isn't," Ian Chisholm says, not looking around to see whom the desk clerk is nodding at. "I heard he just brought in my brother. It's all some sort of *bullshit.*"

Geoffrey Lasalle tells Ian Chisholm that he doesn't know anything about it. The officer is clearly nervous: his voice cracks when he talks and he keeps fidgeting with his pen, which is on the desk in front of him. I don't blame him for his nervousness. Everything about Ian Chisholm is big—big farmer chest and shoulders, big meaty hands, big dirty beard—and he has at least three arrests for assault and battery. Plus, the Chisholm brothers tend to look out for each other. At least two of Ian Chisholm's assault-and-battery arrests have come in the name of defending his younger brother in bar fights.

As for Officer Lasalle himself, he is quite small, which is why he's the desk clerk.

"I want to see Kerry *right now,*" Ian Chisholm says.

"No."

At this, Ian Chisholm moves a little closer to where Geoffrey

Lasalle is standing behind his desk, and slaps the desk clerk right across the face. It is a surprisingly refined blow, like a French nobleman challenging someone to a duel. The desk clerk is stunned by the slap. I am stunned, too. Even Ian Chisholm seems a little bit stunned. He stands there and examines the palm of his hand. Who would have suspected that violence could be so dignified?

What follows is not so dignified. Three cops, who must have been watching the whole thing, come charging out from a doorway to the left of the lobby and slam Ian Chisholm facedown on the marble floor. Then, they beat the hell out of him. To those of us who have never been in a fight—I never have—all beatings look brutal. But this one truly is. One of the cops has his knee in the middle of Ian Chisholm's back; another one strikes him on the back of his legs with his nightstick; the third hits him repeatedly in the back of the head with his closed fist. Unbelievably, Ian Chisholm doesn't make a sound during any of this, and neither do the three cops.

As for the identity of the three cops, I probably know them—I know most of the local police—but during the beating I cannot really focus on their faces, even though they are right in front of me: they are just a blue blur of cops-taking-care-of-their-own efficiency.

Then, just as quickly as they appeared, the three cops drag Ian Chisholm to his feet, and haul him out of the lobby, off to the room they first came out of. Once they are gone, it is absolutely silent in the lobby. You would not know anything has happened except for a small red smudge of blood on the marble floor.

I look at Geoffrey Lasalle, who is still standing there, rubbing his cheek. He looks angry. Embarrassed, too.

"What do you want, Lamar?"

"I forgot."

It is not exactly that I'm afraid that something will happen to me here: after all, I am still related to the chief of police. But when you are in the police department, and you see something you shouldn't, and you are not the police yourself, you leave. I leave.

CHAPTER 3

"WHAT DID you find out?" my father asks when I get back to the office.

"Something I shouldn't." I tell him about Ian Chisholm and the slap and the beating. Like me, my father is shocked. My uncle's department is known for its incompetence, not its brutality.

My uncle calls smack in the middle of our disbelief. I answer the phone.

"Which Lamar is this?" he asks. My father and I have similar phone voices.

"Well?" I ask him.

"Well, what?" he says, obviously now recognizing my voice, and even more obviously not happy to hear it.

"What do you have to say about Ian Chisholm?"

"I don't have to say anything."

"I was there," I say. "He got beat up. Bad."

"He assaulted a police officer."

"Ian Chisholm *slapped* the desk clerk," I say. "I was *there*."

"He assaulted a police officer."

I have hit the roadblock of my uncle's absolute sense of crime and punishment. I look over to my father, who points to himself as if to say: I'll handle it. Then, he makes a twirling motion with his finger, as if to say: Get on with the questions.

"Fine," I say to my uncle. "What about Eric Chisholm?"

"Eric Chisholm is under arrest," Uncle Bart says. I give my father a thumbs-up before I realize that something is not entirely right. I don't hear anything upbeat in my uncle's voice, nothing triumphant at all.

"You arrested him for something to do with Mark Ramirez?"

"No," Uncle Bart says. "It turns out that Chisholm was in Scranton for the whole week that Ramirez first went missing."

"Scranton, Pennsylvania?"

"Staying with a girlfriend. Or someone resembling a girlfriend. This is what he told us when we brought him in yesterday. We called the Scranton police and they checked it out. Chisholm was there for two whole weeks. He just came back to town the day before yesterday."

"What in the hell did you arrest him for?"

"Parole violation," my uncle Bart says.

I hold my hand over the receiver. "Parole violation," I tell my father, who has been waiting, watching, listening to me talk to my uncle. My father waves his hand in disgust at this development and starts typing on the computer again.

"He wasn't supposed to leave the state," my uncle says. "Those were the terms of the parole. So we've got him locked up down here. He'll get three to six months in the county jail."

"But he doesn't have anything to do with Mark Ramirez."

"I didn't say that," Uncle Bart tells me. "All I said was that he was in Scranton. That doesn't mean he doesn't have anything to do with Mark Ramirez's disappearance. After all, he threatened Ramirez in public. I have my theories."

"You arrest Eric Chisholm for no good reason," I say. "And then you beat up his brother who comes in to complain about it. Good work."

"Ian Chisholm assaulted a police officer."

"Whatever you say."

My father must sense that I am on the verge of ending this conversation with my uncle. He grabs the phone on his desk and motions for me to hang up my receiver.

"Lamar told me everything," he says to my uncle, by which he means everything about Ian Chisholm.

My father listens to my uncle's response.

"Don't give me that," my father says. "Christ, Bart, what am I supposed to do with this?"

I get up and go to the bathroom. I don't need to sit around and be witness to the wrestling that goes on between father and uncle, between small-town police chief and small-town newspaper editor. There are only two possible outcomes here. If you are a participant in this wrestling match, then you either end up asking the other participant for a break, or you end up giving one.

When I get back from the bathroom, my uncle has asked, my father given. We will not be publishing anything on the Ian Chisholm incident.

"Well?"

"I've decided not to run a piece on Ian Chisholm," he says. My father takes off his glasses and rubs his eyes with the heels of his hands.

"No?"

"No," my father says. "Bart says they'll hold him overnight and then let him go."

"I see."

"He said they wouldn't file charges."

My father and I do not speak any more about it. We just sit quietly in our chairs. I don't know what to say, anyways. It's not that I am outraged by or ashamed of what my father has done. That's not really the case at all. But I am *wary* of my father. My old man has made his decision about Ian Chisholm and he knows it is a decision that leans toward corruption and he has come to terms with the corruption.

Now, I wonder what other corrupt decisions my father has made, and what decisions he might yet make.

But for the moment, my father has decided to sit quietly and try to forget about Ian Chisholm. I am going to let him try.

After a silent minute or so, my father asks me exactly how it is that Eric Chisholm has violated the terms of his parole agreement. I tell him. I also recount Uncle Bart's idea that Eric Chisholm might still be involved with Mark Ramirez's disappearance. How Eric Chisholm could have kidnapped Mark Ramirez from Scranton is beyond me, beyond my father, beyond Eric Chisholm as well, I suspect. But still, my uncle's logic doesn't escape me entirely. If you remember, my uncle believes that in situations such as our own, one must do the math. And when a true believer like my uncle does the math, and then the numbers don't work out the way he wants them to, then the true believer just rearranges the numbers and *makes* them work.

"And Bart still believes that Eric Chisholm has something to do with Mark Ramirez?" my father asks, a little ache of hope still lingering in his voice.

"Uncle Bart has his theories."

"Yes, he does."

"It certainly seemed like Eric Chisholm *could* have done it."

My father nods. He looks bad: red eyes, splotchy face, mussed hair. I have never seen my father look so beat-up, so old.

"It's unfortunate," my father says.

He hands me a copy of the Utica paper with a follow-up article on the gang-related deaths—also still unsolved—circled in red ink. He means for me to start copying the article.

Instead, I start scribbling notes in my spiral-bound notebook.

The theme of the notes: How to avoid becoming a small-town wrestler.

What exactly is a small-town wrestler? you ask.

A small-town wrestler is someone—like my father, like my uncle—who becomes so wrapped up in the wrestling match itself that he inures himself to certain illegalities: headlocks, eye gouging, match fixing, and the like. A small-town wrestler becomes so lost in the match that he forgets that there is a world outside the ring, forgets that the world does not end where the ring itself does.

Can a man live in a small town, you ask, without becoming a small-town wrestler himself?

In all truth, I wish I knew the answer. But I do not.

I do know, however, that there are ways to delay, if not avoid, the transformation:

If possible, do not become a witness to the wrestling match.

If you do become a witness, then do not let yourself be dragged in the ring, for any reason. Once you are inside the ring, it is difficult to see anything or anyone that is not in the ring with you.

Do not let yourself be put in a position of power. Once you have power, you automatically become a wrestler as well. You have no choice in the matter.

Do not make deals with people who are in positions of power.

Do not believe in the math.

I underline this last one, several times. This, after all, is why my father looks so beat-up, so old: he desperately wants Uncle Bart's math to work. And as long as you put faith in the math, you will never be anything but a wrestler in the ring of small-town futility. You will plug Mark Ramirez into the equation and then expect the properly guilty Eric Chisholm to show himself so you can plug him in, too. The expectation will age you, like excessive financial worry or catastrophic family illness or disappointing children.

CHAPTER 4

A SURPRISE reunion with my aunt Fay. It happens by complete accident, and in the name of romance. While I'm reading over the afternoon paper back in my apartment, I see a notice about a television movie being filmed in Herkimer, outside the Herkimer County Courthouse. The filming is supposed to start in the late afternoon. They are only shooting a few scenes in a two-part miniseries based on Theodore Dreiser's novel *An American Tragedy*. Someone moderately famous is playing Clyde Griffiths, the book's homicidal protagonist. I decide to surprise Glori and take her to the courthouse to watch the filming. Like many women stuck in small towns, Glori is more than a little starstruck.

I call her at work around three o'clock.

"It's me," I say.

"I know who it is, Lamar," Glori says in a voice notable for its scary seriousness.

"I've got a proposition."

"Propose."

I tell Glori about the movie, about the moderately famous actor. I give her a brief synopsis of Dreiser's novel, how the young industrialist impregnates the poor worker, fears that this will hurt his reputation and chances for social advancement, and he kills his lover, gets caught, is tried in the Herkimer County Courthouse, convicted, and later executed.

"Good," Glori says. Her voice is still serious, still scary.

"What's wrong?"

"Nothing."

"I see."

"No, you don't."

This is true. I don't see. But this is one of those moments when it's better not to squint.

"Do you want to go to Herkimer or not?" I ask her.

"Fine," Glori says, sighing. She obviously wants to see the filming and yet not does not want to admit to it. "I'll take off work early. Pick me up in a half hour."

I pick Glori up a half hour later at the Monroe Street Elementary School.

"I got sick," Glori says as she pours herself in the front seat of my car.

I nod. Her cheeks are red enough, her eyes their normal dark blue. Glori doesn't look sick, which must mean I'm still blind.

"Better just take it easy, then," I say.

"Exactly," Glori says. "That's what I told them at work."

"Work," I say.

"The stack of paperwork was this high." Glori raises her hand high above her head, then lets it drop dramatically to the vinyl car seat.

Finally, I do see. Glori is not physically sick. She's professionally sick. This doesn't just mean she hates her job. It means she hates herself for doing the job in the first place. This is a serious illness. Glori has been professionally sick before.

"I feel just *awful*," she says.

You should know here that Glori gets professionally sick twice a year or so. I have learned from experience that when the illness strikes, you should get away from the radio and the scanner, away from anything that reminds her that she's been working the same low-paying, low-skills job for over two years now. Last October, when Glori got professionally sick, I suggested that she take some vacation time and visit her parents. When Glori got back to Ohio, her parents told her that she should move home for good and get a job at Wal-Mart. Maybe a visit to the movie set will prove a more effective cure.

There is no acting, no filming going on at all when we get to the Herkimer County Courthouse. The grunts and gophers have only just arrived and they're setting up their equipment like so many high-tech Egyptian slaves, running around, building the pyramid of cameras and lights and booms, and then tearing the pyramid down whenever a senior slave tells them to. We watch all this for a while, hoping to see someone famous.

Instead, after twenty minutes or so, we see Aunt Fay coming out of the courthouse, looking very tanned, very pretty in a yellow sundress.

"Jesus, there's my aunt."

"Is she in the movie?" Glori asks, not knowing exactly what or whom I'm referring to until she sees my actual flesh-and-blood aunt, standing at the top of the courthouse steps. Glori knows all about Aunt Fay turning in her husband—my uncle Eli—and in the process sending him to prison. Glori brightens visibly. This encounter promises to be better than the movie itself.

The film equipment was obviously not in place when Aunt Fay entered the courthouse. I say this because of the look on her face— more dread than shock—as she exits the building. It is as if my aunt knew that if she came back to the area, something bad would happen: the cameras and lighting equipment can only signify something truly bad. And seeing Glori and me standing on the sidewalk, surrounded by all these cameras, doesn't appear to ease my aunt's dread much.

"Hello, Aunt Fay," I say once she comes down off the courthouse steps and walks over to where Glori and I are standing.

"What's going on here?" she asks.

"They're making a movie," Glori tells her.

"A movie," my aunt repeats, relieved. She is so relieved that she kisses me on the cheek as if this is merely your garden-variety surprise meeting of close relatives who are pleased to see each other after a long separation. She even kisses Glori, whom she has only met once before, at a family Christmas party.

"How long have you been back?" I ask her.

"Two hours," she says. "And I'm not actually back. I'm going right home."

"Home where?"

"I was just here doing a little paperwork," she says, ignoring my question. "Settling property taxes, filing divorce papers. They make you do all that in person." As Aunt Fay says this she turns and looks, for some reason, directly at Glori.

"Is the divorce final?" I ask.

"It will be very soon," Aunt Fay says.

That said, there is a painful little silence that none of knows how to ease out of. Finally, my aunt says, "Have you seen him?"

"Uncle Eli?"

"Yes."

"I have not," I say. "The prison is about four, five hours from here, you know. I've just been too busy to make the drive up."

"Yes," Glori says through her faint crease of a smile. "Lamar has been extremely busy."

"I feel bad about not seeing him," I say.

"I wouldn't feel too bad about it," my aunt says. "Prison is right where your uncle belongs. He's probably very happy there."

This comment aggravates me, even though it should not. This is one of the mysteries of family: that you defend the honor of family members who you know don't deserve your defense.

"Why'd you stay with Uncle Eli so long, then, if he was so awful?" I ask.

This draws a small, mirthless smile from my Aunt Fay. Again, she turns to Glori.

"Why have you stayed with him so long?" my aunt asks her.

"Good question," Glori says, smiling her own mirthless smile.

"Ha!" I say, trying to make light of this dangerous turn in the conversation. "It's a mystery."

"Indeed," Glori says.

"Indeed," I repeat. Mimicry here is my only real option. There is something imbedded in Glori's "indeed," some small, hard piece of meaning that I would prefer to remain ignorant of. That is, if I am allowed the privilege of ignorance.

"We were just about ready to go," I say to my aunt. "Aren't we about ready to go?" I ask Glori.

Glori says we are, even though she has yet to see her moderately famous actor, even though she is probably just as sick as she was before she left work.

"Good-bye, Aunt Fay," I say.

"Lamar, I was married to your uncle for eight years," Aunt Fay says, holding my hand.

"I know," I say. "Eight years is a long time."

"For eight years, I tried to be happy," Aunt Fay says. "But it didn't work."

"I realize that."

"I know now," Aunt Fay says, "that I was never happy."

That said, Aunt Fay turns loose my hand, turns away from us, walks back to her car, and then drives off to wherever home is for her. I don't expect to see my aunt Fay again, but she has made an impression on me. I cannot remember hearing anyone say something so awful in my life: *I was never happy.*

My aunt has made an impression on Glori as well. We do not talk the entire ride home.

GLORI CALLS me four hours later to explain why she has stayed with me for so long. I am in bed, rereading *An American Tragedy.* I've skipped to the part where the industrialist kills his impregnated lover. I read the book in college, and so the edition I have is the critical edition. It has never been clear to me whether the industrialist actually means to kill his lover. It isn't even clear whether he *wants* to kill her. According to one of the critics in the back of the book, this is the tragedy: that the heir doesn't know whether he wants to kill his lover or not. But this doesn't seem to me much of a tragedy. No, the tragedy is that the characters in the novel who know what they want—the girl, for instance, knows she wants the industrialist—don't get it, while the characters who don't know what they want get to call the not knowing a tragedy.

"Do you know why I'm here?" Glori asks me.

"Here where?"

"In Little Falls."

"Because I'm here?"

"I was here before we met, Lamar. Why was I here in the first place?"

"You were here because you went to college here."

"Correct. And didn't you ever wonder why I went to college *here*? Didn't you ever wonder why I came all the way from Heath, Ohio, to go to Herkimer County Community College?"

I have never wondered. It simply has never occurred to me to wonder.

When I admit this, Glori gives me an unexpected lesson in her personal history.

"A year before I went to college my boyfriend was killed in a car accident," Glori says. "I was the one who was driving the car in which he was killed. It wasn't my fault—a truck ran a stop sign and ran right into the passenger side of the car—and so I wasn't really guilty of anything. I'm not even sure if I was in love with him. I never even thought about it at the time. But I was definitely *happy*. I know I was. And when my boyfriend was killed, even though it wasn't my fault, I became unhappy, very unhappy. I recognized it, Lamar. Do you know what I mean?"

I tell her that I do. But I am stunned by all this information. Glori has never even mentioned that she had a boyfriend, never mentioned that she was once involved in a car accident, fatal or otherwise. I feel strangely insecure hearing her story, not because I'm jealous that she might have been in love with someone else, but because hearing one thing I don't know makes me wonder what else I don't know.

"And since I knew I was unhappy," she goes on, "I decided to do something about it. There was someone from my high school, a boy I didn't even know that well, who went to Herkimer County Community College to play lacrosse. I decided that HCCC was as good a place as any to get away from my unhappiness."

"OK."

"But as it turns out, in getting away from unhappiness, I got a useless degree and a job that makes me miserable."

"OK."

"I also got you."

"OK."

"Do you remember the question your aunt asked me today?"

"I'm not sure," I say, even though I do remember.

"She asked me why I've stayed with you for so long."

"That's right," I say. "I remember now."

"Do you know why I've stayed with you so long?"

"Because you love me?"

"I do love you," Glori says. "That's certainly true."

"Why?" I ask Glori, attempting to distract her from the gravity of my aunt's question.

"Because you took me to the movie set, for example," she says. "That's why I love you."

"I'm glad."

"But love is not the real reason I've stayed with you for so long," Glori says. "Ask me the question."

"What?"

"Ask me your aunt's question."

And so I do, even though I would rather do nearly anything else.

"Why have you stayed with me for so long?"

"I have stayed with you for so long," Glori says, "because I'm not sure whether I'm closer to happiness or to unhappiness. It's disconcerting, not knowing for sure whether I'm happy or unhappy. The only thing I can think of is that if I stick around long enough, I might go definitively one way or the other."

"One way or the other," I repeat, zombielike.

"I'm not sure love by itself is enough to make a person happy," Glori says. "Do you understand me when I tell you that?"

"I understand."

"I'm in such a rut, Lamar," Glori says. "I'll call you next week."

Then she hangs up, and I go back to reading my book, from the beginning this time. It occurs to me that there is plenty the novel might still teach me. For instance, I don't remember Clyde Griffiths ever standing up and saying, "I am happy." I don't remember him saying "I am unhappy," either. Was he incapable of definitively saying one or the other? And is that the tragedy?

CHAPTER 5

ON SATURDAY, my second serious phone conversation in two days. This time, with my parents.

First, my mother.

"Hello, Lamar," she says. "I'm in Syracuse."

"Why?" I ask. "What?"

My mother explains that her doctor is concerned about the accelerated rate of her physical deterioration. So he's sent her to Upstate Medical in Syracuse, an hour away, so they can do some tests.

"Tests?"

"A spinal tap, specifically," my mother says, her voice even. "A half hour from now."

"Why didn't you tell me?"

"I don't know."

"I'll be there in an hour."

"That's why I didn't tell you. I shouldn't have even called you now. Don't come up here, Lamar. I will see you when I get home."

And I am grateful. I don't know what a spinal tap is, really, and

I don't want to know. I have a difficult time even imagining it. What I do imagine are scenarios straight out of Edgar Allan Poe. These images cannot be right—I don't want them to be right—and so I stop trying to imagine my mother's spinal tap at all.

But it is too late. My eyes well up. I make an involuntary sniffling sound. My mother hears it.

"Lamar," she says. "Desist."

"It's not fair," I say. "I thought they said you wouldn't need any more tests."

"They lie."

"It seems they do."

"Get used to it, Lamar. They always lie."

Clearly, this is why my mother has called me. She has called me not because she wants me to feel sorry for her, nor because she wants me to pray for her, or anything like that. My mother has called me because she wants me to hear how tough the world truly is. She wants to teach me a lesson in toughness.

I learn the lesson. I stop sniffling.

"You'll be fine," I tell her.

This is the wrong thing to say. I think I have learned the lesson too well, because I hear my mother choke and sob a little on my toughness. She says my father wants to talk to me. Then, my mother is gone, off the phone and back into her hospital room, where she will toughen up again and wait for her spinal tap.

"What did you say to your mother?" my father wants to know.

"I told her she'll be fine."

"Of course she will be."

"That's what I told her."

"Don't come up here, Lamar."

This is my mother's line. My father has apparently learned his lesson, as well. He is smart enough to know that he is not tough himself, so he mimics his genuinely tough wife. This mimicry is prudent. Without it, my father would have to be true to himself, which would be embarrassing: like me, my father is a shameless weeper.

"I won't come up there," I tell him. "Call me tonight and tell me how things go."

"Will do," my father says. Then, having run out of things to mimic, he asks me how I'm doing.

"I saw Aunt Fay yesterday." Then I tell him the whole story. I tell him how pretty she looked and what she said about Uncle Eli being where he belonged.

"She might be right," my father says.

"But still," I whine. "What a thing to say."

"You don't sound so good, Lamar."

Now it's my turn to mimic *my* tough woman. "You're right. Seeing Aunt Fay has put me in a rut. That and some other things."

My father is not sympathetic. As you know, he believes I shouldn't be here in Little Falls at all; Little Falls, in my father's mind, *is* my rut.

"All ruts are man-made, Lamar," he says. "And men can make their way out of the ruts just as easily as they made them in the first place."

This is supposed to be profound, of course, and of course it makes me want to bounce the phone off my forehead. I come close to telling my father that he should stick to mimicking his genuinely tough wife.

Instead, I thank him for the advice.

"Call me once they're done with Mom."

"I'll call you," my father says. His voice is trembling. "Your mother will be fine, Lamar."

"I know she will," I say, my voice trembling, too. My mother will be fine, my father and I both agree that this is a fact, even though she's in the hospital; even though she's in a wheelchair; even though they are going to tap into her *spine;* even though my father's voice is trembling like he's calling from the epicenter of an earthquake. "I know she'll be fine," I say.

"I mean it," my father says.

"I mean it, too."

We are both on the edge of heartbreak. I can hear it in my father's voice; I am sure he can hear it in mine. Time to get off the phone.

"Good-bye."

"Good-bye."

Then we hang up, two tough parrots.

CHAPTER 6

I GIVE myself an assignment: to walk around and get people's opinions on the Mark Ramirez case. After all, we have heard from the police on the matter and they have told us nothing useful. It is time we hear the voices of our fellow citizens.

So over the course of three days I go into bars, restaurants, banks, city parks. I stand in line at the post office and ask people if they think the investigation is being handled properly. I ask them how Mark's disappearance has affected them personally. I ask if they have any ideas or theories about what has happened to Mark Ramirez. I get a consensus opinion from my fellow citizens: They don't care. They don't even care enough to do what Eric Chisholm did back at the track meet in June: don't care enough to mutter "wetback" in the checkout line at Aiello's News or "spic" in the stands at the Babe Ruth game. What my fellow citizens do care about are the rumors that Corrigan's will be laying off workers, about the diocese closing St. Mary's Elementary School because of low enrollment, about the property tax hike, about the black fly insecticide the state sprays every May. And that, I find, is the sum and summit of their concern.

This discovery makes me angry and not a little righteous. By Tuesday afternoon, a pattern develops: I ask my questions and then make furious little notes and aggravating clucking noises as I get my answers.

Finally, on Thursday morning, when an old lady in the P & C says she cares about the escalating price of ground chuck, I lose all hold on my journalistic objectivity.

"*Ground chuck,*" I say. "Are you sure ground chuck is really something worth caring about?"

"I'm sure," the old lady says as she pitches five dollars' worth of plastic-wrapped hamburger meat into her cart. She is wearing loose khaki shorts, the kind you might wear on safari. Her arthritic knees are a riot of raised purple veins and bulbous, knotted scar tissue. "What do *you* care about?" she asks.

It is a startling question. I stop smack in the middle of the meat aisle and stand there, an island in the eddies of old ladies with their food stamps and shopping lists, and their squeaking carts and creaking joints.

I am so struck by the old lady's question that I repeat it out loud.

"Lamar," I ask, "what do you care about?"

And to be true, I am not exactly pleased with the answer. The answer is that I care whether Glori will find happiness and whether I will be a part of it. I also care about my bedridden mother. She gets home from the hospital on Tuesday. When I go up to see her on Wednesday, my mother is in bed, covered up to her chin with a down comforter. It is over ninety degrees outside, and my mother has her bedroom so air-conditioned that I feel like Admiral Byrd without his parka.

"You look great," I tell her.

"I'm just a head," she jokes, flapping the blanket weakly, slowly wagging her head from side to side. My mother looks awful: her cheeks are gaunt, her skin battleship gray. Her hair is bleached-blond, like it always is, but now it looks wrong, completely wrong. For the first time, my mother looks like an old person who is trying too hard to look young; for the first time, my mother looks like a dying person who is trying to convince herself that she is not dying. And she has obviously been crying, too: her eyelids are puffy and her eyes are pink, the color of calamine lotion. My mother looks so tired, so anguished, so *scared*, that there is no longer any possible way I can pretend she is Lana Turner. And if my mother looks so bad from the neck up, then it is unlikely that the rest of her is in any better shape. In fact, still thinking in terms of Mr. Poe, I have the horrific, fleeting suspicion that *they* could have mistakenly removed my mother's spine during the spinal tap. But this is a hysterical, un-reasonable thought, is it not? Mom, tell me you still have a spine; Mom, tell me you're not dying; Mom, tell me that I have nothing to worry about, that everything will be fine.

"I'm just a head," she repeats, still wagging her head. My mother even does this comic, eye-crossing bit that she frequently employed to cheer me up when I was a child. But I do not find it funny just now.

"Don't be ridiculous," I tell her. "You're more than just a head."

That said, I wait for some kind of confirmation from my mother.

Instead, my mother goes on a prolonged coughing fit. I get her a glass of water and sit by her bed while she coughs herself to sleep without telling me that yes, son, I am more than just a head.

"My mother might be just a head," I say out loud in the P & C, causing the old ladies to give me wide berth.

To my mind, this is a truly troubling revelation—not only about my mother, but about myself as well: above all else, I care about me and my own. Can it be, then, that I am becoming a small-town wrestler? Isn't it true that a small-town wrestler, when faced with a large problem, always returns to his own more immediate personal problems? No one I talk to cares much about Mark Ramirez's disappearance in face of their own private pains. Is that true with me as well?

"What do I care about?" I ask again, out loud.

But none of the old ladies answers me. They simply and silently wobble around me on their way up and down the meat aisle.

And so I put my notebook in my pocket and leave.

FINALLY, AFTER the long, crawling week, it is Friday morning. Glori calls me at home. She sounds happy to hear my voice. Can it be that she's gravitated back to me, and in the process, back toward happiness?

"I've been thinking about you."

"I've been thinking about you, too," I tell her. "I've got a question for you."

"Ask," she says.

I tell Glori about my recent assignment, about what I've asked and what I've found. "Two years ago, we have racially motivated arson," I say. "Now, we have self-interest at best, apathy at worst."

"What's your question, Lamar?"

"Does this mean we've evolved or devolved?"

"The evidence is inconclusive," Glori says. "Is that your only question?"

"No," I say. "What do you say about dinner tonight at Ponzo's?"

"I say yes."

So we make plans for our regular Friday night dinner at Ponzo's. I tell Glori that I've missed her; she says she knows exactly what I mean. She says she's missed me, too.

It is a new world! I bound down the stairs from my apartment to the street, two at a time. Somewhere, in some corner of my conscience, I recognize that Mark Ramirez is still missing, of course, and that I am still the reporter pursuing the truth behind his disappearance. But you wouldn't know any of this from the way I take those stairs.

I come busting out of the front door of my building without looking where I'm going. I run right into my cousin, Loreen, and knock a carton of milk out of her hand. She doesn't seem to mind.

"Good news!" Loreen says as she bends to pick up the milk carton off the sidewalk. It must be good news. At family get-togethers, Loreen sees me coming and ducks into the bathroom, where she reads magazines until someone tells her I've gone home.

"Tell me."

"St. Mary's isn't closing!"

"That's wonderful!"

"The diocese found money to keep the school open, God bless." Loreen cut her long sexy hair years ago. She now has a severe bob haircut, which makes her look much like a mushroom.

"Do you hear me, Lamar? I still have a job!"

"Just wonderful," I say.

We stand there, smiling at each other. We stand there for so long, in such dumb, grinning silence, that my happiness loses something of its solidity. This is clearly a situation that calls for talk.

So I ask Loreen her opinion on the Mark Ramirez case.

"Mark Ramirez," she repeats. "I thought Dad said they found him. Didn't they already find him?"

I assure her that they didn't.

"It feels like they found him!"

"I know exactly what you mean!"

Then, we part, full as ticks with our own happiness.

Unfortunately, once you realize that your happiness is tainted by self-interest, then it is only a matter of time before it makes you feel ill. I get in my car, drive down to work, and begin to feel nauseous. I once got food poisoning from a piece of undercooked chicken, and I spent an entire day in the hospital, vomiting into a bedpan, an IV stuck in my arm. But this feels worse. You can be treated for food poisoning; there is no treatment for self-interest. And if there were, I cannot be sure that I would willingly endure the treatment. I'd like to think that I would choose to be cured if given the opportunity. But I simply cannot be sure.

CHAPTER 7

IT IS wedding-announcement day down at the *Valley News*. This means that Sis Harkes, my father's obituary and wedding writer, is busy telling our readers all they need to know about brides, brides-maids, and ringbearers. My father is supposed to be at work as well, but Sis appears to be all alone in the office. I still feel some-what queasy from my tainted happiness, and the queasiness makes me surly.

"What kind of chiffon were the bridesmaids wearing, Sis?"

"Leave me alone," she says. She is a typist's Woody Wood-pecker or John Henry, pecking and hammering violently on the keys of her computer with her two index fingers.

"Were the ringbearers *little men* and *little women*?" I ask her. "Were they stepbrothers and stepsisters, or were they illegitimate children of the bride? Was the bride stunning or was she glowing?"

"Leave me alone."

Sis has worked for the paper for twenty-seven years. She is also a fragile, bitter old woman and I don't blame her. For one, like me, she has a college education (Smith), and unlike me, she thinks she's too good for her job. For another, she has to play the long-suffering, underappreciated employee to the smart-ass boss's son every Friday. If that's not enough, she also has to be a sixty-five-year-old spinster who gets paid eighteen thousand dollars a year to type up wedding announcements. And if *that's* not enough, when Sis isn't writing up wedding announcements, then she's writing up obituaries. On obituary days, Sis chucks her brides and their beaded trains and tells us whether the corpse was a member of the Rotary or the Elks, and how many loving children he's leaving behind as he goes to meet his Heavenly Reward.

Then again, it's hard for me to feel too sorry for Sis, especially since I am only here on a Friday morning to type up the church bulletins. This is one of my responsibilities as a part-timer. I come in every Friday morning and tell you what time the High Mass is at St. Mary's, who the visiting missionary will be at the First Baptist, and whether the topic of his speech will be "Finding God in the Veldt" or "Spreading the Good News in the Lower Congo."

I am not the ideal man for this job. The ideal man would just write; he would not actually want to know anything. He would not want to know, say, what it is exactly that the Unitarians think they are doing in a *church*. Do they sit there and think: What am I doing here? I am not even praying. What exactly is prayer? I should be in the library, reading Emerson or something. What in the hell am I doing here?

"What in the hell am I doing here?" I ask.

"Leave me alone," Sis says, woodpeckering at her keyboard.

"Where's my father?" I ask, because Friday is not only wedding and church bulletin day, it is also pay day. My father owes me one hundred dollars, at least, for my work this week on the Mark Ramirez story.

Sis says, "Your father was here earlier. Then he received a phone call and left. He's not returning until noon. He could possibly return even later."

"My father better have a good reason," I say, thinking of the heavy wet heat and my recovering mother, hoping that my father doesn't have a good reason.

"You have a message," Sis says, pointing in the direction of my desk.

"Why didn't you say so?"

"It slipped my mind," she says. "Now leave me alone."

I walk over to my desk. There is a piece of scrap paper, on which Sis has written down a message from Andrew Marchetti, asking me to call him back at home. On this piece of scrap paper Sis has written URGENT and then underlined it three times.

So I call Andrew back. "What's so urgent?" I ask him.

"I'm bored," he says. "Let's go do something."

I know that when Andrew says, "Let's go do something," it means the same thing it did ten years ago in high school: "Let's go get drunk."

"I'm at work," I say. "I can't go anywhere."

"So what's the problem?" he says. "Just ask your father if you can take the rest of the day off."

"My father isn't here for me to ask him anything."

"Where is he?"

"I don't know."

"You mean he's playing *hooky*," Andrew says.

"Not exactly," I say.

"Lookit," he says. "The teacher is late for class and he doesn't even have an excuse. That means you should be playing hooky, too."

He has a point. This is what drinking buddies do, after all: they play hooky. Andrew and I have done so before. But am I not supposed to be a twenty-seven-year-old adult? Is my mother not horribly ill? Is my girlfriend not this minute working hard as an attendance secretary at Monroe Street Elementary School? Am I not my father's only son and trusted heir? Is Mark Ramirez not still missing? Are people not counting on me? How can I go have a drink and still be the responsible human I'm supposed to be?

The answer to these questions, as is usually not the case, is in the newspaper, the Utica newspaper, which is on my desk. There is a brief article on the front page, announcing that there will be a rally held this morning in front of the Utica police station. The rally, which will be led by the Utica College sociology professor, is in response to the city's racist law-enforcement policies in general, and to the recent murders of the two black men in particular. I read all this to myself while I'm on the phone with Andrew.

"This certainly deserves my attention," I say. "What say we take a little drive up to Utica and do a little follow-up work?"

"What are you talking about?" Andrew says.

"I'll pick you up in five minutes and explain it then," I say, and then hang up.

I'm so pleased with myself that I'm probably glowing like one of Sis's brides. I am not playing hooky after all: I am *working*. I pull up last week's church bulletin on the computer and then print it as is. God is waiting to be found on the veldt again this Sunday and the heathen lions are still hungry. Meanwhile, I am sneaking out of class and I have an excuse. Sis, the embattled old spinster substitute teacher, pretends she doesn't see me. This is what bad boys are good at—being bad—and if one of them is going to be bad somewhere else, then by God the sub is going to let him.

"I'm going up to Utica to do some follow-up work," I explain to Sis.

"Leave me alone," she says.

This I do.

CHAPTER 8

THE RALLY is already at full tilt by the time I pick up Andrew, drive up to Utica, and pull up next to the police station. There are close to one hundred people standing outside the building—some with placards, some without, some singing old civil rights songs, some merely listening to the singing. Not all of the protesters are black: I see several white people my age and younger (students maybe), and a few white men and women my parents' age. But the majority of the protesters are black, and almost all of the black protesters are men. Most of these men are dressed in grave-looking black business suits: except for some exotic headgear—muftis, old-time bowlers, tweed golf caps—they look more like bond analysts than social activists. One man in particular—I assume he is the sociology professor—stands out: he is wearing a pin-striped business suit and a brightly colored mufti, and he's standing halfway up the steps that lead to the police station, yelling chants into a megaphone. The sociology professor is facing the crowd, of course, with his back to the police precinct. His back is also to a row of cops, who are standing in the front entrance to the building, their arms crossed over their big blue chests. The protesters present no clear threat to the station, but the cops appear to be guarding it anyway. The fading, turn-of-the-century limestone building itself hardly seems worth protecting in the first place: the city law-enforcement offices and holding cells are on the first floor, but the second floor of the building is all boarded up because the city can't afford to heat it. There is some frayed, ragged plastic lining peeking out from behind the boarded-up windows, and the strips of plastic are flapping in the wind, beckoning to us like fingers. The whole sight is more than a little spooky. It is as if the cops are guarding a haunted house.

The sociology professor finishes one chant and begins another, something along the lines of, "What do we want?" etc.

I turn off the car, and Andrew and I sit and watch the rally. We do not speak. I have witnessed similar scenes on television, of course, but never in person. Nor have I ever seen, firsthand, so many black people in one place at one time. It is a surprisingly provocative scene, one that calls for you to do something. It does not call for you to join the rally, necessarily, but rather to get out of your car and walk around, to ask questions, and to not miss a trick. Even if you discover, as is possible, that nothing dramatic will come of the rally, that the same old songs will be sung and the same old stalemates reached, that nothing will be taught and nothing learned, you must at least try to learn something.

You must at least get out of your car and try to put yourself in the middle of *something*.

"I should get out of the car," I say to Andrew. I do not look at him because I know my suggestion violates the spirit of our truancy. "Mingle. Ask some questions."

"What are you talking about?" Andrew asks. I've told him that I had to stop off at the rally before we go get drunk, of course, but I've said nothing about actually getting out of the car. Andrew has let me know—through a series of sighs and grunts—that he's got something on his mind and he really needs a drink. He's counting on me. Andrew's not so much angry at my suggestion as he is confused and a little wounded. "I thought we were up here to have a good time."

"We are," I say. "But since we're here, I should at least get out of the car, look around for a bit. Shouldn't I?"

"What are you *talking* about?" Andrew says again.

"It'll just take a minute," I tell him, and then before Andrew can say anything else, I hop out of the car, and walk toward the rally. I must make quite a figure: reporter's pad in my right hand, number-two pencil behind my ear, accomplished look on my face, as if I have overcome great obstacles just to be here. I see myself wading through the audience until I am face-to-face with the sociology professor, and telling him, I could have stayed in the car! I could have just gone off to get drunk with my buddy! *He* stayed in the car. But I didn't! Doesn't that count for something?

Before I get a chance to say anything to the sociology professor, I am confronted at the edge of the crowd by a white woman, a youngish white woman who is pushing a baby girl in a stroller, and an older girl who is standing next to the two others, sucking her thumb. All three of them have blond hair. I notice this much. I also notice that they seem to be waiting for me to do something. But I don't really see them, don't really focus on their faces: they are just a blur of whiteness in between me and the sociology professor.

"Hello, Lamar," the woman says.

"Shit," I say. I actually say this. Because the woman *knows* me, and I recognize the voice from somewhere. So I look at them closely and then they are no longer a blur of whiteness. They are Jodi Ramirez and her two daughters.

"Mommy," the oldest daughter says, "did that man swear?"

"The *man* did swear, honey."

"Sorry," I say. And then I say a second stupid thing: "What are you doing here?"

"What are *you* doing here?" she asks back.

I hold my notebook up in explanation, but as I do so it strikes me as the feeblest of feeble gestures. "I don't exactly know why I'm here," I admit. "It's complicated."

"I don't exactly know why I'm here, either," Jodi says, but she doesn't stop staring at me, and her voice is deadpan, ironic. The two gang-related black men are dead, and her Puerto Rican husband might be dead, too, and Jodi knows exactly why she's here. The Jodi I knew from high school was sweet in the extreme, a complete stranger to sarcasm. But this older Jodi has become expert at it. "Who knows why I'm here?" she says, and shrugs her shoulders in mock confusion.

"Who knows why we're here?" her oldest daughter says and then raises her arms in the air and starts twirling.

"The *man* knows why, honey."

The girl stops twirling and waits for me to tell her what I know.

"Your mother's talking about someone else," I finally tell the girl. "I'm not really a man. I'm a *boy*."

The girl doesn't buy this for a second; she looks skeptically at me for a good long time, and then starts twirling again, chanting, "Who knows why?" over and over. Some of the nearby protesters hear her and take up the chant themselves, which makes the girl very happy. Her twirling intensifies.

"You know," Jodi says over the chanting, "I remember you from high school. You were a real fuckup then."

"That was me," I say, looking back to the car, searching for a way out of the conversation, out of the rally, out of the middle of something.

"It was cute then," she says. "It's not cute now."

"Listen, Jodi," I say, frustrated because I know I'm on the

defensive, and I know I'm in the wrong, but I don't know exactly what I'm supposed to do about it. "I'm sorry about Mark, I am. But what do you *want* from me?"

"I want you to help me," Jodi says. All of the sarcasm drops out of her face and voice, and she can be seen for what she is: a woman who is frightened and lonely and who has achieved a degree of clarity and strength in her fright and her loneliness.

"I'm trying to help," I say. I manage to resist the urge to hold up my notepad again.

"No you're not," Jodi says. "You're doing your job. You're doing what you *have* to and that's all you're doing."

"OK," I say. "I'll try harder. I'll do everything I can to help you find Mark." As I say this, I realize I sound exactly like my uncle Bart making an official police statement.

"I don't just want you to help me find Mark," Jodi says. "What if Mark isn't found? What if he's *dead*?"

With the word *dead,* the oldest daughter stops twirling and starts crying quietly, very quietly. You can barely hear her because of all the chanting. Jodi squats and puts her arm around the girl's shoulders, but the girl doesn't stop crying and Jodi doesn't tell her to. The other daughter, enviably, is asleep in her stroller and has been the entire time.

"Lamar, look where we are," Jodi says. She says it so softly that I have to squat down to hear her. "Do you believe I ever thought I'd be here? At this rally? Do you believe I ever thought I'd have a reason to be here? That I'd need to be here?"

"No."

"I want you to find out what happened to Mark," she says. "That's true. And I also want you to find out why it happened. I want you to help me find out what this rally has to do with me, if anything. I need your help. Please."

"Why me?" I ask. "I'm the fuckup, remember?"

"Your uncle is the police chief," Jodi says. "Your father is the editor of the newspaper. That's got to count for something, doesn't it? Doesn't that mean that you might be able to find out something that I can't find out by myself?"

"Don't be so sure," I say.

"Besides," Jodi says, "you can't be as big a fuckup as you used to be. You must want to be something more than a fuckup, don't you?"

"Of course I do."

"I need your help, Lamar," she says. *"Please."*

And in this way, I find myself faced with a decision: either I do what the smallest of small-town men always do when confronted with something outside the tiny realm of their experience—search out a bar and drink away the rest of the morning—or I surprise myself, and stick close to Jodi and her daughters and help them find out what has happened to their husband and father and why it has happened and attempt to find out how the world has changed for them and how they might go about living in that changed world. And if I am going to do all this, that means I'm going to have to start by attempting to learn something from the rally, even if it is that nothing is really to be learned.

If I really hope to be different than my uncle, my father, then this is a decision of enormous consequence. Perhaps this is why I feel so paralyzed. My limbs tingle, my skin itches.

"I've got another appointment in Utica," I say, and as I do so something comes loose in my conscience: a hook, a clasp, a metal bolt. I look at my watch. I have been at the rally for less than fifteen minutes. "Once I'm done with that other appointment, I'll come right back."

Incredibly, Jodi doesn't give up on me right then, maybe because she doesn't want to give up on herself. Maybe because she really does need me. "Please, Lamar?" she says.

"I'll come right back," I repeat, even though I obviously have no intention of returning to the rally.

"I understand," she says, sighing as if she's just eaten a too big meal. My first feeling: relief that Jodi understands, or says she does. My second feeling: extreme guilt that I have decided not to do the right thing. It is a decision no less corrupt than my father's and my uncle Bart's, and I know it.

But it is too late to change my mind, and I don't want to anyways. After all, I have this other appointment. So without even a good-bye, I turn away from Jodi and her daughters and walk back to my car. Andrew is asleep in the passenger seat. I open the door and slam it, and the slamming wakes him up.

"Let's go," I say.

"About time," he says.

I start my car and we make a beeline for the Cornhill Tavern and Social Club on Genessee Street, six blocks from the rally. I don't see Jodi and her daughters and I don't want to see them. As we drive away, the sociology professor yells something into his megaphone, and the crowd roars in response, but by now we are too far away to hear what it is the professor is yelling. It might be something surprising, might be something entirely predictable. But we are too far away to hear it.

IT IS my first time in the Cornhill, where grown men have been bad boys for almost one hundred years. This is what Andrew, who like most bartenders knows everything about all area bars, tells me. His father, for instance, used to hang out in the Cornhill when he wasn't behind the bar at the Renaissance. In fact, he had an affair with one of the female bartenders at the Cornhill five years ago, and was estranged from his wife and hated by Andrew because of it. As I said earlier, Andrew's father died only two years ago, with a ruined liver and a ruined family, and no doubt with some deep regrets about being so bad in the Cornhill for so many years.

"What are you boys up to?" the bartender asks us. She smiles at Andrew, whom she has obviously seen before. The Cornhill is not

THE ORDINARY WHITE BOY   109

really a club anymore, but apparently some people still belong here. Andrew is one of them.

"We are being *bad*," I say. Considering how quickly I've fled the rally and betrayed Jodi Ramirez, it seems true enough.

Andrew turns and stares at me. It is obvious that he has no idea what I'm talking about. We are not being bad?

"That's what you think," the bartender says. It cannot be Andrew's father's marriage wrecker, but it might be her daughter. She gives us two bottles of Utica Club and stands there and watches us drink them. I confess that I cannot drink beer as fast as a legitimate bad man can. The bartender, I can tell, is not surprised. She is an impassive, red-haired, high cheek-boned, fair-skinned, apron-wearing, black T-shirted Mae West, waiting to see if this junior W. C. Fields can actually walk the walk. When he cannot walk that walk, Ms. West says to herself: I didn't *think* so.

"We are not being bad?" I ask Andrew after the bartender finishes her inspection, gives us two more bottles of beer, and goes down to the other end of the bar.

"We are drinking beer." He says this gravely, and again I become aware that something is wrong with Andrew. It could have something to do with his job at the prison; it could have something to do with his wife, Sheila. It probably has something to do with both. But I've chosen not to help Jodi Ramirez, and I'm sure as in hell not in the mood to help Andrew.

"Loosen up a little," I tell him. "It is the middle of the day and I've shirked my responsibilities and now we are playing *hooky* in a *bar*."

"And we are drinking *beer*," Andrew says.

Perhaps Andrew is right. Perhaps you don't have to be bad to play hooky; maybe you can just drink beer and you ought to do exactly and only that. This is the lesson Andrew learned from his old man's mistakes. If someone is going to let you drink beer with no behavioral strings attached, then you should just drink beer.

So I drink my beer and give the room a quick once-over. All the beer drinkers in the Cornhill this morning are men, all seventy, seventy-five years old, all sitting at a table at the back of the room. These old men are drinking their beer out of scuffed-up water glasses, and from the sound of their voices, I can tell that the old men are angry about something, about many things. After a minute or so, one of them comes up next to me at the bar. He is wearing a shabby-looking black suit and a brown felt hat and has a prominent barrel chest. He doesn't know what to be furious about first.

"Who are you?" he asks me. "Are you Boston?" I am wearing a gray-and-red Boston Red Sox T-shirt. I figure this question makes about as much sense as anything.

"I guess so."

"You *guess* so?"

"I know so," I tell him. "I am definitely Boston."

"Boston, what do you miss?" he asks me. "Don't you miss anything? I miss pinball machines."

Boston does not miss pinball machines, especially since there is one right in the corner. It is called *Juicy Lucy.* Juicy Lucy is spread out Jayne Mansfield–style on the vertical part of the machine's right angle. Her breasts are lit up like Hiroshima and Nagasaki.

"Juicy Lucy's breasts are glowing," I say.

"Never trust a man without a shirt collar," he says. Then he jabs me in the chest with his index finger, right in the dead center of the Red Sox logo. Hard. This, it goes without saying, gives me pause. I do not know what to do with this drunk old man who is a little bigger than me and much drunker and much badder. So I look at Andrew, who *is* wearing a shirt with a collar. Andrews smiles and looks the other way. Junior W. C. Fields is on his own. What would a man with a collar do in this kind of situation? He certainly would not repeat, "Juicy Lucy's breasts are *glowing,*" and then point at the two, thirty-point, double-flipper nuclear explosions. Which is what I do.

"Doesn't anyone dress *up* anymore?" the old man yells.

His question produces an affirmative howl from somewhere deep in the room. My antagonist rambles away from me, back to the other like-minded aggressive old men. These men are also wearing their best shabby suits and their hats, and their cigarette smoke pours like a funnel cloud all the way to the tin ceiling. There is no music in the Cornhill, no jukebox at all that I can see. It is quiet enough that I can hear the roaring old drunks go on about what was once next door to the Cornhill (a bakery) and across the street (an Italian restaurant and another bar) and how there are no buildings there anymore, only parking lots.

"Why do we need so many parking lots?" someone asks. I can't see who it is or what he looks like. "I don't even *drive*."

"The hell you don't drive," someone else says. "How am I going to get a ride home if you don't drive?"

"You could take the bus."

"The bus," the second voice says, "is for the birds."

At this, one of the old men stands up out of the cigarette-smoke funnel cloud, walks by where Andrew and I are sitting, opens the door, and goes outside. I can't tell if it's my antagonist, and I don't really want to know. Whoever it is comes back in the bar about a minute later. According to my calculations, he's been gone just long enough to take a drunken piss in one of those parking lots. When the door to the Cornhill opens, the bright July sunshine illuminates the cigarette-smoke funnel cloud at the back of the bar.

Once the door is closed, it is dark enough inside the Cornhill that we could conceivably be in a *real* funnel cloud.

The man stops behind me and taps me on the shoulder. I sigh, turn around, and see that it definitely is the same old man who jabbed me in the chest a few minutes earlier.

"This fellow," he yells out, slapping me on the back, "ran a marathon. The *Boston* Marathon."

A congratulatory roar from the back of the bar. I have been rehabilitated by this leap in logic. I am like Molotov, out of the gulag and back in the arms of the Kremlin.

"How long is a marathon?" the old drunk wants to know.

"A marathon," I tell him, "is *forever*."

Another roar. The old drunk takes his hand off my shoulder and jabs me in the chest again. Apparently I am too rehabilitated for his comfort. Molotov had better watch his ass.

"What's his problem?" It is Mae West with two more Utica Clubs. She points at the retreating old man.

"He is being bad," Andrew says. Mae West laughs. I laugh too, even though I know the laughs are on me. I drink more beer and yuk it up and watch the cigarette-smoke funnel cloud spin and darken behind me. I laugh and drink until it is obvious that I have become the too drunk, slaphappy third wheel to Andrew and Mae West. I watch and listen as Andrew whispers to Mae West that he's going to work in a prison, and his wife doesn't want him to, and he's going to do it anyway. So this was Andrew's problem after all; this was why Andrew needed a drink and some consolation from his old buddy Lamar. But now he seems to have found consolation elsewhere. I watch and listen as Mae West leans over the bar, whispers something into Andrew's ear about how brave he is. I swear that she seductively grabs Andrew's shirt collar and circles his top button with her index finger. I swear, even, that she winks at him.

So I stop laughing and decide to go. Andrew is going to work in a prison, and his wife is working with my girlfriend, and the second-generation Mae West is telling the second-generation husband to come up and see her some time. That time is now. I don't want to know how any of this has happened. Andrew *is* bad after all. I have been left behind, all alone on the *Good Ship Lollipop*. I don't want to know how this has happened, either. I feel betrayed, somehow, although I don't know by whom and for what reasons. My problem with Andrew and Mae West is not moral, has nothing to do with the betrayal of the sacred vows between husbands and wives. True, I know Andrew's wife, Sheila, true she has always been very polite, very *nice* to me in the way that women are with their husband's friends that they don't quite trust. No doubt Sheila doesn't deserve any of this.

But I don't feel sad for Sheila; I feel sad for myself.

I feel sad for myself because back at the rally I was presented with a choice—do the expected cowardly thing or do something unexpected and brave—and I made the wrong choice and did the expected, and son of a bitch if I'm not being *purged* for it.

But perhaps it is not too late to make another choice. Perhaps it is not too late to reverse my decision. Perhaps it is not too late to help Jodi Ramirez and her daughters and to prove that I can be something more than a fuckup.

"Andrew, I trust you can get a ride home."

"You know I can."

"You know he can," Mae West says.

I do know he can. I turn on my heel and head out of the funnel cloud into the bright summer sunshine. The broken glass in the parking lot catches the sun, glimmering and glinting, and it is like I am walking on *sparks*. This impromptu fire walking makes me feel most hopeful as I get in my car and drive back to the police station.

But once I get to the station, there is no one mingling or rioting or dispersing outside the building. There is no one at all: no cops guarding their turf, no serious black men in serious business suits and eccentric hats yelling into megaphones. There is no Jodi Ramirez or her daughters. I am too late. The rally is over. There is a placard lying on the ground that reads *Change Now!* and that is it.

CHAPTER 9

I RETURN to the office and in doing so, sink more deeply into disappointment.

"Hello, Lamar," my father says. He is sitting at his desk, tapping his pencil lightly against his forehead. "Where have you been?"

"I've been in Utica."

"That is correct. That is the word on the street. You've been doing *follow-up* work."

It is two in the afternoon by this point. Sis is still at her desk, happily pecking away. She does not look up, but I swear I see a smile on her face. The substitute teacher has ratted out the truant. Later on, she'll call her spinster sister on the telephone and say, "I really stuck it to the head honcho's kid today. That spoiled little so-and-so had it coming to him, and he got what he deserved, and I'm glad."

I have no good response for my father. He of course knows that there is really no such thing as follow-up work at the *Valley News*, particularly since it was my father himself who wrote the original article on the dead black men, and even he didn't really write it. Of course, I could explain to him that I had legitimate business up in Utica, that I went there to cover the sociology professor and his rally. But how, then, to explain my failure to actually do so?

So I just stand in front of my father's desk, head down, in a posture of penitence.

"Where is your friend, Mr. Marchetti?"

He is in a bar. He's wearing a shirt with a collar, he's drunk, he's a lech, he's upstairs with Mae West, he's behind the bar with Mae West, he's being his father, he's being bad.

"He's at the movies," I tell my father. I'm not sure why this is any more excusable than anything else, but it does seem to me to be at least more true. On the *Good Ship Lollipop,* bad things only happen in the movies.

"The movies," my father repeats. He nods as if this makes perfect sense.

A copy of today's paper is lying on my father's desk. I can see that his daily story on the Mark Ramirez case is on the front page. The headline reads, "Ramirez Still Missing: Police Still Following Up Leads." My father has chosen to run his most unflattering file picture of my uncle Bart: his eyes bugged, his jowls hanging down like mud flaps. I see the article and the photo, and I decide to distract my father from how irresponsible I've been with a little choice information that I've just remembered from earlier this morning.

"Did you know," I ask my old man, "that no one in this town gives one damn about Mark Ramirez being missing? I ran into Loreen on the street this morning and she thought they'd already found him. She said that 'Daddy' told her so."

My father doesn't answer me, doesn't wonder about the city's apathy toward Mark Ramirez's disappearance, doesn't tell me if he expected the lack of reaction or not. My father just sits there in silence and pretends to casually open up and read the copy of today's paper that has been lying on his desk. Specifically, my father is looking over the church bulletin that I have not deigned to update.

The sight of my father, slowly and theatrically perusing the dated church bulletin, the vision of him flapping and folding the documentation of my failure, leads me to do the most unconscionable thing I have ever done.

"How is Mom?" I ask my father. I even wrinkle my brow for effect. "Is she feeling OK?"

This is the worst kind of juvenile diversionary tactic, and I regret the questions the second I ask them.

"Your mother," my father says, "is *awful*."

There is nothing to say to this. I know she is awful, that is why I asked. And since I asked, I am awful, too. I am worse than awful. I am *mud*.

"Do you know that you are twenty-seven years old?" my father asks after he has told me that my mother has barely gotten out of bed in the two days since I last saw her; that she is in so much pain that she starts sobbing every time she has to get up and walk to the bathroom. "Do you know that you are supposed to be a man?"

I do know this, I assure him. I really do.

"Do you know that this is a newspaper?" my father asks. "Do you know that this is a *real* newspaper?"

This is not strictly true, of course. Real newspapers do not emphasize the church bulletins, nor do they so prominently feature marriage and funeral announcements. Besides, no one really wants or needs a real newspaper around here anyway, and my father knows it. But I don't say any of this. I have said too much already.

"I'm sure this is my fault, somehow," my father says, leaning over his desk, rubbing his temple with his index finger and thumb. "I've never been as good a father as my father was."

This is one of my father's favorite lines. He wheels it out whenever the mother lode of his grief or disappointment becomes too weighty for fresh sentiment. I was eight when he first said the line in my presence. It was after an office Christmas party and my father, who is not a big drinker, came home slightly loaded. The drifting snow was so deep and the west wind so fierce that he got his car stuck a half-mile down the road. My father was drunk enough to leave the car there, halfway off the side of the road, and walk the rest of the way home. When he got home, my father drank some more bourbon. While my mother called the city road crew, asking them to watch out for our car once they started to plow the road, my father sat me down and told me about his father, who was killed in a combine accident when my father was fourteen. I had heard the story before, but I had never heard its accompanying moral.

"Lamar," my father said, "my father was a great man."

"He was?" I was only eight, but I knew plenty of farmers already, and none of them seemed to court greatness. Even my uncle Lee, whom I liked, did not seem great.

"He was," my father said. "I'll never be as good a father as my father was."

There was some element of truth here, some depth of adult sorrow that I didn't want to plumb when I was eight, and I don't want to plumb now, either.

"Lamar," my father says after I have not responded to his *mea culpa*, "you should just get the hell out of here. You should just *go* somewhere."

"Where should I go?" I ask.

"Just *leave*," my father says.

At this he throws down his copy of today's paper and leaves the room. My old man might be crying, I'm not sure, but I am definitely crying, once again, the way a drunk son cries at every familial disappointment that is his fault. First, I cry silently, fat tears dribbling down my slack cheeks, then in small trying-not-to-be heard gasps, standing next to my disappointed daddy's abandoned desk.

Sis is still sitting at her desk, still typing. There is no way she cannot hear me crying.

"This has been a disappointing day," I say to Sis by way of explanation. "I've disappointed *myself*."

No response.

"Maybe my father's right," I tell her. "Maybe I should just leave."

Still no response. But Sis is not even trying to hide that smile now. I have never seen the miserable old maid so happy. I can just picture her later on, calling her sister on the phone, and saying, "And listen to this: the head honcho's kid even *cried*."

"Leave me alone," I say.

But Sis does not leave me alone: more smiling, more typing.

And so I leave.

CHAPTER 10

IN MY experience, men do one of two things when they are in trouble: they get themselves in more trouble, or they make lists. For instance, after my uncle burned down the Rohals' house, he got his gun, went out, and shot up mailboxes. He even shot up my parents' mailbox, which was decorated with a hand-painted mural of a deer preparing to jump over a white picket fence. I had drawn the mural when I was a child. Out of the deer's mouth came a cartoon dialogue bubble with the name *Kerry*.

My uncle Eli hated the mailbox and the deer: I know this because I was visiting my parents, looking out the house's front bay windows the day he pulled up alongside the mailbox, took out his shotgun, and blew the mailbox right to hell. He didn't even bother getting out of his car.

My father was also witness to the destruction of our mailbox. In fact, he was standing only ten feet away from this assault. He'd been raking gravel off the grass and back into his driveway.

"Eli. Nice shot."

"You are a piece of work," Eli said to my father. "How do you think a deer would even know your name? Do you think he looked it up in the phone book?"

"That," my father said, "is an interesting point."

The mailbox was knocked off the side of its post, hanging on by a thin strand of its sheet-metal vertebrae. The deer had been a jaunty deer; now, if the deer was anything at all, it was blackened metal and smoke.

"A deer can't even read the phone book," Eli said. "He can't even fucking *talk*."

As Eli peeled away, my father chalked his bad behavior up to ordinary drunkenness. And Eli was drunk. But my father didn't know that his brother was also in serious trouble and he was making it worse.

I do not have a gun and I have no stomach for the kind of trouble you find after purchasing one. So after betraying my father's trust and breaking his heart and his hopes, I break into Glori's apartment (I have a key, so it is a subtle break-in), break open a bottle of her rum, break out a vacuum cleaner and a mop and cleaning solutions, and I throw myself at her apartment. I also make a list. The theme of the list is how to make myself useful.

I have dusted Glori's black-and-white photos of Canada geese in midflight, mopped her kitchen floor, vacuumed her throw rugs, and am eyeing the dirty Corning double-pane insulated windows, feeling like the king and conqueror of all self-improvement, when Glori gets home from work.

"Those windows," I tell her, "are a disgrace."

"What are you doing, Lamar?" She sees the three-quarters empty bottle of Myers's Rum on the kitchen counter. Seeing such a thing does not exactly inspire confidence in the judgment of your lover and uninvited domestic help.

"I am being useful."

"I can see that."

It is the first time we've seen each other since our run-in with Aunt Fay, since Glori told me about her possible unhappiness. I should not be drunk on such an important occasion, I know this. But knowing this does not make me sober. I consider apologizing, immediately, before anything else happens.

Glori throws her keys next to the bottle. She puts her arms around my neck and kisses me. Then Glori pulls back from the kiss and wrinkles her nose, not so much like a rabbit but like a rabbit who has just stepped in something. I have been drinking since this morning and it is now 5:30 in the afternoon. I have not brushed my teeth once since I woke up. If you are drinking all day, you need to brush your teeth and brush often. That goes on the list, too.

"Don't worry," I say. "I'm going to brush my teeth right now."

"I'm not worried," Glori says as I walk into her bathroom so I can use her toothbrush, so we can kiss again, and so I can cross the toothbrushing off the list. "When you're done, how about we get something to eat?"

Which makes me realize that I forgot to get my one hundred dollars from my disappointed father. One hundred dollars goes a long, long way at Ponzo's, but it goes nowhere if you don't have it. Remember to get one hundred dollars from father also goes on the list. Remember to first redeem yourself in father's eyes before asking for money. The list is getting out of hand, and suddenly I'm a panicky drunk who is in trouble again and I'm looking for my shotgun. This is not just a figure of speech. I am banging around in the bathroom, opening cabinets, drawers, and toilet seats with Glori's toothbrush in my mouth, and I find myself actually looking for the shotgun that I don't own. I am outraged that I can't find it. I am also, it goes without saying, much drunker than I realized. A moratorium on rum is going on the list, if I can remember it. A rumatorium is definitely going on the list. Definitely.

"What are you doing in there?"

"I am running a marathon," I tell Glori. "The *Boston* Marathon." This blast from the not-so-distant past makes me feel like laughing and so I do. Little breathless giggles. I have run the Boston Marathon and I am so tired that I am loopy.

"You are doing what?"

I am clearly running out of chances to make sense. I go back to being panicked again.

And so I decide to tell the truth.

"I'm looking for my shotgun."

"One more time, Lamar."

I try my last remaining truth. "I'm chewing your toothbrush all to hell," I tell her. "I'm so sorry."

This *is* the truth. In my panic I have gnawed instead of brushed, and I am now spitting out bristles like sunflower seeds all over the bathroom rug. This is how Glori finds me once she opens the door, delicately spitting out tiny white bristles all over her blue shag bathroom rug. I am the picture of diligence. I do not stop spitting, even though I know Glori is standing there watching me in absolute disbelief. I do not stop spitting until all the bristles are gone, removed from my mouth and deposited on Glori's rug, and the job is done and I can cross it off my list.

"IT'S FRIDAY," I say. I am in Glori's bed, just waking up from a nap I did not know I would take and do not remember beginning. The day of the week has some meaning here. As you know, every Friday night I go out to dinner with Glori, my treat.

I pick my head up off the pillow and see Glori sitting in a hard-backed kitchen chair, her feet propped up on the radiator, her back to me. She is smoking a cigarette and staring out at the river.

"I had to put you to bed," she says, not looking back at me. This putting-me-to-bed development does not make Glori happy. I don't blame her. She has mothered me and I made her do it. I do not know where men get the idea that women like to mother the men they sleep with, and I do not know where men find such women who actually like to do so. I don't want to know. Mothering, as it is popularly defined, does not belong in bed.

"I guess you did."

"And I know it's goddamn Friday." She looks at her watch, still smoking, still not turning around to face me. "*Was* Friday."

At this, I look over Glori's shoulders, out her windows, and focus on the red, blurry sun coming up over the south walls of the valley. I have apparently slept all the way through Friday night. It is now Saturday morning.

"Was Friday," Glori repeats.

I do not ask her what time it is, exactly. It is inexactly late: too late, of course, to go out to dinner, too late for a great many things. To state the obvious: I fucked up. I fucked up at the rally, at the Cornhill, with Jodi Ramirez, with my father, and now with Glori. Glori wanted to spend Friday with me and now it is gone and I made it go away. And in making it go away, did I reverse the tide of her happiness?

"Have you been up all night?"

"I have," Glori says. "Do you know how that makes me feel?"

"I've reversed the tide of your happiness, haven't I?"

"I'm too tired for your shit, Lamar," Glori says. "Don't you know how tired I am?"

I do know: by the rough, phlegmy, choked-up sound of Glori's voice, I can tell that she is exhausted. I also know that she is too tired to hear me merely say, "I am sorry." As for me, I am not tired, maybe because I slept for so long. But I don't feel exactly rested, either. I feel dull. There is no other way to describe it. My heart, for instance, is not heavy but it is not light, either. My heart is definitely *there*. If you wake up and you are already aware of your heart, then you better do something to make it go away.

"Glori," I say. "Will you please come over here?"

"No."

"I'd like you to feel my heart," I say.

The strangeness of this request moves Glori to get up out of her chair, walk over to the bed, and lie down on top of the covers. She props herself up on her right elbow, hair down, staring at me with red, exhausted eyes.

"Feel my heart."

This she does, still staring.

"Is it still there?"

She nods. Hair down, eyes open and red.

"Damn," I say. "I was afraid of that."

Glori nods again, eyes still red, staring.

"I could give you an excuse," I say. "For last night."

"You could."

And so I tell Glori everything that happened yesterday: about my father and the rally and Jodi Ramirez and Andrew and Ms. West and the Cornhill and the list and the whys and wherefores of my drinking so much that I am accidentally in her bed, long after Friday is ruined and gone. I don't leave anything out. I even tell her that I made my father cry, maybe.

"You know what your problem is?" she asks.

I tell her that I would like to know. I truly would.

"Your problem is that you think you are better than other people. You believe that just because you're not as bad as Andrew Marchetti, just because you didn't cheat on *me*, that you are better than him."

Glori is on to something. I *do* think I'm better than Andrew Marchetti. And I am on to something, too. I would have thought that Glori would be outraged about what Andrew has done to Sheila, who is after all Glori's friend. But Glori doesn't mention Sheila. Either this means that Glori isn't surprised by how untrustworthy Andrew is and how cruel the world is in general, or it means that she doesn't care about Sheila just now, that first and foremost she cares

THE ORDINARY WHITE BOY   125

about herself. This self-interest doesn't make Glori seem selfish; it makes her seem strong.

"And it's not just Andrew Marchetti," she says. "You think you're better than everybody. Your uncle Eli for instance. You think you're better than him, don't you?"

"I do," I say. There is no point in telling Glori I don't believe I'm better than my uncle when I so obviously do.

"Why?" Glori asks. "Because he's in prison and you're not? Because he's an arsonist? Is that *it*?"

"That's some of it."

"Lamar, your uncle isn't the man who listened to me tell him how unhappy I might be, and your uncle's not the man who then got drunk on *my* rum in *my* apartment and passed out on me."

"OK."

"And you weren't too far off before," she says. "You are coming mighty close to reversing the tide of my happiness."

"I'm sorry."

"If you're not part of the solution, then you're part of the problem."

"Heard that."

"I might *already* be unhappy. I might just be too tired to realize it."

"I hope not."

"You left that rally to go to a *bar*. You lied to Jodi Ramirez and left her and her kids standing there to go to a fucking *bar*. I wonder if even your uncle would have done that."

"I know," I say. "It's unconscionable."

"You're not better than *anyone*."

"You're right," I say. "I'm ordinary."

"Shut up."

"OK."

"From where I'm sitting," she tells me, "Andrew Marchetti and your uncle are looking pretty good. From here, Andrew Marchetti and your uncle are a couple of crown princes."

"I can see your point."

"But I don't want you to be a prince, Lamar. This is my point. My point is that I don't mind having low expectations of you. I don't want much of anything. I just want you to be a little bit better. Can't you even do that for me?"

There is a little mother left in this request, but after all I've said and done, I can't really complain about being talked to like a little boy. I can be better, I tell her. I won't even try to be better. I will just *do* it.

"I hate to say it, Lamar, but we've nearly run out of reasons to stay together," Glori says, and then, inexplicably, she smiles. It is a very tired, very reserved smile, but I know it is the best I can hope for. The smile makes me want to say something excessively romantic.

"Glori," I say, "I am going to take it to the limit for you."

Why I make this particular promise, I could not tell you. I must have heard someone say it on television once. It is most embarrassing. Fortunately, Glori doesn't hear me: she's already asleep. I watch her. Watching her, I feel absurdly optimistic. If there is anything that can give you greater sense of false hope than giving the woman you love a little peace of mind after giving her a lot of pain and then watching all the residual mothering pour out of her as she falls asleep, finally and fully falls asleep with her hair spread out fanlike on the pillow in the still early Saturday morning, then I do not know what it is.

CHAPTER 11

I DO NOT take it to the limit, whatever the limit might be in this day and age. After I leave Glori's place, I go home, shower, eat some breakfast, and then turn on the television. The national news is on, and the woman at the news desk is doing a piece on a recent murder in Texas. The newswoman explains that three white men kidnapped a black man, shot him, tied his body to the back of their pickup truck, and dragged him around the back roads of east Texas until they were sure he was dead, that he was well beyond dead.

The newswoman says that three murderers were caught almost immediately after the black man's body was found.

I know what my reaction should be here. I should be reminded of Mark Ramirez's disappearance and what's at stake in my investigation of it. I should be reminded of how I abandoned Jodi Ramirez and how I need to make things right with her again. I should be outraged over the viciousness of the crime in Texas. I should be sick at the sight of the bloody corpse. I should be happy that the murderers have been caught and that they will be punished.

And I am all of these things.

But I am also confused.

I am confused because the murder in east Texas seems far more concrete, far more *real* to me than Mark Ramirez's disappearance, even though, of course, I know Mark and do not know the murder victim in Texas. Why is this? It's not only that the man in Texas is dead, definitely dead, and that I don't know what has happened to Mark yet. It's not just the extreme horror of it all: the camera shots of weeping relatives, the file photo of a Klan rally, the film of the black man's body being hoisted into the coroner's van. There is something else in the images they're showing on the television: a picture of the battered old truck, then the three blond, bearded, tattooed white men in shackles, then a still photo of the dead black man. The news shows these images over and over: truck, white men in shackles, dead black man; truck, white men in shackles, dead black man.

Then, I get it. Truck + white men in shackles = the dead black man. I am reminded of my uncle Bart's earlier request that I do the math. The black man's murder in Texas is real because his murder adds up, whereas Mark's disappearance doesn't add up at all.

And I want it to.

And so all my theorizing comes to this: I am sitting on my couch, bone-dry of original thought or complex worldview, and I desperately want Mark's disappearance to make sense, no matter what the consequences are for Jodi or her kids or anyone. Because I am sick of trying to be surprised by how the world works. I can no longer pretend otherwise. Yes, I want Mark Ramirez's disappearance to add up. And like my father and my uncle Bart, I want Eric Chisholm or someone like him to reveal himself and complete the equation.

In this fashion, I, Lamar Kerry, Jr., am finally faced with the ugly truth: I have become like my father, my uncle Bart. And that is not the worst of it. Is it possible that I am something worse than my father and my uncle Bart? After all, what am I saying here? In order for Mark to become real, does he have to be murdered like the man in Texas? It is a sentiment worthy of my uncle Eli. But then again, now that Glori has brought it to my attention, I'm not even sure that I'm any better than uncle Eli. As Jodi Ramirez and my father and Glori have all made perfectly clear, I am a fuckup who is no longer cute. And does a fuckup who continues to be a fuckup after he is no longer cute eventually become a dangerous fuckup? Isn't this exactly what my uncle Eli is: a dangerous fuckup? Am I any different than my uncle Eli?

I cannot say for sure that I am different.

These are all extremely tough epiphanies. My junior varsity high school football coach was fond of saying that when the going gets tough, the tough get going, by which he meant that the tough aren't going anywhere except back on the goddamned field to break their collarbones, which is what happened to me.

I am not tough, and I am going. I am going north.

I AM GOING north with Andrew Marchetti. It is his idea. He drops by my apartment as I am in the self-pitying aftermath of my epiphany.

"What do you want, Andrew?" I ask, letting him in my apartment.

"I want to be better."

"Get in line."

"I'm serious, Lamar." Andrew does look serious. He is certainly serious as he tells me that Sheila threw him out this morning, when he came home after being out all night. Andrew seems genuinely pained by his wife's reaction. He speaks of atonement, responsibility, a husband's sacred vows, and the like. He speaks of his father's rotten example and history repeating itself.

"But the shit stops here, Lamar. I am not my old man. I do not believe in the inevitability of history."

"I didn't think you did," I tell him.

"I mean it, Lamar. My father was a bad man, plain and simple. I don't want to become the same kind of man."

"Of course you don't."

"My father *never* would have worked in a prison," Andrew says. "He didn't have the *balls* to do the job I'm going to do."

"Whatever you say."

"Not that I'm not scared," Andrew says. "Because I am."

"What are you doing here, Andrew?"

"This is why I'm here," Andrew says. "I have a plan. The plan requires that we go north."

I tell him that I'm listening.

"We are going up north," he says, "and we are going to find out something about our true selves. Me, I'm going to go visit that prison. I start working there in a week, and I want to see it before I start." Andrew tells me that he's called the prison, and found out that there is a tour of the place, open to the public, that starts tonight at seven o'clock. Andrew says, "What kind of man do I have to be to work in a maximum-security prison? This is what I want to know. This is what I want to see. You, you can see whatever it is you need to see. The point is, when we come back, we're going to be better men. Much better men. We're going to be worth something when we come back."

I am, of course, already inclined to sympathize with Andrew's theory. If you fail to meet everyone's expectations, even your own, then you might as well go somewhere where you can hide from that failure. North, for instance. When you go into exile, you go north. Siberia, after all, is north. There are disappointed fathers, sad-eyed lovers, sick mothers, unsolved mysteries, and complicated racial and family politics in Siberia, maybe, but they are not mine.

"All right," I tell him. "Let's do it."

"Are you sure?" Andrew asks, surprised that I'm so easily won over to his plan. "What about Mark Ramirez? What about Glori? What about your parents?" Andrew is testing me. In this he is prudent. If you are looking for a traveling partner-in-exile, you better make sure he is a properly self-interested, cowardly son of a bitch.

"Are *you* sure?" I ask back. "What about your wife? Your family?"

"They'll be better off without me," Andrew says. "At least for the time being."

If this is not the whole truth, it is close to it. So I run into my bedroom and stuff some clothes in a backpack. Then, cowardly sons of bitches that we are, Andrew and I grab a cooler and a twelve-pack of beer out of the refrigerator and pack up his Chevy S-10 pickup and prepare to head north on the road to self-improvement.

IT SHOULD be obvious that I am the irresponsible one here, even though, like all deadbeats, I try to convince Glori that I am not. Andrew is outside, waiting in his truck, revving the engine; I am inside, on the phone, telling Glori that it would be irresponsible for me to stay even though I love her. I love you, I say, but I am no good for you or anyone right now. So I'm leaving you. When I get back, I tell her, I will be better. I promise.

"Get better, then," Glori says. She does not have any questions, demands, or threats. She just hangs up. It is obvious that Glori does not believe this stuff I'm saying.

It makes me sad, for an instant, knowing Glori thinks me a liar. For that instant I picture Glori staring at the phone and continuing our conversation. Life is short, she is saying, and you have just made it that much shorter. I don't so much hate you for shortening life as I do love you less than I could have. I have loved you and you have not taken advantage of that love. If you were smart, you would know that love dissolves into other, less impressive sentiments—mild affection, friendship, apathy—when it is not taken full advantage of. But you are not smart.

That is what Glori is saying, staring at the phone on a Saturday that I have ruined just like the Friday before.

It makes me sad.

Then, the instant of sadness is gone. After all, I am stepping outside the real world of consequence and conscience and into the world of self-imposed exile. When you are such an exile you can make yourself believe anything. One of the things I make myself believe, drinking beer in Andrew's truck as it climbs out of the valley, north into the Adirondacks, is that I am leaving Glori because it will be good for us. When I come back I will be a better man, and Glori and I will be together again, and life will be easy.

THREE

CHAPTER 1

FOR AN hour Andrew and I drive north, toward and then into the mountains. We don't speak much and we don't need to. I am happy until north of Piseco, when Andrew steers the car into a gravel pull-over, just past a causeway that joins Lake Pleasant and Sacandaga Lake.

"What's going on?"

"I'm going to do a little fishing before we head on up to the prison."

"You don't fish."

Andrew says that I'm wrong; he tells me that he has fished his entire life. Either I knew this about Andrew and forgot or he's lying. I suspect he is lying. I suspect that he has read a book about how someone like him, some lost, self-destructive Man in Crisis, was saved through fishing. Does this actually make any sense to anyone? If you can save yourself through fishing, then you probably were never very lost to begin with. And if you were really lost, you would not find the proper moral or spiritual compass by hooking a rainbow trout, even if you threw the trout back, which is what these soul-saving, angling orienteers all recommend. This doesn't make any sense either. If you are not going to eat the fish, then you might as well save the fish the agony of being caught and save yourself somewhere else.

I voice these opinions, and others, but all my bitching does no good. Andrew gets his rod and his tackle box out of the back of the pickup, and he walks back to the causeway, leaving me behind. It is not a particularly busy causeway—there is not much car traffic—but Andrew does have some company: there are three fishermen already on the causeway, wearing their Orvis vests and holding their state-of-the-art fiberglass rods and their souped-up jitterbug lures. These men are at least twice as old as Andrew, but Andrew is bald enough and doughy enough to look like their peer. Andrew nods to the three others and they nod back. It is a community of men but it is an ambivalent community. Clearly, the four of them feel validated that they are not all alone in the soul saving and in their expensive gear that they bought at their Orvis fishing clinics. But Orvis told them that if they paid their four hundred dollars and bought their gear and took their lessons, then they would be able to go out into nature and fish. Now, they are in nature and nature looks a lot like an Orvis clinic. This is a letdown, obviously, but they are here to fish and after all it is *important* that they do so. So they fish, in resentful, staggered distances from each other on the causeway.

Me, I set up a folding chair in the truck bed and grab a warm beer. My attention drifts, lazily, from the quartet of Orvises, to the blue herons soaring overhead, their spidery legs dragging behind them, to the east shore of Lake Pleasant, which is congested with rusting trailers, crumbling cabins, and all the other sorry second homes of the lower middle class. Finally, I focus on three pickup trucks parked next to Andrew's. Looking at the trucks, I realize that I have become part of a community of women. This community is composed of what must be the three wives of the three other men. The wives are sitting in folding chairs in the back of their men's pickup trucks, drinking beer.

"I'm Bea," one of them says. She is in her sixties, I'm guessing, and there is a neglected pile of yarn in her lap and a beer in her right hand. Like the other two women, Bea has white, tightly curled hair; she's wearing a white sweatshirt with an intricate, unidentifiable sequined design on the chest. It is a sweatshirt, sure enough, but it is clearly an expensive sweatshirt. The other two women are wearing shiny matching workout tops and bottoms. These getups, I'm guessing by their impressive shininess, are expensive, too. These three women have reached an age where casual and formal clothes meet, and the common ground is glitter.

"Good to meet you. I'm Lamar." I raise my beer at Bea and she raises hers back.

"Doing some fishing, Lamar?" Bea asks.

"*He's* doing some fishing," I say, gesturing with my beer in the general direction of Andrew. "*I* am in exile."

This gets a big laugh from Bea and the other two women. "I know just what you mean," Bea says. "We're in exile, too."

It turns out that the three of them—the other two women are named Helen and C.J.—have been dragged around by their husbands for years, from lake to lake, causeway to causeway, up and down the Adirondacks. The three women have never even met each other before, but wherever they go it's the same. Their husbands, each of them says, are looking for something, something they apparently cannot find in Albany, Schenectady, or Amsterdam. Albany, Schenectady, and Amsterdam are exactly the *problem,* the men tell their wives. So the men pack up their trucks and look up north for solutions to the problem of small-city life. But the men are scared to look alone, so they bring their wives. The wives are supposed to look at the mountains and be at peace. What the wives *actually* do is sit in the truck, commiserate with each other, and wait for their lesser halves' soul-search parties to pack it in for the night. It is obvious from the way Bea, C.J., and Helen talk that the wives themselves are not looking for something. If anything, they are looking to be left alone as they slip slowly into old age. But within the parameters of their marriages, being left alone is not an option. So they get dragged into exile while their husbands fish and look.

"They," Bea says, hooking her thumb in the direction of the four fishing Orvises, "think we like being in exile."

"They don't know what they're talking about," I say.

"They sure don't," Bea says.

"The fish know more than they do," says C.J. "The fish are god-damned geniuses."

No one disagrees.

I don't tell Bea, C.J., or Helen, but I'm discovering that this particular moment in this particular exile is turning out to be not half bad, although not in the way any of the Orvises might think. Unexpectedly, I am learning something as I sit here in the truck bed, drinking this one beer slowly and talking with these women at least twice my age as the summer sky dies and cools a little. I am learning that these women-in-exile are better company, much better company, than their soul-searching, self-involved, son-of-a-bitching men. I learn that their husbands are looking for something because they are spoiled, and they are the ones who have done the spoiling. They have pampered themselves and now they are looking for something that will straighten them out. The women are not spoiled, and they have not had the chance to be spoiled. They have found all they need to know, maybe all there is to know, without even announcing the search. Looking for something, indeed, is what I learn.

But there is a limit to my learning here and I know it. I may be temporarily in a community of women, and I may prefer the community to my own. But in the final accounting I am a man, on the run with another man, and like it or not I am spoiled. Like it or not,

I, too, am looking for something to straighten me out. To be true, if I could go back and choose to be not spoiled, to live the hard, smarten-up-quick life of these women, I would not choose to do so. That is the fundamental difference here between myself and the women whose company I prefer: if you were given the choice to be spoiled or not to be spoiled—which the four Orvises and myself have been given and which Bea, C.J., and Helen have not—then you are already spoiled, by virtue of having the choice in the first place. Once you have that choice, then it is just a matter of time before you buy the fishing gear, drive north, and make your one-woman, sequined search party sit in the truck while you look for life the way it was before you had the choice, which was never. I am sorry when Andrew comes back, but he does come back. And once Andrew shows up at the truck, holding his fishing pole and his tackle box and smiling like he has just learned something meaningful and he can't wait to *share* it with me, we are once again two pampered men on the lam, in the company of each other. There is no helping it.

"I caught two trout," he tells me. Bea, C.J., and Helen are looking at him, waiting for Andrew to introduce himself. But Andrew either ignores them or doesn't see them, I cannot tell which.

"Super," I say. "Where are they?"

"I did the right thing," he tells me. "I let them go."

This is his meaningful news. The meaningful news draws another big laugh from the heretofore ignored or unseen wives.

"They always let them go," Bea says. "I've never tasted fresh fish in my life."

Andrew hears this comment and finally looks in the general direction of Bea's voice. He smiles thinly, uncertainly at Bea, who from Andrew's angle is probably just a soft shadow against the bright backdrop of the sky and the truck. The beads on Bea's sweatshirt catch and reflect the late afternoon sun. Andrew nods in Bea's direction, but still doesn't greet her or introduce himself.

"Let's go," Andrew says to me, turning his back on the women and throwing his stuff next to me in the truck bed. It's obvious that Andrew does not know what Bea is talking about. What can he think she is talking about?

What she is talking about is that it is obviously time for the two of us to go. This we do. I get down from the truck bed and into the cab. I don't even shake hands with the three women. I don't even say good-bye.

ANDREW STOPS at a Nice 'N' Easy to get gas and directions to the prison. So like all boys who run away from home, I go to a pay phone and call my parents to tell them I am all right and not to worry about me. Of course, I've been gone for less than six hours. My parents probably don't even know that I'm gone yet. But still.

My mother answers the phone.

"Guess where I am?" I ask her.

"Where are you, Lamar?"

"I'm in a campground in the middle of the Adirondacks," I tell her. "Don't worry about me."

"I'm not worried about you," she says.

"It's a state campground," I tell her.

"Even better," she says. "I'm still not worried."

My mother would be worried, maybe, if she knew that I am not in a state campground at all, that I am on my way to a maximum-security prison and then who knows where after that. But I don't tell my mother any of this because I don't want her to worry. I also don't tell her any of this because I'm afraid she won't be worried at all, which would be disappointing. There is no point in running away from home if no one is going to worry about you.

"How's Dad?"

"Your father is fine," she says. "Lamar, tell me the truth: Are you running away?"

I tell my mother that I am not running away, even though this is not really the truth and she probably knows it. "I am having an *adventure*," I tell her.

"Can I tell your father that? He's always wanted you to have an adventure. It will make him so happy."

I tell my mother that she can.

"Wonderful," she says.

"How are *you*?"

"I am me," she says. I have no idea what this means, and neither does she, I am guessing. *Me*, for my mother and her erratic synapses, unpredictable body parts, and intrusive medical procedures, is a wait-and-see proposition. "I'll be me when you get back, too."

"I hope so." The bright light of my adventure flickers and dims a little with the thought of my mother and her wheelchair and her spinal tap, and I feel a fear, an unreasonable fear that I won't ever see her again. Suddenly, I wonder if this trip is such a hot idea; suddenly I really am a boy, a scared little boy who misses his mother, who can't imagine life without her, and who will run back to her in a hot second if she asks him to. "Seriously," I say. "How *are* you?"

"Don't be a sap, Lamar. You're having an *adventure*."

Then she says good-bye and we hang up.

My mother is right. I am running away from difficulty because it is scary and I am calling this flight an *adventure* and it feels good. Besides, you cannot run away from home on the doorstep of adulthood and then find yourself in the middle of the Adirondack Mountains, your belly already full of beer and on your way to a maximum-security prison, and then not have an adventure. If you can't have an adventure under these kinds of ideal circumstances, then there is obviously something wrong with you.

CHAPTER 2

WE DRIVE to the prison, which Andrew tells me is about ten minutes away. I'm excited, thrilled even, at the prospect of going to the
prison, because I've never seen one before, and isn't this the point
of my going on this kind of adventure in the first place? Isn't the
whole idea of the trip for me to see something that I have never
seen, to get away from the deadening sameness of ordinary life? In
fact, this wasn't the idea of my trip, but my conversation with my
mother has convinced me otherwise. Just talking to my mother has
gotten me jazzed *up*, so much so that I have this crazy idea that I'm
doing this all for her sake. My mother is in a wheelchair, my theory
goes, trapped in the same body in the same wheelchair in the same
house in the same town day after day. My mother obviously can't
have an adventure, so I will have one for her. And while I'm at it,
why don't I also have an adventure for Glori and my father and
Jodi Ramirez and anyone else who's trapped in a job, a body, a
town, a *life*? I actually think this stuff, and I also convince myself

that I'm doing something important here, something absolutely unique.

"Faster, Andrew, faster," I say, and then clap my hands.

Andrew doesn't say anything. He just keeps driving at the speed limit, forty-five miles per hour. There is something wrong with him, clearly. Andrew is hunched over the steering wheel as if he's just been kicked in the stomach. His face is baking soda white and his right eye is twitching and he's gritting his teeth. Andrew is obviously trying very hard to empty his face of all expression. In doing so, he comes off as a man who looks afraid to look afraid. The drive is over soon enough and we're at the prison and Andrew still hasn't quite conquered his face.

"Are you all right?" I ask. I have known Andrew for over fifteen years, and I have seen him tired, happy, hungry, peeved, outright angry, sullen, and, of course, drunk. But I have never seen him like this before.

"I'm fine." The prison looks like a prison: from where we're sitting in the truck we can see a gray tower and high gray walls topped with rolls of razor wire. The prison also looks cold; I don't know how else to describe it. There is a lazy breeze blowing and it is warm out, agreeably so: it is the sort of weather people who have never been to the tropics (I haven't) call "tropical." But just looking at the prison gives me the shivers. "I'm fine," Andrew repeats. He sits up straight, adopts what is supposed to be a military bearing, hops out of the truck, and marches toward the entrance. I follow. At the entrance there is a man, a boy really, a probably nineteen-year-old boy who is wearing a uniform that is somewhere between military and police. The boy is holding a clipboard. We tell him we're there for the tour. He makes some sort of mark on the clipboard and then lets us in.

I HAVE been to institutional openings before: elementary schools, hospital wings, community college gymnasiums, public libraries.

But as I said, I have never been to a prison. As I wait for the tour to begin I remember my mother wanting me to have an adventure for her, and I let my imagination get away from me completely. I expect to be horrified—iron bars, sinister mustachioed guards, and violent clanging lockdowns. I expect to see something that I have never seen before.

But I don't see much of anything. For one, the prison is empty. There are no actual prisoners and no guards working there yet, just the twenty or so of us on the tour and the guide himself, who is a frail, meek prison liaison wearing an L.L. Bean windbreaker and brand-new blue jeans. As a result, the prison is empty of actual menace, too. Once the tour begins, I either lose Andrew, or he loses me. I am near the front of the tour, so I figure he must be in the back. The twenty of us—ordinary citizens all, curious about the final resting place of our tax dollars, even more curious about life on the other side of the penal fence—lag behind the tour guide as he tells us how much more humane prisons are than they were in the past, how the Hamilton (this is what he calls it, as if it were a luxury apartment building with uniformed doormen) is escape-proof, and how the Hamilton will be a vital part of the local economy. We are shown the gleaming white cells and the sterile, sanitized cafeteria and the whitewashed exercise yard. It feels like we are taking a tour of an extraordinarily security-conscious nursing home. Up close even the razor wire doesn't look dangerous; it just looks new, like it has just arrived in the mail, just been taken out of its protective plastic packaging. I close my eyes and try to hear the horrible sounds of prison life, the shouts and screams and alarms and grunts; I try to imagine what it would be like for Andrew to work in a place like this, for my uncle Eli to live in a place like this. But all I can hear is the squeaking of our moderately priced shoes and sneakers as we walk down the perfectly clean corridors. I feel like I could be anywhere in America: a mall in Kansas, a nursing home in New Mexico. Is there nowhere in America that isn't exactly the same as anywhere else? This is the way I feel. I also feel an idiot for being so jazzed up about seeing the prison in the first place. But mostly, I feel like I've once again let down my mother, my father, Glori, Jodi Ramirez, everyone.

After the tour is over we are directed to the front gate. The tour guide even buzzes us out, "releases" us two-by-two, for effect. I find myself walking next to a fit, middle-aged white man, fifty or so years old, with thinning brown hair and a thick, graying mustache. He looks like the kind of man you wouldn't mind having as your father-in-law.

"I didn't think it would be so clean," he says.

"America is moving hopelessly toward sameness," I tell him. "I'm not afraid to say it."

"You might be right," he says, nodding agreeably, the good-natured, reasonable father-in-law who doesn't especially want to argue with his opinionated son-in-law. "I imagine it'll be different once it's all full."

"I don't imagine *anything*," I say. "It's terrifying."

He nods again as we pass through the prison gates and step out into a spectacular orange sunset. The model father-in-law and I stop to admire the sight of the fat, bulging orb hanging so low in the sky, its blurry edges streaking and flaring against the dark blue flaking clouds. It should make me feel better, being out of the antiseptic prison and into the beautiful glowing world. But it does not. It seems that you might be able to keep the beautiful world safe from the prisoners, but not from the prison itself.

"It is terrifying," I say again.

The model father-in-law smiles. He extends his hand and we shake the way men do when they pretend to understand each other, and then we part.

I walk to the truck; Andrew joins me a minute later. He has lost his military bearing entirely: he walks the way my uncle Bart did in the months following his hip replacement surgery. Andrew takes the truck keys out of his pocket and hands them to me.

"Could you drive?" he asks.

"Sure," I say. "Where to?"

"Wherever. A bar."

"OK."

And so we get in the truck and I drive north. Andrew and I don't say anything. Even without saying anything, I know that Andrew has seen a potential for violence, danger, adventure, *something* in the prison that I have not. I know this because after five minutes of silent driving I hear a strange repetitive noise. I look over to the passenger seat and Andrew is slowly and deliberately bouncing his forehead off the dashboard—*thump, thump, thump*—as if keeping time to a song that I can't hear.

CHAPTER 3

WE PASS several bars, but I don't stop driving until we get to a log cabin joint with the promising name of the Stumble Inn. From the outside it looks like the kind of bar where you could easily get into a brawl, or end up in some cinder-block local hoosegow, or get in your truck after the bar has closed and drive drunkenly into the Ausable Chasm and then live to laugh about it. It looks like the kind of place where you could not help but say the wrong things to the right women, or the right things to the wrong. And I figure Andrew needs all of this to happen if he's to forget about the maximum-security prison and if we're to continue on with our adventure.

But the Stumble Inn is not what I had in mind. First, you should know that while the Stumble Inn may look like a log cabin from the outside, inside it is something else completely. Inside there are no logs at all, just a graying formica horseshoe bar with rust rings on the surface. The ceilings and walls in the Stumble Inn are made entirely of unfinished particle board and are covered with old, ratty

NASCAR posters and beer lights from brands of beer that no longer even exist, I don't think. The Stumble Inn looks less like a bar you might find adventure in, and more like the clubhouse you abandon when you are twelve years old.

Another thing about the Stumble Inn: it is *light*. Both ceiling lights are on, plus those obsolete beer lights, all of them bouncing off that light-colored particle board. It is like Andrew and I are sitting inside an eighty-watt bulb.

"It is blinding in here," Andrew says. He looks a bit steadier than he did back in the truck: his eye isn't twitching; his face isn't any paler than normal. There aren't even any marks on his forehead from his beating it against the dashboard. He doesn't look as petrified as he did, but he isn't what you would call happy, either.

"It's not so bad," I say, trying to make the best of it, trying to get Andrew and his mind away from whatever he saw in the prison.

"You could read in here. You could do surgery."

"It's not so bad," I say, and then, oddly, I make a sweeping gesture with my left hand, as if to invite Andrew to survey the bar. We do. It is empty except for us and the bartender, a beefy, bearded guy in a red flannel shirt and a John Deere hat who somehow hasn't gotten around to bringing us a beer yet. Finally he does. Our choices are Utica Club in a can or a Canadian beer named, for some reason, Old Vienna. Old Vienna comes in midget bottles that are too dainty to be conducive to any kind of adventure. I take the can. So does Andrew.

"It's not so bad," I say.

"Give me a break," Andrew tells me. He chugs the rest of his beer, slams the can on the bar, and as in the movies, motions with his index finger for the bartender to give him another. "Give me a fucking *break*."

So I give him a break and don't try to make the bar any better than it actually is. We sit there, silently, and drink beer after beer.

We watch the hirsute bartender pop open one of those tiny Canadian beers and drink it down in one gulp, pinky lifted, much in the manner of a steroided English matriarch at tea time. The bartender immediately opens a second beer and drinks that one, too, his pinky again lifted against the backdrop of his ratty red flannel shirt and his John Deere hat and his absolutely gigantic hands.

"Tell me," I say, once the bartender is out of earshot. "What is it that you saw in that prison that scared you so much?"

In our fifteen years of friendship, this is the first time Andrew and I have had what might be called a heart-to-heart. I feel strange even asking him such a straightforward, intrusive question. But Andrew seems to be ready for the question and the heart-to-heart, both.

"I saw big black guys," Andrew says without hesitation.

"Say again?"

"I saw enormous black guys with barbed wire tattoos around their big knotty biceps," he says. "I saw them all together in the exercise yard, all hunched down together like in a football huddle. I saw them inside their cells, whispering something to me, I don't know what. I saw them in the laundry room, smoking cigarettes."

"They don't let people smoke in the Hamilton," I say. This is one of the things I learned on the tour.

"That's what I'm talking about. They're in the laundry room smoking cigarettes, and I'm supposed to tell them to stop, but I don't. Because I'm scared of them, of what they'll do to me, and they know it."

"You don't sound scared," I say. And he doesn't. Me, I get little ulceric waves of pain just listening to Andrew. But Andrew doesn't sound scared at all.

"I'm fucking terrified," he says. "I'm terrified because one day I'm going to have to tell them to stop smoking their cigarettes. And then they're going to stab me."

"With their cigarettes?"

"Cigarettes, sharpened toothbrushes, switchblades, nail files, whatever."

"You only scared of the black guys?" I ask.

"I'm scared of all of them," he says. "But especially the black guys."

"I understand," I say, and I do. Or at least the racial theorist in me understands. And as the racial theorist, I nearly attempt to explain away Andrew's fears for him. I nearly say to him that he's more afraid of the black guys because he doesn't know any black guys. But I suspect Andrew knows this, and I also suspect that simply knowing why he's afraid of black men in particular isn't going to make the fear go away. So I make the racial theorist in me disappear and let the lifelong friend take over. "Listen," I say. "Let's just get out of here. Let's keep driving. Tonight we sleep in the truck; tomorrow, we keep driving. You can fish some more and I will sit in the truck and pass the time with the wives-in-exile. I will compliment them on their sequined sweatshirts, and you will pull in the trout hand over fist. And when you catch the fish, we are going to *eat* them. We are going to eat them and we are not going to feel guilty about it. We're going to have a good time."

"We could do that," Andrew says.

"Those fish are going to taste *great*."

"But what about the prison?" Andrew asks. "I have a *job* there. I made a commitment."

"Forget the prison. Forget the job."

"I'd like to," Andrew says. "But that's what my father would have done. He would have forgotten about the prison and his job. He would have backed out of his commitment at the last minute. That's exactly the kind of irresponsible thing he would do. Did do."

Andrew is most likely right about his father. I don't want to pretend otherwise. So I say the only thing I can, the only thing that Andrew wants me to say.

"Forget your father."

It is the right thing to say. What a satisfying thing it is to absolve someone of the obligation to remember. I feel almost holy.

"What county are we in?" Andrew asks the bartender, who is staring off into space at the other end of the bar. Andrew has an inspired look on his face; you can very nearly see the glowing lightbulb hovering above his head.

"Hamilton County."

"Hamilton County," Andrew says. "My father never was in Hamilton County, I bet. He never went any farther away than Utica. I'm already doing something he never did."

This is a pathetic piece of rationalization, but I don't say this to Andrew—mostly because I, too, am guilty of the same kind of pathetic rationalizations. "That's right," I say. "You're nothing like your father."

"Forget him," Andrew says.

And so we do. We forget Andrew's father and we forget the black men, and like the ordinary white boys we are we get spectacularly drunk and make a big production out of forgetting all the things we are afraid of. We put the Stones on the jukebox and shout over Mick Jagger's singing and play air guitar when air guitar is called for. We get into loud, theatrical arguments over professional athletes whom we care nothing about. If there were anyone else in the Stumble Inn we would try to pick fights with them, or seduce them, or both. But there is no one else, and this makes us even more desperate in our high times.

Finally, it is two in the morning, and the bartender wants to close up. He wants us to get our asses off our bar stools and to close the door behind us on our way out. And in this way, we find a focus for our desperation. We will refuse to leave the bar. We will pick a fight with the bartender and we will lose the fight and will wake up faces bruised and noses bloodied, and in this way we will have some proof of our adventure.

"No way," I say. "We're not leaving. We won't do it."

"We won't do it," Andrew says.

The bartender has one of those tiny beers in one hand, a mop in the other. I think I see a smile crease the dirty brown mask of his overgrown, mountain-man beard.

"You'll do it," he says.

And before we know it, he puts down his mop and his beer, spins us around, pushes us out the door, and shuts it behind us. He is the father and we are his sons and he has put us to *bed*. We have been manhandled and have no bruises or blood to show for it.

"What happened?" Andrew asks.

"We've been manhandled," I say. Add this to the list of things we try to forget as we climb into the truck and pass out.

CHAPTER 4

SO WE continue to drive north, crisscrossing the Adirondacks, and the farther we drive the further we slip into disappointment. It shouldn't be this way. Now that Andrew has been liberated from the prison, we should let loose. We should be carefree, and we want to be, we try to be, but it all feels so desperate, so sad. Each day is the same. Each day we wake up badly hungover from the night before; each day we feel vaguely guilty, not because we were drunk and wild the night before, but because we weren't drunk and wild enough to make us forget all the people and things we are running away from. Each day, we drive into the nearest town—Inlet, Long Lake, Keene, St. Regis—to get something to eat. Each town has an old, fading red-brick high school and unpruned forsythia bushes in the overgrown, unmowed municipal park, and a regal white mansion that now serves as the Folts Home. In each town the Folts Home's front lawn is carefully manicured, dotted with empty green plastic chairs, next to which sit all the docile, withering old invalids in their wheelchairs. Each town has its crumbling downstreet, thriving bars, and its one sorry daily newspaper—the Inlet *Telegram,* the Long Lake *Herald,* the Keene *Evening Times.* Each town has a river, a beautiful, wild, churning river where Andrew fishes and broods about how guilty he feels about the night before and life in general. While he fishes, I sit in the truck bed and drink beer and talk with the wives-in-exile and brood about how guilty I feel about the night before and life in general. Then, at night, we go to bars to try to forget our guilt by getting drunk—but not drunk enough, never drunk enough—until we're kicked out at two in the morning by a big hillbilly bartender with a one-syllable name: Ted, Bud, Sam.

The only difference from town to town is that the farther north the town, the more permanently it is on the fringes of the world, and therefore that much closer to complete failure. St. Regis, the last town we get to, is far enough on the fringes of the world that its citizens haven't yet moved from bold ugly racism to apathy: the newspaper police docket is full of felony arrests for public drunkenness and assault and battery, the result of fistfights and major vicious brawls between men with local white names and men with foreign Spanish names. Also, I read in the paper that the town's one lumber company, its largest employer, went under three years ago after several years of layoffs. Unemployment is ruinously high; or rather it was high. I read in the same newspaper article that in a week the majority of the town will be employed by the Hamilton Maximum-Security Prison, the prison Andrew is supposed to be working at, which is almost two hours south of here.

It is in St. Regis that things change for Andrew and me. First, we decide to get a room at The Traveler's Rest Motel on the outskirts of town. Our room has a rusty sink and rusty tap water and no cable TV, but Andrew says it doesn't matter; he says he feels crappy enough as it is and he can't stand to sleep one more night in the truck. And since he's paying (he pretty much pays for everything; I'm completely broke and have been the entire trip), I say, "Fine."

So we get our motel room, get something to eat, get in the truck, and drive to the St. Regis River. Andrew fishes and I stare dumbly into space. This is what happens when you slip into the pattern of drinking and feeling guilty and scared and drinking some more to forget the guilt and the fear: you get dumb. You get dumb so that, hopefully, you forget what it was like to be smart. You get dumb so you forget all the people you're hurting by being so dumb.

But even dumb people get tired of staring off into space; even dumb people get tired of watching other dumb people fish. And so in the early afternoon I decide to go for a long walk, and a half hour into my walk something horrible happens. Or rather, a horrible thing has already happened and I stumble upon its even more horrible ramifications. A half hour away from the river, I come upon a farm accident. A tractor has tipped over on its driver. I walk to about twenty feet away from the accident scene. It is not difficult to figure out what has happened here: the man was working his fields and running the tractor a little too fast when he hit a slight slope in the field, and tipped the tractor over upon himself. As I mentioned, my grandfather died in a similar accident. It is not an uncommon accident at all, although it is the first time I've seen one firsthand. Both of the man's legs are caught underneath the tractor and he is screaming for someone to get the tractor off him. The two paramedics are screaming at each other to get something—I don't know what—from the ambulance. The three migrant workers, who are trying to push the tractor off what must be their boss and who are covered in the blood from his crushed legs, are screaming at each other in Spanish.

The noise and panic, the opera of screaming, must be contagious, because I nearly start screaming.

But there is an even more horrible part. The screaming stops, just stops as if the whole accident and rescue effort are hooked up to a public address system and someone has pulled the plug. The stopping of the noise is so abrupt—like an amusement ride that comes to a jerking halt when it's not supposed to—that I nearly vomit. A little trailing noise—a moan or a not fully formulated question—comes from the man underneath the tractor. Then nothing. One of the paramedics jumps up and runs to the back of the ambulance and then the other one yells after him, tells him to forget it. The remaining paramedic says something to the migrant workers and they walk away, toward the barn and silo at the south end of the field. The other paramedic goes around to the front of the ambulance. I hear him talking on the CB.

I walk up to where the other paramedic is still squatting next to the man's body.

"God, what happened?" I ask him.

"Where'd you come from?" It occurs to me that the paramedics and the farmworkers were too busy to notice me standing there, twenty feet away, watching.

"I was walking by and saw the accident," I say. "Did he just *die*?"

"He had a heart attack," the paramedic says.

"Can people just *die* like that?"

"Some people can."

I sneak a quick look at the man on the ground. He looks to be a middle-aged man with a big, curly head of hair. His whole bottom half is still underneath the tractor, flickers of blood licking his belt line and little streams of blood on the ground. The man's face is so waxy, so sickly yellow, that it is difficult to think of him as a real person my parents' age who was screaming a minute before. Instead, he looks more like a mannequin made up to represent that real screaming person. This is a strange, inappropriate thought to be having, so I look away from the dead man. His baseball hat is on the ground next to him. I pick it up, hand it to the paramedic.

"What do I want with *that*?" he says. The paramedic—who is about my age—is very upset: his face is red and he's pulling and then smoothing his hair, and sniffling a little bit. This behavior surprises me. I had assumed all paramedics were stoics by profession, if not nature.

"Sorry," I say, and put the hat back down where it was. I don't know what else to say, and so I tell him, "My grandfather died in a combine accident. I never even met him. He died before I was born." A pause. "My father says he was a great man."

"We would have had to amputate his legs, at least," the paramedic says, trying to compose himself.

"Sure," I say.

"He most likely would have died from the blood loss even if he didn't have a heart attack."

I don't say anything to this piece of rationalization. There is a small space of emotion growing between myself and the paramedic, the kind of distance that grows between people who have seen the same thing and yet who have different reactions to that event, who feel different levels of implication. The emotion I feel toward the paramedic is something between sympathy and resentment.

"Where'd the three men go?" I ask, trying to fill up the space between us with information.

"They went to get another tractor so we can pull this one off him."

"I see."

We fall quiet again, quiet enough to hear the other paramedic still talking on the CB, speaking in jargon and code to the dispatcher, who is asking him to repeat the jargon and code, which he does. The whole exchange seems very cold to me. It is the first time I have actually seen someone die and I feel very cold myself, because now that the man is dead, I feel less sad, much less like screaming than I did when he was dying. Is it normal to feel like this after you have seen someone die? To feel this cold? The only person who does not seem cold is the paramedic squatting on the ground in front of me, whom I'm starting to resent for his emotion and his unprofessionalism.

"There was nothing you could have done," I say as I begin to make my retreat back to the river, to the bed of Andrew's truck. "It wasn't your fault."

"Jesus, what the hell is that supposed to mean?" the paramedic asks, slipping back into a fit of hair pulling. "I *know* it wasn't my fault. Is that supposed to make me feel any better?"

And would you believe that I find this confession the most horrible part of the accident? Innocence is meaningless, this is what the paramedic teaches me. What an awful thing to say; what a terrible lesson to learn. It occurs to me while I'm walking back to the river that I must be the last person on this earth to realize that innocence is meaningless. Glori, who is innocent of her old boyfriend's death, knows this. My father, who is innocent of his father's death and his brother's crime and my ordinariness, knows this. My mother, who is innocent of her own illness, knows this. Mark Ramirez, who is innocent of being kidnapped or worse, knows this. Jodi Ramirez, who is innocent of everything except marrying someone who isn't white, knows this. The dead man under the tractor, who is probably innocent of all real evil and is guilty only of driving the tractor a little too *fast* when he shouldn't have, knows this, if he knows anything anymore.

Me, I have not known that innocence is meaningless, and I've just watched a man die, and what now? After all, I am innocent of so many things: infidelity, murder, kidnapping, arson, ambition, so many meaningless things. Of course, I am *guilty* of many things as well, and have counted on my innocence to redeem that guilt, or at least to protect myself from it. But if innocence is meaningless, then you are guilty of everything. And if you are guilty of everything, then what do you do to find meaning and redemption? Where do you go for self-protection? And more immediately, where do I go to protect myself from the image of the waxy, bloody corpse wedged underneath his own tractor?

I go back to Andrew's truck, lie down in the bed, put the newspaper over my face, try to go to sleep.

CHAPTER 5

WHEN I wake up it is already early evening. My memory of the farm accident and the dead man and my worthless innocence is fuzzy—not like a dream, but like a memory of a real thing that I wish were a dream. My jaw hurts from grinding my teeth in my sleep. I sit up in the truck bed, see that Andrew is still fishing in the river. I grab a beer, and as my head clears I become aware that I am not alone. I have company, but I am not in the company of women, as is usually the case. This time, I am in the company of two men who are watching their buddy fish next to Andrew on the bank of the St. Regis. The two men are sitting in the bed of a black S-10 pickup truck. The truck is almost identical to Andrew's.

"Nice truck," I say, tipping my beer in their direction.

"I know it's a nice truck," one of them says. He has a beard; the other man in the truck and the one fishing are clean shaven. All of them are about thirty, thirty-five, forty years old. All of them have short hair, cropped close to their heads much like mine, and are wearing relatively decent-looking flannel shirts. All of them are also drinking beer, including the fisherman. None of them is intimidatingly big, nor sinisterly runtish, nor dangerously hillbilly. In other words, they fit my definition of normal, and I'm not real scared of them, despite the bearded guy's possible hostility.

"Your truck looks the same as his," the clean-shaven one says. "That's what he means."

"I know what he means," the bearded one says. "Is that what you mean?" he asks me.

I tell him that it is.

"I *know* it's a nice truck," he says again, tipping his beer at me to show me that there are no hard feelings yet. "It's my nice truck."

That said, we sit there and watch our men fish for a while. Unlike the wives and their soul-searching husbands, I am guessing that these men live around here. They seem perfectly at home, sitting in their truck, watching the deep, black river roar by, much too comfortable to actually be men on the lam. This being their turf, I decide not to speak again until spoken to. I will act comfortable and watch the river, as it appears to be the thing to do.

After a minute or two of silent, contemplative beer drinking, I am asked something.

"That your Tommy?" the bearded truck owner asks me.

"My what?"

"Is that Tommy *yours*?" he asks again and points at Andrew, who is fishing thoughtfully in the St. Regis, twenty feet away from the other man.

"That's the Tommy I'm stuck with," I tell him. I have no idea what we are talking about, but I am smart enough to know that when you are on someone else's turf and you are spoken to in code, then you talk back in code, too. "That *your* Tommy?"

"That's my brother."

"What's his name?"

"His name?" Apparently this is the wrong question. The man with the beard seems offended.

"I don't have a brother," I say by way of apology, which the bearded man seems to accept.

"Martin," he says after a few more minutes of silent drinking.

"Your brother's name," I guess.

"*My* name," he says slowly, deliberately, as if he's just realizing that I might be retarded. "*His* name is Tommy," pointing at his brother, who has just caught a fish—a perch, I think. Tommy lifts the lid of his white Styrofoam cooler, puts the fish inside, and closes the lid. I see Andrew cast a dismayed sidelong glance at his unwanted companion and his Styrofoam cooler. Andrew himself doesn't have a cooler; he has a leather pouch, which smells of leather, not fish.

"I understand," I say.

"My name is Russell," the other guy says. He explains simply that they're all three of them brothers.

"I'm Lamar."

"Lamar does what?" Martin asks. Despite this sinister-sounding, oddly phrased question, Martin doesn't sound so much aggressive as curious. So I answer the question.

"I work for my father."

Martin doesn't respond immediately. So I wait. It is getting to be night and it will be clear and cold—the distant black-and-blue, star-cluttered sky tells me so—and so I put on a jacket, waiting for Martin or Russell to divulge some personal information.

"We don't work for anyone's father anymore," Martin finally says.

"What do you mean?"

"We got fired," Martin says. "We got fired because of Tommy."

Martin doesn't elaborate, but Russell tells me that three Fridays ago they took the day off from their jobs on the Franklin County road crew to watch Tommy fish while they drank beer in the truck.

They didn't call the foreman of the Franklin County road crew to say they *weren't* coming to work, Russell admits, but then again, they never bothered calling in sick before, either, and there had been no repercussions. Until now. As for Tommy himself, Russell tells me with disgust that Tommy doesn't work at all; he just fishes. When he and Martin went to work on Monday, they had already been fired. Unemployment being as high as it is up here, the foreman had no problem replacing them immediately.

"Good job?" I ask Russell, knowing that it is probably not a good job.

"Only job," Martin says.

"Only job," Russell says.

"I'll kill whoever it is who took our jobs," Martin says, and then, for some reason, stares right at me. "I truly will," he says.

"I believe you," I say, and I do.

Just then Tommy returns to the truck. He has a cooler full of fish, packed in ice, which he places in the truck bed.

"You know what Lamar likes?" Martin asks Tommy, pointing in my direction. Tommy, who is obviously Martin and Russell's younger brother, is a good-looking guy, maybe five years older than myself, with sandy brown hair, a ruddy, sun-chapped face, and a small scar under his left eye. He doesn't look like a Tommy at all; he looks more like a young, genuinely rugged version of Robert Redford.

I turn to Tommy to see if he does know what I like. I myself am eager to know.

"Lamar," Tommy says, "likes baseball."

Apparently, this is the correct answer. The two older brothers get out of the truck bed and into the cab of Martin's truck. Tommy gets in with them. Have I been invited somewhere or have I not? I don't move for a second, just to see what will happen. Nothing does. They are obviously waiting for me.

I hop out of Andrew's truck.

"I just have to talk to my Tommy for a second," I yell. The real Tommy turns around, gives me a thumbs-up from the truck cab.

So I scramble down the riverbank to tell Andrew that I'm abandoning him.

"Fine," he says, not even asking where I'm going or how I might be getting there. It occurs to me that this is the first time I've ever actually spoken to Andrew while he's been fishing. He seems to be in a trance, or something very close to it, standing on the riverbed, casting and reeling, casting and reeling.

"I'm going to a baseball game, I think."

"Fine."

"Do you want to come with me?"

"No, thanks."

Andrew doesn't even bother to look at me: he just stares at the river. He is either in deep soul-search, or he is in a deep depression. Perhaps they are the same thing.

But I am sick of all this, sick of sitting in the truck and brooding, etc. I scramble back up the bank and am about to leap into the bed of Martin's truck when I remember my own cooler of beer. It seems like I might have actually found adventure, and I don't want to be lacking for the proper provisions. I run back to Andrew's truck, grab the cooler, and throw it in the truck bed next to the fish cooler. Another thumbs-up from Tommy. I hit the top of the cab twice with some fine, old-boy gusto. And then we're off.

THERE IS no better way to understand the complete spookiness of a place than to bounce around on its dirt roads all alone in a truck bed in the cool, moonlit darkness. After we leave the river we drive east, away from St. Regis. Martin is not a conservative driver. He takes corners like they are not corners, fast, the big tires of his truck spitting out dirt and rocks and other mostly unidentifiable debris. He hits at least one small animal and the carcass comes flying out from underneath the tires. I think it's a muskrat, I can see the tail. I hold on the best I can, watching the world whip by in the darkness. Or rather, we are whipping by and the world stands still and it looks absolutely strange. The mountains are everywhere, standing out in jagged relief as we pass through deep forest, through apple orchards, over causeways, back through forest again. We occasionally pass a trailer or a shack, and these trailers and shacks occasionally have a light on in a window, smoke dribbling out of the chimney or stovepipe. The world we're going through feels old somehow. Sitting in the truck bed, I imagine I am witness to a kind of domestic forest primeval, with its attendant gnomes and hoary cottage dwellers, and I feel very young, imagining these old lives being lived in these strange mountain homes. In front of one trailer I see a big buck deer, standing completely still. It might be plastic.

Then, Martin takes a bad turn badly. I end up hugging one of the coolers, which turns over on me when Martin takes a sharp turn in the other direction. It is the fish cooler. I stop trying to imagine the old primeval lives being lived in their strange mountain homes and start picking the dead, slimy, cold perch and trout off me and putting them back in the cooler. The mountains and orchards and cabins are still spinning by and I smell fishy, like the beach. It is extremely disorienting.

Martin drives for a little longer. I open a fresh beer and try to ignore my own powerful fish smell. The truck climbs a small hill, then crests and descends. On our descent, I can see what appears to be the baseball field.

Tommy taps on the window. "We're here," he mouths. I give him a thumbs-up.

"Here" is not what I expected. I mean, it is a real baseball field, and yet, it is not. The field looks like it has been abandoned, and then recently cut by a drunk groundskeeper with a dull rotary mower: there are big shocks of uncut grass here and there in the outfield. The base paths are gravel, not dirt. There is no outfield fence—the outfield ends where the pine and oak woods begin. I can see light poles around the edges of the outfield, along the far foul lines, and behind home plate, but the lights themselves are dead. In their place, there are dozens of trucks and cars parked around the edges of the field, and their headlights are on, making the field look much like a dimly lit parking lot. And there is a game being played. The team in the field seems to be entirely composed of Puerto Ricans, or at least men who have darker skin than I do. The batter at the plate is white like me, white as white gets. He's wearing an International Harvester hat. So is the pitcher. No one seems to be wearing any uniforms, unless it is the generic work boots and dark blue jeans uniform of the rural working class.

Martin drives the truck down to the field and parks it along the first-base line. He leaves his lights on, of course. The three brothers get out of the cab, but I stay in the truck bed, stunned.

"Who is playing who?" I ask.

"You smell like fish," Tommy says.

"You look more like Robert Redford than Tommy."

"Heard that," Tommy says. Then, without saying good-bye or explaining his departure, he heads off down the first-base line, into the thick congregation of cars behind home plate.

"Who's playing who?" I ask again.

Russell explains that the local migrant workers are playing a team from the now-defunct local bar league. The bar's name is The Last Shot; this is also the team's name. The migrant workers' team, Russell tells me, doesn't have a name as far as he knows.

"They're Puerto Ricans," he says. "At least most of them are."

I can see what Russell means as my eyes focus a little through all the beer I've already put away and through the bad lighting. I think the third baseman might be Vietnamese.

"Where are the umpires?" I ask.

"A luxury the league can't afford," Russell tells me.

"What's wrong with the real lights?"

"Utilities are expensive."

"Where are the bleachers?" I ask.

"You're sitting in them," Martin says. "Scoot over."

I scoot over. We drink beer in the truck bed, and the brothers bitch about my fish smell, and Tommy comes back to the truck and the other two brothers leave, and Tommy continues to bitch about my fishiness. I am defensive enough about the bitching that I don't ask about all this coming and going. When I am not defending myself, I watch the game. Watching the game, I wish I were someone else. I wish I were not the rank ordinary white boy shanghaied by three other ordinary white boys to watch this bizarro version of the American pastime. Instead, I wish I were an American documentary filmmaker who has turned his camera's eye on the true heart of sports-crazy America. There are two options here in my wishing I were a documentary filmmaker. One, the filmmaker finds what he's looking for here in the hillbilly fields of play of upstate New York: he finds the economically disadvantaged local whites and the economically disadvantaged imported nonwhites coming to a mutual understanding through baseball. The understanding is this: they are poor, but they are super athletes and sportsmen, which somehow takes some of the sting off the poverty. There is plenty of hand shaking after the game, which both teams seem to have won. Someone's wife brings a covered dish. The racial-remediation teacher, who is in the stands, cheers loudly; her white students have finally and fully learned their lesson. The documentary filmmaker plays Woody Guthrie as the credits roll.

My other option as the documentary filmmaker is that the poor whites are not such super sportsmen. The poor whites are such bad sportsmen that they try to inject their racism and jingoism into the pure democratic heart of the game. Fortunately, the democratic heart of the game is so strong that the poor but incredibly graceful nonwhites humiliate the whites on the field of play. The game is still democratic. The documentary filmmaker still plays Woody Guthrie.

But I am not that documentary filmmaker, and even if I were, I suspect I would find my subjects unacceptable. For one, no one on the field of play seems to know how to actually play baseball. Both teams are horrible. This is not that surprising from the white team: in my experience, true country boys cannot play sports, their fine motor skills made crude from bailing hay or shoveling manure or milking cows ten hours a day. But I expect something different out of the migrant workers. Is Latin America not even more baseball crazy than the United States? I once read an article that said that Latin America was—so crazy, in fact, that in the article they used dried fruit for a baseball in the trash-filled lots of Santo Domingo. We are a long way from Santo Domingo. The white guy at bat hits a weak little dribbling grounder and trips over his big shit-kicker boots running down the first-base line, and he's still safe. He's safe because the second baseman throws the ball over the first baseman's head, over even the trucks and cars that light up the field.

"Not so good," I say.

"Not that bad," Martin says. He has just come back to the truck with Russell. Martin sits down next to me in the truck bed. "Last week the ball didn't make it over the trucks. Busted someone's windshield."

"What happened?"

"Windshield busted the shortstop's nose."

"Puerto Rican?" I ask.

"White nose," Martin says. "White windshield, too."

The first baseman goes after the ball, running and ducking through a barrage of garbage and beer bottles. Martin throws a perch at him. The first baseman swears something in Spanish, retrieves the ball, and hurls it in the direction of second base. The ball goes over the second baseman's head into left field. There must be a small stump out there, because the ball hits something and bounces back toward center field. The documentary filmmaker throws Woody Guthrie back into the pile of compact discs and looks for a song featuring a kazoo.

"What inning is it?"

"What's the score?" Martin asks back.

"Get me a beer," Tommy says, tracing his scar with his pinky finger. He opens the beer, and then he leaves again, with Russell.

"Where they keep going?" I ask.

"College," Martin says.

"What's that?"

"Did you go to college?"

"Indeed."

"You talk like it."

This cannot be a compliment, but Martin's voice sounds as completely neutral and even as a hum.

"I went to college," he says.

"Community college?" I ask.

"Cornell," Martin says. There is no note of triumph in his voice, only a lazy, long stare that is meant to make me realize that I have fallen victim to my own assumptions.

Finally, Martin stops staring and explains that he got a free ride to the Cornell agriculture and forestry school by virtue of a state regent's scholarship.

"Did you get your degree?" I ask.

"You know I did."

"So why'd you come back to St. Regis?"

"Where was I supposed to go?"

This is a treacherous exchange, I know. I once had a similar conversation with my father, immediately after I graduated from college. My father asked me the same superior question I have just asked Martin—Why do you want to come back *here*?—and I gave the same defensive answer that Martin has given me—Where else am I supposed to go? This experience tells me to shut up and drink more beer before I say something I shouldn't.

"Women," Martin says after a long pause.

"Women what?"

"Tommy and Russell went to find women."

"There are women here?"

"There are."

"What kind of women?"

"What *kind*?"

"Prostitutes?" I guess. It is not exactly an educated guess: I have never even seen a prostitute before. But I have never seen a spectacle like this before, either.

"Wives," Martin says.

"Whose?"

"Theirs."

Sure enough, Martin points down the third-base line, where I see Russell and Tommy in the distance talking with two women. The two women are leaning against the side of a car, parked behind home plate. Russell's and Tommy's wives don't look a thing like prostitutes: they appear to be perfectly normal women who have a reasonable mass of hair and the proper number of limbs. Tommy kisses one of them on the mouth and she smiles, then she kisses him on the cheek. Then she and the other woman get in the car and slowly make their way out from behind home plate.

"Where they going?"

"The wives?"

"The wives."

"Home."

"You have one?"

"I do."

"Where is she?"

Just then, as the wives are backing out of their spot from behind home plate, a foul ball hits the roof of their car. I think it's the same inning; the whites are still at bat.

"The wives don't really like baseball," Martin says.

"Neither do I. I don't think I can watch this anymore."

"Agreed."

So we stop watching the game. This is not unusual, of course: men never go to sporting events to actually watch the sport. They go to find expression for their fierce, inexplicable animosity toward other men. They go to develop grudges against men four rows down, or in this case, two vehicles away. Two vehicles away, two Puerto Ricans are sitting on the hood of a beat-up Dodge Duster. The Duster has only one working headlight. The two Puerto Ricans are dressed in flannel shirts and jeans and mesh baseball hats; they would look exactly like Martin and his brothers were race not largely in the way.

"You see that?" Martin asks.

"See what?"

"Over there." He gestures over at the Puerto Rican men, by which I mean he points right at them and they see him point. One of them smiles and points back.

"You see that?" Martin says to Russell and Tommy, who have just gotten back to the truck. Tommy has a smear of red lipstick on his right cheek. The two Puerto Rican men point at the smear and laugh.

"I see it," Russell says. He leans over and whispers something to Tommy. Tommy nods, then spits on his hand and rubs the lipstick off his cheek, all without taking his eyes off the Puerto Ricans.

"What are you seeing?" I ask.

"I see *them*," Martin says, a little louder than before. He again points his finger at the Puerto Ricans. It occurs to me that Martin is *drunk,* not just because he's speaking loudly and pointing at complete strangers, but also because he starts arguing, with conviction, that these two Puerto Rican men are the ones who have taken his and Russell's jobs. Why he believes this, I have no idea; I also have no idea how I have gotten myself in this suddenly dangerous situation.

"How do you know they're the ones?" I ask.

"I know."

"Those guys are migrant workers," I say. "They don't work for the road crew. They pick apples."

"They took our *jobs*," Martin says, still pointing.

"He's speaking figuratively," Russell tells me.

"Of course."

And despite my drunkenness and my disorientation, I do understand now what Martin is talking about. Martin doesn't literally believe that these two Puerto Rican migrant workers literally took his and Russell's jobs on the road crew. What Martin does know is that he went away to Cornell to get his degree so that he could come back to a good, middle-management job in the lumber industry. Four years later, he comes back and finds there is no more lumber industry. Instead, he finds a minimum-wage job working on the road crew, and he finds Puerto Rican migrant workers where ten years ago there were none. Then, there isn't even the minimum-wage job anymore, just the migrant workers. This is what Martin sees.

What *I* see is a potential race riot. The three brothers have gotten out of the truck and are standing in the headlight beams of Martin's S-10, staring down the two Puerto Rican men who have gotten down off the hood of their car. Two other Puerto Rican men get off an adjacent car and stand next to them. The racial relations instructor appears behind me, whispering in my ear, asking me if I have ever seen a race riot before, asking me if I can imagine *West Side Story* without the dancing and Natalie Wood.

Suddenly, I am very sober and very afraid.

I am afraid because I do not want there to be a race riot, but nor do I want to sit around and just let it happen. The tractor accident has taught me at least something. I don't want to act like I'm innocent and not take any responsibility for the actions of my fellow ordinary white boys Martin, Russell, and Tommy. Of course, I don't want to be responsible for anything, which is why I'm up here in the first place. But it seems that one can't help but be responsible for something.

So I decide to be responsible for my own beating. I decide to lie and tell Martin and Russell that I'm the one who took their jobs.

"You are the what?" Martin asks. This new information doesn't distract him or his brothers as much as I hoped. They continue to stare the Puerto Ricans down; they don't even bother looking back at me, still sitting in the truck bed.

"I took your place in the road crew. Me and my friend Andrew."

"Who?"

"Andrew. My Tommy who was fishing."

"Whatever you say."

My false confession is clearly not having its intended effect. It doesn't even distract Martin and his brothers all that much. After all, the jobs are already gone, but the migrant workers are still here.

So I try again. I remember Glori's complaint about my supposedly superior attitude, and how angry it made her.

"You stupid son of a bitch," I say, climbing out of the truck and pointing at Martin specifically, and at his two brothers by association. "Don't you know that I am better than you? Don't you know that that's why I have a job and you don't?"

This has its intended effect. Martin and his brothers forget all about the Puerto Ricans and beat the living crap out of me. I even lose a tooth. I can hear the Puerto Ricans clapping, laughing at something, I can't tell what. I can hear Woody Guthrie singing as someone, Russell I think, bloodies my nose. The blood flows and the Puerto Ricans clap and laugh some more as I get what I deserve. It is a very democratic moment.

CHAPTER 6

IN THIS fashion I, Lamar Kerry, Jr., receive my first beating. By virtue of this one-time experience, allow me to make the following generalization: There is nothing initially dramatic or earthshaking about getting beaten up. This is particularly true if you have asked for the beating and if your request has been honored. Martin and his brothers pounding me into the cold, hard dirt is something like an unusually painful business transaction. They are very efficient. It takes about two minutes. When they are done, they leave. I get hit with some more dirt spraying out from underneath Martin's truck tires as he peels away from the baseball field.

I stay on the ground a little while longer. I find that is difficult to lie to yourself when you are flat on the ground, bleeding. So I take an honest accounting of my situation. First, the physical. My ribs are sore, and my mouth throbs and beats from where I lost the tooth, but other than that, I don't feel so bad. My nose has stopped bleeding, and strangely, it doesn't hurt at all. I think about looking for my missing tooth, but it is dark and besides, what am I going to do with the thing if I find it? I decide to let the tooth stay missing.

Then, the intellectual self-assessment. Lying gap-toothed on the ground, I close my eyes. I can hear the game still staggering on behind me. There will probably be more fights, racial and otherwise, before the game is over and the game will never be over, really. Worse, I know now that my false confession was neither brave nor noble, and I am no martyr except to my own half-assed sense of responsibility. Lying on the ground with my eyes closed, I know that what I did was stupid, very stupid, and nothing else. And if I am this stupid, I obviously am not better than Martin and his brothers.

I suddenly and passionately miss my tooth. I miss it enough to say so out loud.

"I miss my tooth."

"What did you go and do that for?" It is a woman, standing above me, and her voice is familiar enough to make me open my eyes. She looks much like the bartender way back in the Cornhill— red hair, attractive weathered face, blue corduroy shirt, and big, tough shoulders—except she is chewing gum, blowing impressive pink bubbles. I don't remember Andrew's Mae West blowing bubbles.

"Excuse me?" A whistling sound—something like the last bit of steam coming out of a kettle that's been taken off the burner— comes from and through my gap tooth.

"You got yourself beat up on purpose," she says, blowing another big pink bubble. "Why?"

"I'm stupid."

"Knew that."

"Who are you?" There definitely is something familiar about her, the clipped manner of her speaking, but I still can't quite place it.

"Wife," she says, and then I know who she is.

"Martin's wife," I say.

"Obviously."

"Obviously."

"I'm making a phone call," she says. "You need to make one?"

I tell her that I do.

"Get up," she says, and I do and we get in her truck, which is cobalt blue to her husband's midnight black, and we leave the field of play and my tooth behind. Leaving the field, I have the unreasonable premonition that my tooth will be of some future significance to someone. Maybe some archaeologist will find the tooth thousands of years from now, buried next to the fossilized remains of an Adirondack wooden baseball bat, and maybe that archaeologist will wonder about these artifacts and their juxtaposition, wonder about their seemingly violent relationship, wonder about what kind of civilization has been lost.

And the archaeologist's conclusion, if he is smart, will be this: No kind of civilization at all.

Martin's wife drives us to a pay phone outside a Nice 'N' Easy. During the ride I keep my eyes closed, my mouth shut.

"Wait here," Martin's wife says after stopping the truck. I open my eyes and watch her as she walks over to the pay phone and makes a call. She comes back after a few seconds, or maybe minutes; it might be an hour. I accidentally fall asleep waiting for her. My nose has started bleeding again during my sleep, and I notice a thick streak of blood on the vinyl seat back when I wake up.

"Sorry about the mess," I say, wiping the blood streak off with my jacket sleeve.

"Coast is clear," she says.

"You make your phone call?"

"I made *your* phone call," she says, and holds up the keys to Andrew's and my motel room, which she has evidently taken out of my front pocket or off the ground. The motel's phone number is on the plastic key chain. Martin's wife—who appears to be experienced in aiding helpless, wounded men—tells me she has called Andrew, given him directions, and that he's on his way to pick me up. Where I am, I have no idea. The Nice 'N' Easy is at a V in two roads that have no signs to identify them and that lead to no houses that I can see. Martin's wife throws me my keys, then motions for me to get out of the truck. I do. I walk over and stand next to the pay phone, which is directly underneath the store's sign. The sign is illuminated by a sick yellow light, which must come from bulbs within the letters of the sign. The bulb in the 'N' is out. I have the definite feeling that I am at the intersection of two roads not taken, and I have the feeling the roads are not taken for a reason. There is no one in the store that I can see, and only one car in the parking lot, which must be the clerk's. I wonder for whom the Nice 'N' Easy is a convenience.

"Made my phone call, too," Martin's wife tells me as she climbs into the truck.

"Safe to go home?" I ask.

"Always safe," she says. "Of course, I never told Martin I was better than him."

"I didn't really mean it," I say. On cue, my nose throbs and beats like another heart.

There is that uncomfortable pause that occurs before two people who don't know each other part company forever. The electrified store sign hums ominously.

"Working at the prison next week," Martin's wife finally says.

"Martin?" I guess, thinking that this is some sort of explanation for his violent tendencies.

"Both of us," she says. "Martin's brothers, too."

"All of you," I say.

"But not you," Martin's wife says.

"True."

"We're going to work in a prison," she says. "What's *your* excuse for acting so stupid?"

Then, before I can give Martin's wife a satisfactory answer, which of course I don't have, she drives off down one of the roads not taken. I feel dizzy, something close to what love is supposed to feel like. Maybe I have a concussion; or maybe I am merely suffering from the delusion—which men like myself always seem to have under the right circumstances—that my life would be immeasurably better if I had fallen in love with someone like Martin's wife: someone who is tough, unwilling to take any shit, and who drives a pickup truck. Either way, I am dizzy enough to momentarily think that Martin's wife might be in love with me, even though I am the pip-squeak whom she has just insulted and who has been beaten up by her husband. I am dizzy enough to actually believe that given the right time and place Martin's wife and I could have fallen in love. This would have been my unsatisfactory answer to Martin's wife's question: "I might have fallen in love with you if..." If what, I do not know. This is another road not taken for a reason: the road is closed.

I sit down underneath the pay phone and take a nap.

CHAPTER 7

ANDREW WAKES me up by punching me lightly in the arm.

"You lost something," he says.

"My wallet," I say. I look around on the ground, panicked. Then I shift a little from where I am sitting, and pat my left back pocket. My wallet is there, in my pocket, where it's supposed to be. I feel extremely confused. I look up and, for a minute, I think the sky has somehow turned yellow, that we've been nuked or that Martin and his brothers have done some real damage to my ocular nerve. Then, I realize that it's the sickly light from the yellow store sign. The sky beyond the sign is its normal pitch black. I have no idea what time it is. I look down at my wrist. Where is my watch? My watch is what's missing: I must have lost it somehow at the baseball field.

"My watch," I say.

"Your tooth, Lamar," Andrew says. "You're missing one of your front teeth."

"Oh." I run my tongue through the vacant socket. It hurts

enough—pain like little electric currents running through my mouth, into my jaw and cheekbones, up into my sinuses—that I make a mental note not to do so again. *"That."*

"What happened?"

"I fell down."

"You fell down *hard*."

"Obviously."

Andrew and I are not longtime pals for nothing: he knows when his traveling companion doesn't feel like talking about the fate of his missing tooth. Andrew doesn't even ask me who it was that called him, telling him to come pick me up at the Nice 'N' Easy. Maybe Martin's wife has already told him everything he needs to know. Whatever the case, Andrew and I get in the truck and he drives us back toward our motel and doesn't ask me any questions that I don't feel like answering.

"What time is it?" I ask after a few minutes.

"Around two."

"That's it?"

"You thought it was later?"

"Much."

Another long silence. We drive past the St. Regis River, where Andrew and Tommy were fishing just a few hours ago. Things— buildings, trees, road signs—begin to look familiar. We are nearing home, or at least what temporarily passes for it. Andrew turns on the radio. The farm report says that we need more dry weather. Bad. And that we're not going to get it. And how the farmers can't take any more rain. Andrew turns off the radio. We pass by a bar that seems to be open—cars in the parking lot, beer lights still glowing in the windows. Bars are allowed by law to stay open until 4 A.M. in Franklin County.

"We could go get a drink," Andrew says, slowing down slightly, putting on his blinker.

"We could," I say. But to be honest, I just don't feel like having a drink right now. To be even more honest, I fear the way a beer might feel passing through the exposed nerve of my tooth. More little electric currents just thinking about it.

"No, thanks."

"Another time," Andrew says.

"Sure."

But even as I say this, I have the feeling that there won't be another time. I have come to the end of something. Sitting in Andrew's truck, tearing through the mysterious mountain night, through those rows of pine trees and rusted cars and apple orchards and crumbling old lumber towns on our way back to our sorry little motel suite, I know the adventure is over. I know the adventure is over because the thought of sitting in the truck bed even one more time—drinking beer, conversing with the wives, waiting and brooding—while Andrew fishes makes me want to stick a Phillips head screwdriver right into my exposed socket.

Maybe Andrew feels we've come to the end of something, too. Maybe this is why we end up in a truth-telling session while parked in front of our motel suite.

"I want to ask you something," I say.

"Ask," Andrew says.

"Why did you do what you did with Mae West?"

"Who?"

"The bartender at the Cornhill."

I expect Andrew to take his time answering this question, or to not answer it at all. But he answers immediately.

"I did it," he says, "to see if I was capable of doing it."

"To see if you were like your father."

"To see if I was capable of *being* like my father."

"And you were."

"Apparently."

"Another question," I say, the *s* whistling painfully through my missing tooth. "Why did you run away?"

"Why did I run away?"

"I'm just curious," I say. Another *s*, another agonizing whistle. "I'm just wondering what you're doing up here."

Andrew nods. Again he doesn't take any time at all to answer my question. It seems likely he's been asking and answering these same questions while he's been fishing.

"I ran away," Andrew says, "so I could forget what I'm capable of."

"Fishing supposed to make you forget?"

"Supposed to."

"I see."

"Your turn," Andrew says. He turns on the ceiling light in the truck cab. I am briefly blinded. I feel like I'm in an interrogation room. In that harsh light, Andrew is less a friend and partner-in-crime than he is homicide detective.

"OK."

"I had my reasons for running away," he says. "What were your reasons for coming with me?"

It is a doozy of a question. I get a low, throbbing ache in my jaw just thinking of all the possible reasons. Oh, beautiful, sad-eyed Glori Burns, oh, disappointed Daddy and dying Mother, oh, missing Mark Ramirez and pleading Jodi Ramirez, oh, dead uncles and jailed uncles and crooked uncles and part-time jobs and burning houses. These are exactly the reasons I ran away, of course: because I didn't want the responsibility of helping Jodi Ramirez and watching my mother die and seeing my father's disappointment and identifying and maybe alleviating Glori's unhappiness. I did not want all these people to need me. And now I know that this is exactly what I want, and why I want to go back home. I want to go back and tell everyone that I'm no longer innocent and that I never was, and I am a better person for accepting my guilt. I want to go back and say: I am here if you need me. I want to go back so people—Glori, my parents, Jodi Ramirez—will tell me that they need me, and I want to go back so they won't stop needing me. And I was needed before I left, I am sure of it. So why was it again that I left in the first place? Why was I so afraid of being needed? Why do I miss everything that I was so scared of before my exile? I would sacrifice another tooth—all my teeth—just to see my mother again in her wheelchair, to see my father in his disappointment, my Glori in her unhappiness, Jodi Ramirez in her desperate need for me to help her.

This is what I feel. But how do you say any of this stuff? How does anyone say, "I want to be needed," to his good buddy with a straight face?

Andrew is waiting. He has asked a real question. Am I honest enough to give him a real answer?

"I came with you," I say, "because I wanted to sit in the truck and watch you fish."

Andrew nods, as if this were exactly the kind of smart-ass response he expected from me. I feel momentarily ashamed.

"It's not working," Andrew says.

"What's not?"

"The fishing," he says. "It's not working."

"I didn't think it would."

"Good for you."

"Fishing isn't helping you forget *shit*," I say. "So let's just go home."

"No."

"The fishing isn't working. You said so yourself."

"I'm not going home, Lamar. Not ever."

"Why the hell not?"

"Why the hell should I?"

"Your family," I say, and even as I say this it strikes me as a worthless answer, a desperate answer. I am, it seems, going back to

Little Falls without Andrew, and it is difficult for me to imagine one without the other, the sad-sack town without the sad-sack friend, and I feel wrong and desperate about it, the way you feel when you're driving on a very familiar road, a road you've driven on all your life, and suddenly you know you've missed a turn that you can't possibly have missed. So I persist with my worthless answers. "What about your wife? Your job?"

"I left Little Falls because of those things," Andrew says. "Why should I go back now?"

"Why should you stay here?"

Andrew shrugs, says nothing. But he doesn't need to. I know the reason. Andrew felt lost back in Little Falls, and so he wanted to go find himself somewhere else. But if you have to run away to find yourself, then you are probably so lost that you are never going to find yourself, no matter how hard you look, no matter where you run. Still, anything is better than the humiliating retreat back to the place where you lost yourself. So you keep running and running.

As for me, I *have* found myself, but then again, it is possible that I was never really that lost to begin with.

Good-bye Andrew.

"Are you sure you won't come back with me?"

"Positive."

"What are you going to do?"

"I'm going to go to bed," Andrew says, nodding in the direction of our motel suite.

Fine. Andrew is going to bed. And he should: his face looks hollowed out, he's so tired. But me, I'm not tired at all, and I'm not going to bed. I am going to see my uncle in prison, about three or so hours from here. I have a question or two I need to ask him. But how am I going to get there?

"Before you go to bed, I have a favor to ask."

"Ask."

"I need your truck to get where I'm going."

I expect Andrew to say no. After all, he probably needs the truck as badly as I do. But he surprises me.

"You can have it on one condition," he says. "You can't tell anyone where I am or what I'm doing. You can't tell them that I'm not working at the prison. You can't even tell them that the fishing didn't help me any."

"I won't tell."

Of course I won't tell. It is the very least I can do. The very most I could do would be to stay with Andrew, stick close to him, help him ride out whatever trouble he needs to ride out. But I won't do this, whether because I'm too selfish or too smart or too scared, I don't know. No, I won't do the thing that I should for Andrew. But I will do the least I can do.

I say it again. "I won't tell."

"I believe you."

Andrew gives me the keys. We get out of the truck. I walk over to the driver's-side door, where Andrew is standing, and we shake hands. Then I get back in the truck, and Andrew walks toward the motel, opens the door to the motel room, walks in, and closes the door behind him. I busy myself with the truck, making a big deal of turning up the heat, fidgeting with the radio, adjusting the seat, the mirrors, because I don't want to see Andrew alone in the motel suite. Because you should never look at the sadder version of yourself; you should never look at your best friend for whom things don't work out. But I finally do look at Andrew; I have to. He is standing at the window. The room is dark except for the television flickering behind him, and the silhouette of him is staring at the silhouette of me. I almost wave, but it seems silly, so I don't. Andrew must be thinking the same thing: his hand comes up to his waist, then it drops back to his side. Andrew turns away from me, toward the television. So I drive on.

CHAPTER 8

MY UNCLE Eli is not especially happy to see me. I didn't think he would be.

"How are you, Lamar?" he asks. "You look god awful."

"I feel fine," I say.

But my uncle is right, I know: I do look god awful. I don't feel so fine, either. I have a week-old scratchy, patchy beard and my eyes are heavy and pink with fatigue and niggling allergies, and I still feel a little shaky from the tractor accident and my beating and from leaving Andrew back in St. Regis. Then there is my missing tooth, which my uncle must see but doesn't comment upon. And being in the Clinton State Penitentiary doesn't make me feel much better: like the Hamilton, there isn't a great deal of menace in the room where I meet my uncle, but there is something—a smell, maybe, the approximate odor of old, stale food—that makes me uneasy, and a little nauseated. My uncle and I are sitting across from each other on either side of a metal cafeteria-table-looking thing. The benches we're sitting on are attached to the tables, which themselves are riveted right into the concrete floor. In fact, the room itself looks just like an elementary school cafeteria, minus the screaming kids and the bad food. Instead of militant female lunch monitors with bathroom passes and clipboards, we have militant male prison guards with .38s, batons, and handcuffs, one at either end of the cavernous room. Aside from the guards, the two of us are the only ones in the room, even though it is smack in the middle of visiting hours. No, I do not feel fine at all.

"I feel fine," I repeat. "But forget about me. How are *you* doing?"

"Not too terribly bad."

"Making any friends?"

"Not many."

"I understand," I say. "You're part of a transient population."

"I am," he says, his voice flat, bored.

"You make a friend and then he's out on parole. Then what are you left with? What do you do then?"

My uncle doesn't respond to this smart-ass comment, which is probably what he remembers and expects from his overeducated nephew, son of his overeducated older brother. Uncle Eli just sits there and stares at me, his fingers drumming on the table. He is thin, like most of us Kerry men; but his is a winnowed down, survivalist's gauntness. My uncle's eyes, like his prison clothes, like his hair and even his skin, are ash gray. I cannot tell if this is just a trick of light or whether his eyes are actually gray. Can eyes actually be gray? Can your natural-born blue eyes turn gray?

"Best not to make any friends," I say. "Best to stay unattached."

"What do you want, Lamar?" My gray-eyed uncle wants me to stop beating around the bush. He was never a favorite uncle, nor was I a favorite nephew. As you know, I have never even been up here to see him before this, not one time in the nearly three years of his imprisonment. Why am I here now?

"I don't want anything. I'm just visiting."

"Sure you are. You were just in the neighborhood."

"That's right. I *was* just in the neighborhood."

The gray eyes jump a little. My sorry beard, tired-looking eyes, missing tooth, and shaky hands are making sense.

"You've run away from home."

"Not so much. I'm seeing the world, doing a little bit of this, a little of that, having myself an adventure."

"Don't give me that," he says. "You're running away."

"Fine," I say. This, after all, is the truth. I have not been having an adventure. I have been running away. Why can I not admit it? "Yes. I'm running away from home. Happy?"

"Yes," he says. "It makes me very happy."

"I'm glad."

"I wish *I* had run away from home."

"Why didn't you?"

"Didn't seem to be an option. At the time. Now it seems pretty clear to me that it was an option."

"Where would you have run to?"

"Anywhere."

"But now it's too late."

"I could have not burned down that house. I could have just run away."

"The black family's house."

"I should have just run away."

"The *Rohals'* house."

"Just got up and run off."

"But now it's too late."

"Correct."

I'm not sure that this admission would wash in racial-remediation class. In racial remediation, my uncle's admission probably would not be good enough because it wouldn't clearly recognize the hot little racist heart of the problem. The teacher would not be satisfied. Where is the admission of guilt? The teacher would press my jailbird uncle to get under the hateful rock of his own reasons. Why was it wrong for you to burn down *that* house for *those* reasons? the teacher would want to know. The teacher of racial remediation is always a big believer in the Socratic method. Is it enough to wish you hadn't done what you had done? Is sorry, the teacher would ask my uncle, good enough?

Maybe not. But we are not in racial-remediation class and I am no Socrates, and my uncle Eli's confession is good enough for right now.

"If you had run away," I tell him, getting up to leave, "you wouldn't have shot up our mailbox."

"You're wrong," my uncle says, grinning. It is the first I have seen him smile in my whole visit. I think I even see a little bit of blue peeking out around the edges of his gray eyes. "I would have shot it up and *then* run away. I still hate that talking deer."

We both get a big, hearty laugh out of this shared piece of Kerry family lore. He and I shake hands and part company on good terms. What has happened here? Has this really turned out to be a light-hearted occasion? My uncle is in prison and will be for at least four more years, and he is still a violent, shotgunning brute at heart, and we are laughing about it. If there is anything more mysterious in its cause and effect than two relatives yukking it up over an old bit of family history, I do not know what it is.

SO THIS is me, once again. At the end of my trip north, I go to visit my uncle in prison and I get what I am looking for. My uncle says that he did not *have* to burn down the black family's house, that he could have just picked up and run away and not done what he did. Whether he *would* do so given one more chance is another question entirely. But it is a moot question. My uncle did not run away, and he did burn the house down, and he cannot go home again, at least not for another four to six years. The prison in my uncle Eli's case is at least the temporary end of possibility. But I have not burned anything down and I am not in prison. True, I have run away and abandoned the people who need me. But I can go back and still be needed. This is why I have visited my uncle. I have visited my uncle to find out what I still have that he does not. What I have is the ability to go home and be needed. So I do.

FOUR

FOUR

CHAPTER 1

I MAKE the four-hour drive south from the Clinton Penitentiary, through the middle of nowhere, to Little Falls. My father's white pines and his rusting trailers and his fallow fields are still where they should be, and so are the Corrigan's Paper Company smokestacks, which I can see as I make the quick descent out of the hills and into the Mohawk Valley. Most people don't make the return trip home—not because things change but because they do not—and sure enough, everything looks the same as I left it a week ago. But unlike most people, I'm glad. The consequences of my sabbatical, it seems, are nil.

The discovery that the world you abandoned has not changed in or because of your absence will make you boyish. I feel like a boy. There is no other way to describe how unreasonably happy I am. It is August, and the day began hot, but now, well after nightfall, it turns cold outside, as it sometimes does, and the wind is whipping around like it is October, and I don't care. Let it be fall. Let it be summer, too. Let it be all seasons at once, for I am feeling like a man, or at least a boy, for all seasons, and I am home.

I CALL my parents immediately once I get back to my apartment. My father answers.

"I'm home."

"Well, hello."

"I am *home*," I say again, stupidly. "I hope you didn't worry too much about me."

"We didn't worry," my father says, matter-of-factly. "You've only been gone a week."

"True."

"Did you have a good time?"

"Not that good."

"Sorry to hear that."

This is followed by a silence. The silence worries me. Suddenly my sabbatical does have consequence, only I cannot tell what that consequence is and whom it has affected. I imagine my father holding the phone with one white-knuckled hand, the other hand a fist in his pocket, punching his thigh through the thin material of his khaki pants. I imagine him trying to tell me the thing that he does not want to tell me. I don't imagine my mother at all. What has happened to my mother? Is she sitting next to my father, waiting eagerly to talk to her only son? Is she in the hospital? Is she *somewhere else*? Where is my mother?

"Where is Mom?"

"Your mother is in bed. She's fine."

"In bed," I say.

"Absolutely fine," he says.

I look at my kitchen clock. It is after eleven at night. Of course my mother is in bed. The prodigal son is still inconsiderate, but other than that, is it possible that the prodigal son's homecoming is not spoiled after all?

"I'm sorry for calling so late."

"Don't worry about it," he says. "Are you really home for good?"

"It appears so."

"I'm glad."

He does sound glad, my father, the force of whose disappointment I fled into greater disappointment. Now that I am home and my father is glad about it, I find myself willing to do anything my father wants me to. I will even be extraordinary, if that's what my old man still wants.

But there is this one problem. It is, after all, after eleven o'clock. My father should be with my mother, in bed.

"Dad, why are you up so late?"

"I'm doing some work."

It is a dramatic moment. I swear that I can hear the air leak and whistle out of my father and into the phone receiver.

What, I wonder out loud, is so important that my father has to be working on it at eleven at night? He is the editor, after all, of an *afternoon* paper.

"They found Mark Ramirez's body," he says.

I can definitely hear air now, although it might be my own and it is not a leak or a whistle, but a whoosh.

"His body," I say.

"Yes, Lamar, his body. Mark was murdered. That much they know. They don't know who did it, though."

"It wasn't Uncle Eli," I say. My saying this is ridiculous, I know, but for some reason it seems important, even urgent that my father know that his brother had an alibi—me—and that he is not a murderer. He is not even a full-fledged arsonist anymore. He is an arsonist with *regrets,* even if they are not sufficiently introspective or self-critical.

"What are you talking about?"

"I saw Uncle Eli earlier today. He didn't kill Mark Ramirez or anyone else."

"I know he didn't," my father said. "Jesus, Lamar, your uncle has been in *prison*. Mark Ramirez was not killed in prison. He was killed out in the woods, a bullet through his forehead, another in his chest. A farmer out in Paine's Hollow was cutting down trees when he found Mark's body. It happened two days ago."

"All right, all right," I say. "I just thought you should know about your own brother."

"Fine," my father says. "Now I know."

"Now you know."

"We published a picture of Mark's body that the police took," my father says. "It was awful."

"You published a picture?"

"In yesterday's paper."

"Hold on," I say. I put down the phone and run out into the hallway, where one of my neighbors always dumps his old newspapers. On top of the pile is yesterday's *Valley News* with the picture my father spoke of. The photo is mostly a tangle of crime-scene tape and police legs, but there is definitely something visible within the tape. It is definitely a body, its feet sticking out from underneath the coroner's white sheet, the rest of the body giving real human contour to the sheet itself. Strangely, there are no shoes on the feet, just a pair of dark-colored dress socks. I feel sickened, ashamed of myself, standing here in the hall, looking at Mark's stockinged feet. It is much too intimate a detail for me to be looking at. I have no right. I can't help but think that the picture would be much less grisly if Mark were wearing some shoes. Where the hell are Mark's shoes?

"I just saw the picture," I say, returning to the phone. "Where the hell are Mark's shoes?"

"I don't know. They weren't found at the crime scene."

"You were right. The picture is awful."

"Just awful," my father says.

"I'm so sorry," I say. Why I'm offering my condolences to my father, I have no idea. Maybe because it is easier to offer condolences to someone who does not need them than to someone who does.

There is a contemplative, silent moment between my father and me on the telephone. I recall the picture of the dead black man in Texas, how concrete he was, how I was looking for Mark to take on some of that concreteness. Now that Mark has been *killed* much in the same way and for apparently the same reasons that the Texan was, and now that I have seen the picture of the body, Mark has become much more concrete. And now that Mark has become more concrete, I wish that he was back to being abstract again.

I also wish that my wishing weren't so *worthless*.

I'm sorry, Mark. I'm so sorry, Jodi.

"Do you need my help down at the paper?" I ask my father, breaking our silence.

"I do, but get some sleep first," my father says. "If you came in tomorrow afternoon, that would be fine."

Another silence, this one shorter than the first. My father has work to do; he does not have time for the properly dramatic pause.

"Call your mother tomorrow morning before you come to work," my father says, trying to return us to the high emotion of my homecoming. "We are both eager to hear all about your *adventure*."

Then my father hangs up, leaving me all alone in my apartment, and I am *cold*.

I am cold not because of the weather, but because I have already remembered why I ran away in the first place. I ran away because I finally realized how truly unsatisfactory I was. I could not find Mark, and I would not help Jodi Ramirez find him, either. Now, Mark is found, and not by me and not in the condition I had hoped. He is dead, shot dead, and his wife a widow, his kids fatherless, and what am I going to do about it? I will have to do something to make the concreteness of Mark Ramirez's death actually mean something.

But Mark Ramirez's murder is not the only problem, even if it is the most serious one. This is just *one* way in which I was unsatisfactory, one reason why I ran away from home. When there is one reason, there is always another. If you remember one thing, you cannot help but remember the other.

CHAPTER 2

THOSE OF us who do not want to realize the consequences of our sabbaticals will always choose drama over substance. This is what I choose. I do not call Glori to tell her I am back in town and to beg for any real, honest understanding. I do not tell her that I will wait until kingdom come for her forgiveness, either. I do not tell her to take *all the time in the world* or anything like that. Instead, I go work at the *Valley News* for a couple hours, then wait outside the Monroe Street Elementary School for Glori to get out of work. My hope is that the surprise sight of me leaning against my car, James Dean–style—minus the swooping haircut, minus the rolled jeans, minus the sexy car to lean on, minus a full set of teeth, minus everything—will jolt her into forgetting all my offenses. My hope is to surprise her right past the long, halting, healing process straight into reconciliation.

Glori leaves the school at five and immediately sees me leaning against my car. Glori does not seem surprised. She does not seem disappointed or enraged, either. She doesn't seem concerned about or even aware of my missing tooth. If Glori is anything, she is neutral.

"I'm home."

"I can see that," she says, shouldering her bag. "What do you want me to do about it?"

"I don't exactly know."

"I didn't think you did."

This exchange isn't encouraging. Despite what you hear about absences and the heart growing fonder, Glori does not look beautiful. She doesn't look beautiful not because she is not beautiful, but because I am scared. Fear damages your vision, like cataracts. I cannot even look at Glori, I am so scared. And when I do look at her, she is a vague, fearsome blur, arms crossed over her chest, staring me down.

"I'm glad you're still in town," I say. "I was afraid that you'd be gone."

No response. More staring.

"Moved away," I say helpfully.

"Why would I move away?" Glori says. "I was here before I met you." She is a model of stiff-upper-lip righteousness.

"Mark Ramirez is dead," I say.

"I know that, Lamar," she says. "I was in town when they found him, remember?"

"We can do anything you want," I say, changing the topic.

"Let's go for a walk."

"If that's what you want."

"That is what I want."

So we walk, silently, a cold, distant foot separating us. We walk around the eastern end of the school, up Arthur Street, up a steep, lung-clearing hill, and then past Monroe Street Cemetery.

"Are you better?" Glori finally asks once we reach the northern end of the cemetery.

"Am I what?" I ask, breathing hard from the walk up the hill.

"When you left, you said you were going to be better when you came back. Are you?"

"I am better," I say, my wheezing to the contrary. I believe what I am saying is the truth, even though I could not tell you how I have improved or whether the improvements will stick. I nearly tell Glori that I saw a man die, and that his death is part of my improvement. This is the truth, or at least part of it. But even *I* have enough substance not to use someone else's death for my own dramatic purposes.

"I am definitely better," I tell her.

"Fine," Glori says, still neutral. "I believe you."

"I didn't stop thinking about you."

"I believe you again."

"I mean it. I did not stop thinking about you. Not a bit."

"I know you didn't."

"I need you."

"I know you do."

This *does* make me hopeful. We are by this point at the end of Arthur Street, at the west end of the cemetery. Despite my breathlessness, I am feeling a little bit better. Perhaps drama is better than substance after all.

Or perhaps it is not.

"Did you miss me?" This is my self-serving boyish question, and I get the answer that boyishness deserves.

"I did miss you," Glori says. "I also thought about you constantly. When I thought about you, I hated you. So I stopped thinking about you altogether."

"And now?"

"And now nothing. Not even hate. Not even *unhappiness*. I'm not even thinking about you, not even now. I hope you had a good vacation. I truly mean that. Good-bye, Lamar. Don't call me or anything. Good-bye."

Then Glori leaves me standing there at the top of Monroe Street

Cemetery. She walks briskly down the hill with her bag slung over her shoulder, bouncing athletically against her back. The fog of fear, although not the fear itself, has lifted, and I can see Glori clearly as she charges down the hill, jumps in her car, and drives off, tires squealing. It is a dramatic, final gesture. I have been taught a lesson on the relationship between substance and drama.

The lesson is this: There are some of us who choose drama over substance, and then there are some of us who do not have to choose. There are some of us who are already people of substance inclined toward substantial gestures and decisions, not inclined toward beating hasty retreats north or toward shallow emotional shortcuts. When you are this kind of person, you do not take sabbaticals of any kind. When you are this kind of person, the kind who thinks out and accepts the consequences of your decisions, then you do not have to worry about drama. Drama will always follow substance.

I have been taught a lesson.

CHAPTER 3

THAT SHOULD be that for Glori and me. I have been taught a lesson and the lesson is a final Get Lost. Fortunately, for those of us who were bad in school, no lesson or its accompanying grade is permanent. Sooner or later, the bad student will say: I received a D *three months ago*. I received a D three months ago on a test on the French Revolution, which was *hundreds* of years ago, at least. Enough already. This is how the D student becomes an A student, or at least an A student in limbo. An A student in limbo decides that nothing is permanent, not even the grading system. Especially not the grading system.

And so Glori's lesson is not permanent, even though its basic meaning does stick. I decide that I will, for now but not forever, do what Glori has asked me: I will not call her. Instead, I go to work for my father, full-time.

"Are you sure this is what you want to do?" my father asks when I request for him to put me on full-time.

"I'm sure," I say. "Are you sure you want me as your full-time employee?"

"I'm sure."

That said, my father asks me to proofread one of his articles, and we do not speak anymore about our new professional arrangement. But a few minutes later, I glance up from my work and I catch my father looking at me, smiling furtively, as if he's found a twenty-dollar bill on the ground and isn't yet certain that the owner won't appear and demand that my father give him the money back.

I am reminded of the time, about four years ago, when my father was in his greatest denial about my ordinariness. I'd just started working for him at the paper. My first assignment was to go out to Kansas City and interview for a job at the *Kansas City Star*. The features editor of the *Star* was my father's old college roommate; my father told his ex-roommate that he had a hot journalistic prospect on his hands named Lamar Kerry, Jr. Would the ex-roommate give me an interview? The ex-roommate said he would.

"I don't want to go to Kansas City," I told my father.

"You'll love it," he said. "It's the home of the blues."

"Jazz," I said.

"Either way," my father said, "you're going."

So I flew out to Kansas City (my father paid for the ticket) wearing my only business suit (which my father also paid for). I got to the *Star* building early, and so I killed time by walking around downtown Kansas City. This self-guided walking tour killed any desire I might have had to live in Kansas City in the first place. The buildings were all tall and glassy and evenly spaced. The streets were clean and absurdly wide, so wide that I half expected a stampede of cattle to appear at any moment, running toward me down the great dull boulevards of the old slaughterhouse capital of the Midwest. The fear of stampeding cattle will leave you breathless. So will the great dull boulevards of Kansas City. By the time my interview came around, I was wheezing like an asthmatic. And of course, a newspaper as great as the *Star* would never be interested in hiring a hysterical asthmatic. So I didn't even bother with the interview. I jumped in a cab and spent seven hours drinking at the airport bar, where the bartender convinced me that I had done the right thing. The *Star,* he told me, was a crappy paper that didn't run the best comic strips or anything. I was truly grateful. I left him a huge tip out of the spending money that my father had given me.

I called my father at work when I got home.

"I'm back," I told him.

He asked me how my interview went.

I told him that it went fine. I also explained that his ex-roommate suggested that I should work for the *Valley News* for a bit until I got enough experience. Then, the ex-roommate suggested, I should apply again.

"He was very gracious," I told my father.

My father was silent for a second. Then he told me that he had just received a call from the ex-roommate, saying that I never showed up for the interview. My father said that his ex-roommate wasn't mad, wasn't mad at all, but, in the great laconic Midwestern style, the ex-roommate told my father that he was extremely *disappointed.* My father was disappointed, too, and he said so, repeatedly.

But this is not Kansas City and I am not the me I was, and my father appears to be on the verge of swallowing his disappointment. And so I work whenever and do whatever he asks me to, even if he asks me to type up the church bulletins and wedding announcements on Fridays, the obituaries the rest of the week. In my absence, Sis has assumed a more prominent role at the newspaper; my father even has her covering the more important board meetings and developing pictures. Sis has chucked the role of spinster second banana. That is now my role—I am responsible for the obituaries and wedding announcements—and I don't complain much.

"The brides are glowing in their taffeta," I tell Sis on Fridays, "and their grandparents are headed with their hot shopping carts toward their heavenly reward."

"Leave me alone," she says. But Sis is obviously happy when she says this, because she knows I *will* leave her alone. I will do what she says because I have determined that this is what a person of substance does: he listens and he learns. I am listening and learning and I am also *working*. Glori has never asked me to work, never asked me to join the full-time workforce at all, but this is another thing I've decided that a person of substance must do: he must anticipate and preempt the request, even if it never comes.

CHAPTER 4

MY FATHER'S first significant request of his new full-time reporter? To go to Mark Ramirez's funeral with him and my uncle
Bart. This is a promising, highly visible, highly dramatic assignment
for someone who is striving to be a person of substance. I am not
sure I'm up to it.

"Is this official business?" I ask him.

"In a way."

"Should I bring my camera?"

"You should not."

I get it. We are not reporters covering a funeral; we are two
men, father and son, representing the local family-run newspaper
at a funeral. My uncle is representing local law enforcement. He
picks us up down at the *Valley News* building in his squad car.

"Well, well," Uncle Bart says as I slide into the backseat. "I hear
you've been on a little *vacation*."

It occurs to me that my uncle doesn't know exactly where I've
been the past week or so; I only told my parents about all the details

of my trip two days ago, when they saw my missing tooth and demanded to know the wheres and hows. I owe my uncle no such explanation.

"It's true," I say. "I've been something of a tourist."

"A *tourist*."

"A temporary condition," I say. "Now I'm back to real life."

"Yes," my uncle says. "And look what's happened."

As he says this, we arrive at the Shells Bush Cemetery, where the memorial service for Mark Ramirez is being held. My uncle makes a sweeping motion with his hand and repeats, "And look what's happened," as if to say that I am somehow responsible for Mark's death. This is an idea, of course, that I have already entertained. Whether I'm guilty because I left Little Falls in the first place, or because I came back, is not quite clear.

"Innocence is meaningless," I tell him. "You're not telling me anything I don't already know."

"Well, well," my uncle says again.

"Give it a rest, Bart," my father says.

My uncle mutters something back at my father. He pulls into the gravel cemetery lot, parks the squad car, and the official delegation of Kerrys—my father and I in our black suits, my uncle in his formal dark blue police uniform—gets out of the car and walks to the grave site. To the uninformed, we must look like a serious, unified bunch.

Upon reaching the grave site, I feel compelled to risk another religious generalization: Catholics do not fear dying so much as they fear death itself. Or rather, they are afraid they will somehow do death an injustice, that they will *offend* it by honoring the dead incorrectly. This is the only explanation for the obsessiveness of the Catholic funeral service and burial. This is the only explanation for the complicated ritual use of the incense and the candles; the specific, topical prayers and readings; the expensive flowers and caskets; the prolonged, bleeding organ music; the ornate tombstones.

Yes, there is only one reason why Catholics insist on holding the funeral within three days of the death, and there is only one reason why Catholics insist on being there when the body is buried *immediately* after the funeral service: they don't want to screw it up.

So you can imagine my surprise once we get to the site of Mark Ramirez's memorial service and find out that everything is out of order. For one, Mark has already been buried, his modest tombstone already carved and etched and Mark placed under it. I quickly do some math: I have been home for four days; Mark Ramirez's body was found two days before that. That means it has been six whole days between Mark's death and his memorial service. My sense of ritual is deeply confused.

"What's going on here?" I ask my father.

"It's a Presbyterian service," my father says. "The Ramirezes are Presbyterians."

"So?"

"We're in a *Protestant* cemetery." This is my father's only explanation; he has never attended anything but a Catholic funeral before, either. My father is as bewildered as I am.

But there is *something* familiar about the grave site: like funeral services at St. Mary's, Mark Ramirez's memorial service is empty, as empty as the great outdoors can sometimes be. I suspect this has something to do with the person being memorialized. There are three rows of folding chairs arranged in a horseshoe design in front of Mark's grave. My father, uncle, and I sit in the third row, all the way to the left, where we have a good view of the sparse crowd. Jodi Ramirez is there with her two daughters, and with an older man and woman who I'm guessing are her parents (my father and uncle confirm that yes, they are her parents). Five chairs away from them is a Puerto Rican man—maybe Mark's long lost, estranged father; he looks to be about the right age. In the second row there are people in scattered groups of twos and threes who have various connections to Mark—some of the kids on Mark's track team, a couple teachers from the high school, two or three adults I don't recognize at all. Plus we three Kerrys. And that is it, no more than fifteen people, total. It is the kind of crowd you usually see at the funerals of extraordinarily old people who have outlasted their friends, even their own families. The cemetery feels very sad, of course, but it also feels so *empty*. I can find no other word to describe it.

After a few minutes, the Presbyterian minister who is to lead the service appears. He is a hip young man, a regular *dude* with a goatee and gold stud earring in his left ear. I get a glimpse of blue jeans and tan cowboy boots underneath his robes as he strides around the horseshoe chair arrangement and stands in front of Mark's headstone.

The hip young minister's last name is Miller. Neither my father nor my uncle Bart knows where the minister comes from, although my uncle speculates, whispering, that he's possibly from *California.* Wherever he's from, the minister—as one says in the entertainment business—does not appear to know his audience. True, the service begins traditionally enough: an announcement of why we're here—the death of the dearly departed—followed by the familiar prayers and scripture readings. There's even a funeral hymn, accompanied by a sundressed woman playing an acoustic guitar— the kind of woman whom as a child (and I can do no better now) I would have called a "hippie." In short, it is, at the beginning, a comfortable, orderly service. This is what an audience of mourners wants.

What an audience of mourners does not want is for someone to make them uncomfortable. But the hip young minister seems unwilling to give the mourners what they want. I say this because instead of a homily, the minister steps out from behind his wooden podium, and asks for *testimonials* from the congregation.

"Think on it for a moment," he says. "We will begin when you're ready."

An audible wave of concern rises, peaks, and breaks over the crowd. Does the minister know where he is? Does he know who is being buried and for what reasons? What exactly is a testimonial? Are there instructions somewhere in the memorial service program? This shit might fly in California, the congregation is saying through their squirming and muttering, but it doesn't fly here.

So we sit there. The minister stands, looking at us, waiting patiently. I start perspiring, little beads of sweat dripping and dancing on my forehead, even though it is not yet ten in the morning, not yet warm enough to sweat. I wipe my forehead. A full thumping minute of silence.

Then, something unusual happens.

Jodi Ramirez's father stands up and simply says, "Mark will be missed."

When he says this, Jodi's father, who is a fierce-looking, short, overweight man in a blue sport coat and gray flannel trousers, keeps his loose, turkey-flap chin buried deep in the center of his sport-coated chest. Jodi Ramirez's father doesn't look like the kind of man who would miss *anyone,* let alone the Puerto Rican man who married his white daughter. When he is done with his simple, one-sentence testimonial, Jodi Ramirez's father sits back down in his folding chair. It is an honest gesture, a genuinely surprising moment. It is so surprising that immediately afterward I wonder if it has actually happened.

The problem with having a genuinely honest, surprising moment, however, is that everyone wants one of their own. After the congregation has recovered from its surprise (even the minister seems a little shocked), the funeral is positively hijacked by testimonials. A fellow jeweler from Ilion testifies to Mark's high standing among local jewelers; a social studies teacher from the high school remarks that Mark always had an impressive work ethic, even as a student; one of Mark's string-bean long-distance runners, overcome by the flurry of testimonials, stands up and, finding that he has nothing really to add, simply repeats Jodi Ramirez's father's testimonial, with one slight modification, "Coach Ramirez will be missed."

It is difficult to sit through such an event without wondering whether you yourself should stand up and say something about Mark Ramirez. After all, everyone else appears to believe that it is important that one do so. A person of substance would certainly have *something* to say. Would he not?

I have absolutely nothing to say. I think back to high school, flipping through my memory for some revealing anecdote, some memorable catchphrase or piece of advice that Mark once gave me, or me him. There must be *something*. I remember once seeing Mark sitting alone at a cafeteria table, eating an orange and drinking a can of Adirondack Cola. Mark's popularity had dried up by this point, the way the lone minority student's popularity always does, but Mark didn't seem upset by his new isolation. I remember him watching me pretending not to watch him, just eating his orange and staring at me as if to say, That's right, I'm sitting here all alone. What are you going to do about it?

Mark already knew the answer to his own question, I'm sure. He knew I would choose, after some contemplation, not to sit next to him.

So this would be my testimonial: I saw Mark all alone and did *nothing* about it. And I could add, while I'm at it, that Mark's wife asked me to help her and I refused. These are not things you share at a memorial service, unless you intend to reveal the worst part of yourself. I have no such intentions. After all, the worst part of my-self—of ourselves—has already been a conspicuous part of Mark's disappearance and murder.

Fortunately, I am saved from further contemplation of my awful, empty heartlessness by my uncle and his own vast empty spaces. I am grateful, for the only thing worse than no testimonial is a completely inappropriate one. My uncle stands up, introduces himself as the chief of the Little Falls Police Department, and promises that he will catch whoever has done this to Mark. My uncle is overcome by the occasion and its high emotional pitch; his face gets quite red, blood vessels popping and exploding like so many unseen firecrackers. Uncle Bart doesn't say anything in particular about Mark's fine enduring qualities; instead he explains in great legal detail about what will happen to the so-and-so *perpetrator* once he is apprehended. It is a surreal, heady moment. Imagine the president of the American Workers Party standing up in the middle of Trotsky's funeral service and explaining at great length all the available legal recourse against his real murderer, Stalin.

"Well, well," I whisper to my uncle as he sits down. My uncle Bart is not completely thickheaded. He obviously suspects he's said the wrong thing at the wrong time. For one, his little speech has stemmed the testimonial tide. The audience once again sits in stunned, uncomfortable silence. I don't even try to stop myself from smirking.

"Well, well," I say again.

"Don't you have a conscience?" he whispers back, his fleshy, already brilliant ruddy face reddening even more until there is nearly no white skin left at all. "Why don't *you* stand up and say something?"

"I have my reasons," I hiss. I turn back to the minister, who has resigned himself to the cessation of the testimonials and is completing the service.

And I do. True, I lack the appropriate memories to make a real testimonial, but there is another reason why I don't say anything. Perhaps, as my uncle has shown, any testimonial is inappropriate if it lacks meaning. And if something actually is meaningful, then perhaps it doesn't need saying. This, perhaps, is why Jodi Ramirez doesn't say anything during her husband's memorial service; she doesn't make a testimonial to her dead husband and neither do her daughters. Neither does the man who I assume is Mark's father; in fact, he leaves immediately after the hip young minister has completed the service. Perhaps all of them—father, wife, daughters—know what it means to have too much meaning, to be sick of meaning.

The end of the service, and with it, one final religious generalization. Catholics are so fearful of mishandling death that they carry their ritual out of church and the cemetery, and into the postfuneral reception, where the lighting of the candles and the singing of hymns becomes the drinking of cheap bourbon and the consumption of catered finger foods. These Presbyterians have no such ritual. These Presbyterians are more than willing to stand around uncomfortably in the cemetery long after the service has been brought to a close. This we do: no booze, no miniature egg salad sandwiches, no ritual of any kind. If it were up to me, we would just leave, just get back in the squad car where I would gladly endure my uncle's snide interrogation. But my father has chosen to go over and speak to the hip young minister; my uncle is saying something inappropriate to Jodi Ramirez and her family. He is shaking her father's hand, no doubt congratulating him on his testimonial. I am left all alone. Left alone, I feel weepy once again, not only because I feel sad about Mark, about Jodi, about myself, about *everything*, but because I have nowhere to put the sadness.

So maybe *this* is why Catholics want ritual: maybe it is not because they are afraid of death, not because they are afraid of grief, either, but because they are afraid they won't have a place to put the grief once it finds them.

My uncle and father are very experienced grievers, which is why they have engaged themselves in idle conversation and condolences. So I take their lead, and try to find a place to put my grief. Consider the day itself: dancing warm sun, tough, steady breeze, clear view of the heaving, buckling hills and green valley. It is the kind of day when you wonder why so many people would have ever left this place for other, less beautiful places. More sadness. I consider the memory of my uncle Lee's funeral. No good at all. I consider Glori, who is working right now, less than two miles from here, and whom I may never get back. Oh, boy.

I consider the crowd and the implications of its sparseness: Mark is dead and murdered and is no longer abstract, and most of the people in town are still apathetic. How awful it is to be killed, to be *dead*, and not have people care about it.

Finally, right as I am on the verge of once again giving myself up to shameless weeping, I consider the sight of Jodi Ramirez, who is standing there with her family. She is listening to my uncle's vague promises to catch her husband's killer, but she is not looking at him while he speaks. No, Jodi is staring over my uncle's shoulder, staring directly at me. I don't hide my eyes; I look right back at her. There is nothing to suggest that Jodi has forgotten or forgiven me. She hates me, of course she does. But there is something other than hate that Jodi Ramirez wants me to see: she is not crying, even though she has earned the right. This is true of her daughters as well: they deserve to be weeping, have earned the right to do so, yet they are not. They make me ashamed of even thinking of crying.

So I decide to put my grief into this promise: I will not cry again until I have earned the right to. I nod at Jodi. I want her to know that I get her meaning, but she does not nod back. Jodi simply turns her attention back to my uncle, who is still blathering on.

I am relieved to see my father disengage himself from the hip minister and walk my way.

"Ready to go back to work?" my father asks.

"I'm ready," I say, and I am.

CHAPTER 5

A CONFESSION: I have a fantasy in which I find and then interrogate Mark Ramirez's killer. In my fantasy, the killer resembles my uncle Eli in looks and in his racist worldviews. He is unrepentant and stonewalls a great deal when I ask him my questions.

"Do you have any idea how many lives you've ruined?" I ask him. "Do you have any idea how many lives you're *still* ruining?"

At this point, my fantasy merges with that of the racial-remediation instructor's: the murderer admits to the evil of his racism, repents, and submits himself to the whim of my tutelage.

This fantasy is so satisfying that it leads me to spend more time than I would like with my uncle Bart, who lets me tag along as he continues his investigation of Mark Ramirez's murder. Why does he agree to let me do so given our history of mutual antagonism? Maybe my father has browbeat him into it. Or maybe my uncle, like me, wants to find the killer and yet does not believe he can do so. Maybe my uncle, like me, does not want to fail alone.

In any case, I accompany Uncle Bart as he visits and revisits the crime scene, confers with his deputies and patrolmen, sends out updated press releases to newspapers and post offices asking for information leading to the arrest of Mark Ramirez's killer. This goes on for two weeks. Nothing comes of it. At the end of the two weeks, the murder is still unsolved, my fantasy unfulfilled, and I divest myself of any and all involvement with my uncle Bart.

But two significant things do happen while I am in the company of my uncle. One, Ian Chisholm files a lawsuit against my uncle and the Little Falls Police Department for police brutality. This happens two days after Mark Ramirez's funeral. According to the legal papers, Ian Chisholm wants $2 million in damages.

I am at the police station, looking over the official file on the Mark Ramirez case, when my uncle gets wind of the lawsuit.

"Two million dollars," he says, coming out of his office.

"Two million dollars what?" I ask, and he tells me.

"Justice!" I say. "Right here in the police department."

"Not now, Lamar," Uncle Bart says. "Don't you know what this means?" My uncle immediately breaks out into a forehead sweat. He untucks his short-sleeve shirt and uses it to wipe off his forehead. I pay close attention to all this detail so I can tell my father about it later on.

"It means that you're very sorry that your boys beat up on Ian Chisholm in the first place."

"No," my uncle says. "It means that if he wins the lawsuit, I'll never get reelected. It means I'll be out of a job."

"If you lose your job, that's because your three idiots beat up Ian Chisholm. That's what you should be sorry about."

"I'm sorry because I'll be unemployed," my uncle says. "Ian Chisholm struck a police officer. He got what he deserved."

"You're wrong."

"Jesus, I don't have time for this, Lamar." That said, my uncle turns away from me and runs back into his office to call the city attorney.

I put down the Mark Ramirez file, find a pay phone inside the police station, call my father, and tell him about the lawsuit. I go into great detail about my uncle's reaction, his profuse sweating, and his lack of proper regret.

My father is curiously unimpressed by the news.

"What did you expect him to say?" my father asks me.

"I wanted him to say he was sorry and mean it."

"Sorry for what?"

"Sorry for Ian Chisholm getting beaten up in the first place, and sorry for letting his three cops get away with it."

"Well."

"I at least wanted him to be sorry about the lawsuit for the right reasons."

"No one is ever sorry for the right reasons," my father says. We have slipped into a familiar father–son groove here: my father once again is the experienced wrestler in the ring of small-town intrigue, and I am again merely his naive flunky. It is a relationship I've been hoping to outgrow.

"In any case," I say, "at least Uncle Bart will get what he deserves."

"What are you talking about?"

"He's going to lose his *job*."

My father laughs, a harsh cynical chuckle. "I hope you're right," he says. "But I doubt it. They'll probably settle out of court."

"Oh."

"Lamar," my father says, "you still don't know how the world works." Then he hangs up.

My first reaction is anger: *you still don't know how the world works.* My second reaction is surrender: it's probably true that I don't know how the world works and my old man does.

Or maybe he does not. True, as my father says, my uncle and the city attorney do try to settle out of court. But, surprise of all surprises, Ian Chisholm won't do it: his brother Eric is in jail for two more months and word is, Ian Chisholm is irate about his brother's jail time and about his own beating. He wants his $2 million, and he wants my uncle unemployed.

So a judge sets the court date to hear the lawsuit: February 18 of next year.

I am right! Or at least, I haven't yet been proven entirely wrong. But I don't gloat over my father's misplaced confidence, mostly because my father is actually relieved that he's possibly misjudged the Ian Chisholm case. I think I know why: my father hopes that the world *has* changed, that he does not really know how the world works any longer. I mean, what an awful thing to know. I can picture myself in fifteen years, feting my old man at his retirement party: *I will never be the man my father is: I am a naif, but my father, he knows how the world works.* What a horribly final thing to say about your father on the eve of his retirement. A gold watch would be preferable.

THE SECOND significant thing happens two Wednesdays after Mark Ramirez's memorial service, when Uncle Bart and I take a ride out to Richfield Springs, a small town south and east of here. We do so because Uncle Bart finds out that Mark's father lives in Richfield Springs.

"Mark's father the one at the memorial service?"

"The very one," Uncle Bart says. "Jodi Ramirez told me so; she told me that she thought he lived somewhere out toward Vickerman Hill."

"Why didn't she tell you before?"

"She did tell me before, right after Mark's funeral. Mark's father talked to her before the funeral, told her where he was living."

"But that was two weeks ago."

My uncle shrugs. "I just remembered her telling me about it." As you might imagine, I find this response frustrating in the extreme. My uncle is most absentminded for a police chief, and Ian Chisholm's lawsuit has only made him more distracted.

"What's Mark's father's first name?" I ask.

My uncle's loose face droops a little. "She didn't say," he admits. "I forgot to ask."

"Did Jodi think he might know something?"

"She didn't know," he says, rebounding a little. "But I do. Fathers *always* know something." Uncle Bart scowls at me meaningfully. The ten-year-old memory of my potential ravaging of his daughter, Loreen, must still be prominent.

We find Mark's father in a small, clear-cut lot about a mile north of Richfield Springs. When we pull up in the squad car, Mark's father is resting on his haunches, watching a backhoe spin, strain, and struggle to drag a gray, dirt-spattered double-wide trailer home out of a gully. It has rained hard overnight and part of Vickerman Hill has washed away, twisting the trailer off its cinder-block foundations and leaving it sticking end up out of a gully.

My uncle and I get out of the squad car.

"That your trailer?" Uncle Bart asks.

"That your cop car?" Mark's father asks back, still squatting. The backhoe sputters, dies, then starts back up again. There is someone in the backhoe cab at the controls, a white guy wearing a baseball hat. There is a name painted on the backhoe: Kelly Construction.

"It is."

"I'll sell you it," Mark's father says from his squat. He points at the dirt-caked trailer, and looks up at my uncle. "Hundred bucks."

"I don't want to buy your trailer."

"Guess it's mine, then."

"Whose backhoe?" my uncle asks.

"Kelly's."

"Kelly the guy in the cab?"

"I'm Kelly," Mark's father says. "That guy works for me."

"Why Kelly?"

"*Ramirez* Construction?" he says. I get his point.

I consider the figure squatting in front of us. He is the same man who was at Mark's memorial service, all right, the same man who I assumed to be Mark's father. But up close, there is no resemblance aside from the ethnic. Mark had short, thinning gray-flecked black hair; this man has long hair, thick and very black. Mark was tall and thin; he looked like a track coach. This man is short, squat, not athletic at all. Mark always was dressed neatly, like a bank officer; this man is wearing a stained white sweatshirt that reads *Herkimer County Trust*. It is the kind of shirt you get for free when opening a checking account. It occurs to me that we might be talking to the wrong man altogether, and that Jodi Ramirez has given my uncle some false information just so that he would leave her alone.

"Are you really Mr. Ramirez?" I ask.

"Who are *you*?"

"He's my nephew," my uncle says, annoyed that I have interrupted his interrogation.

"You bring your *family*?" he asks my uncle.

"I'm also a reporter," I say.

"I know who you are."

"I was at Mark's funeral," I say. "I saw you there."

Mark's father nods and turns away from my uncle and myself, back to the trailer and the backhoe. The backhoe is making some progress. Its big wheels catch and take hold on the gully bank, and the trailer shudders and something snaps underneath it—an axle maybe, or some other piece of support—as the double-wide makes some inching headway up the bank. All looks good for the salvation of Mr. Ramirez's home. The trailer just about reaches the once-level place it slid down from in the first place when the backhoe loses its grip on the bank and slips back down, skidding sideways, its wheels whirling uselessly. The chain attached to the trailer loses its mooring, and the trailer itself slips straight down the hill again, coming to rest with a fine, solid *thud* at the bottom of the gully.

"Saw *you* there, too," Mark's father says, apparently unaffected by the sorry fate of his home. The backhoe operator gets out of the machine's cab, hops down, reattaches the chain to the trailer. He gets back in the backhoe, which starts spinning and jerking up the hill again. Mark's father continues to watch, paying no more attention to me and my uncle.

Something has been accomplished here, some understanding reached. I saw Mark's father at his son's funeral, and he me. This is an established fact. Moreover, I have seen the way Mark's father lives—in a trailer in the middle of the woods, away from the migrant workers he abandoned years before, away from white people, away from his family, away from everyone. In seeing all of this, I am supposed to see a great deal more. Do you think I would be here if I knew anything about who killed my son? This is what I think Mark's father wants my uncle and me to see. Do you think I would be here if I had choices in life?

"We'd like to ask you a few questions about your son's murder," my uncle says. He's obviously not seeing what I'm seeing.

Mark's father turns back to us. "You still here?" he asks.

"Did your son have any enemies?" my uncle asks. This is a standard police question; I have heard my uncle ask these kinds of pat questions repeatedly over the previous two weeks, with no results.

"You left your family when Mark was still in high school, isn't that right?" I ask, once again commandeering the interrogation.

He nods.

"Why?"

"Mark didn't like me much."

"Didn't like you why?"

Mark Ramirez's father stares at me, smirking, as if I should know the answer to what must be an obvious question. But I truly don't know the answer, don't even know why the question is obvious, either.

"I had no work," he finally says. "We were very poor. This embarrassed him."

"So you ran away?"

"He was ashamed of me."

"So you ran away."

"Correct."

"You ran away to Richfield Springs?"

"It was far enough."

"And when was the last time you saw your son alive?" I ask.

"June."

"June. Where?"

"Track meet," Mark's father says. "Junior varsity meet against Mohawk."

"Mark coached junior varsity track."

"No kidding," he says. "That's why I was there."

"Did you sit in the stands?"

"I stood up on the hill and watched Mark."

"You didn't watch the track meet?"

"I watched everything."

"Did Mark know you were there?"

"I don't think so. Maybe."

"Why were you spying on him?" my uncle says, sensing something sinister.

"Not spying. *Watching.* You ever watch someone?"

Mark's father stands up slightly, pulls out a pack of cigarettes from his front pantpocket, lights one, takes a long, deliberate first drag, and turns away from Uncle Bart and myself, back into a squatting observance of his dislodged home, which is still crawling up the bank behind the backhoe.

"Do you have any idea who murdered your son?" my uncle asks, switching back into the routine interrogatives. He is obviously getting frustrated. I even feel a little sympathy for him.

"Who do *you* think did it?" Mark's father asks, still not turning away from his trailer.

"We think it might be racially motivated."

"A white man did it."

"We think so."

He nods. "Of *course* a white man did it," he says. His eyes return briefly to my uncle, then back to the trailer.

"Thanks for all your help," my uncle says. He spins on his heel and I follow him, back to the police cruiser.

"He's not telling us something," my uncle says once we are back inside the car.

"You might be right," I say. We are in the last dying moments of our partnership, and I feel no need to start arguing with my uncle now. Besides, my uncle might actually be right for once in his law-enforcement career: there is likely a great deal indeed that Mark's father has not told us, a great deal we will never know about Mark's father.

But does he know anything more about what happened to his son? That is another question entirely. Do fathers ever really know what happens to their sons?

We wheel around in the mud that passes for Mark's father's driveway. As we're leaving I see him still squatting, still watching the backhoe's tires spin and the trailer once again break free and careen back down the gully. Mark's father has an expression on his face, a very patient, resigned look that I have witnessed before, on my uncle Lee's face during a summer-long dairy industry crisis several years ago. That summer my uncle would wake up, look out at his barns and milking parlors and his cows and hope that milk prices would rise, that the government would come through with greater subsidies and tax breaks, even though he knew they would not. My uncle's simple blank stare told me that one must expect the inevitable to happen, even if one hopes it does not.

"We'll be back," my uncle yells out the window. We still haven't learned Mark's father's first name. "You'll be seeing us again."

Mark's father doesn't react to my uncle's promise. I wonder, somehow, if it is an unnecessary piece of information.

ONE MUST expect the inevitable to happen, even if one hopes it does not. This is what I've learned over the last weeks and months. True, I give up on my uncle, but I do not give up on the Mark Ramirez case itself. I keep at it, calling my uncle Bart down at the station, pumping him for information, calling reporters at other local newspapers, calling Jodi Ramirez (she is curt with me, officious, but she doesn't bring up my abandonment of her at the rally in Utica). Nothing comes from all this calling, but I keep at it, because this is what people of substance do: they do not give up on hopeless cases because they're hopeless. This is what I have learned.

CHAPTER 6

LABOR DAY, and with it, the Kerry family reunion. The day begins with the horror of horrors. I pull into my parents' driveway around nine in the morning and see my mother lying facedown on the driveway. Her wheelchair is a foot behind her. My mother has fallen out of her wheelchair onto the gravel driveway. And she isn't moving.

Do I scream? Of course I scream. I'm screaming my mother's name before I even get out of the car; I'm screaming things I would be embarrassed to hear other people scream. I scream, "Please don't die," and "Jesus, oh, fucking Jesus." I don't even turn the car off; I just slam it in park and run to where my mother is stretched out on the driveway. I am ashamed to say that once I get to my mother, I am already thinking of her as my dead mother, my poor dead mother, and I am her loving, bereaved son, and what in the fuck am I going to do *now*? I'm even more ashamed to say that I examine her the way a coroner might examine a corpse. The first thing I notice is that my mother is wearing madras shorts, and how small and withered her legs are, like wilted albino green beans. Then I notice how strong and knotty her arms are from manning her wheelchair. Then I see that my mother's head is turned in my direction, and she is looking at me: not smiling at me, not laughing at me, not pleading with me, simply staring at me placidly as if to say, Help me up, please.

"Help me up, please," my mother says.

I help her up, back into her wheelchair, help her brush the gravel and dirt off her strong arms, her withered legs. By this point, my father—who was inside shaving during all of this—is outside, flecks of shaving cream still on his ears and neck. I tell him what has happened.

"Don't overreact, Lamar," my mother says to my father. She reminds him of the new medicine she's on, and how the doctor said it might cause momentary blackouts, like the one that my mother has just had.

"There's nothing wrong with me that wasn't wrong with me before," my mother says. She has her hands on the wheels of her chair and makes ready to go back into the house. My mother has a reunion to run, after all. But my father is holding the handles of the wheelchair, and he isn't letting my mother go anywhere. In this way, right in the driveway, my mother, father, and myself hold a conference. Picture Roosevelt, Churchill, and Stalin convening in Yalta. Yes, it is the morning of the conference and it is *hot*, visible waves of heat hovering and dancing over the valley. Roosevelt has just fallen out of his wheelchair and doesn't want to talk about it. Churchill and Stalin are wiping their brows, and delicately, very delicately reminding Roosevelt to attend to his considerable physical limitations.

"I am fine," my mother says, twisting and shifting in her wheelchair. "Don't worry about a thing."

"Just don't push yourself," my father says.

"He's right," I say. "You just blacked out, remember. You were lying on the driveway like you were *dead*. You have to take it easy."

"Why do I have to take it easy?"

"What's that?"

"Why do I have to take it easy?"

"Because you're *sick*."

"That's right," my mother says. "I am so sick that I am in a wheelchair. And no matter what, I'll be in a wheelchair tomorrow. Or maybe I'll feel so bad that I'll have to get out of my wheelchair and into bed. And the next day or the day after I'll feel better enough, just enough, to be able to get back in this thing again." She pounds on the wheelchair arms. "So why should I take it easy?"

"Because."

"Because why? Because it will make you feel better?"

"Yes." After all, this is the truth: my mother taking it easy will make me feel better. Whether it makes her feel better is nearly incidental. I am about to say this when my father steps in.

"All right, then," he says, acting as the mediator. He is definitely Churchill, intervening and putting a stop to the debate before Stalin and Roosevelt start speaking other truths.

Stalin throws up his hands, turns his back on Roosevelt, and goes to find some vodka.

Surprisingly, despite this ugly little rift, and despite my drinking vodka tonics very early in the day, the reunion turns out to be a mostly happy, well-run affair: the initial getting-caught-up ritual is satisfying and congenial, and we don't run out of potato salad or beer or anything. The only potential trouble occurs during the softball game. My uncle Bart, who is playing first base, makes the mistake of starting up a conversation with a distant cousin from Batavia. The Batavia cousin has just hit a single to left field. Uncle Bart has drunk just enough beer to start talking, apropos of nothing, about Mark Ramirez's murder. My uncle tells the cousin, who

is utterly baffled by the drift of the conversation, that he will definitely find the killer.

"You will?" the Batavia cousin asks.

"I'll find him," my uncle says, loud enough to be heard
throughout the reunion. Uncle Bart is wearing a too large Little
Falls Mounties Varsity Club T-shirt that has come untucked and is
hanging almost to his knees. With his red, drunk face and his
ridiculously large shirt, he looks like an obese child who's been out
in the sun too long, and who has been given his father's overlarge
T-shirt so that no material will brush up against his burned skin.

"Give me enough time," my uncle says, "I'll find him."

"Give you the murderer's name and address," my mother says,
"and you still won't find him."

My mother is the first-base coach. She says this loud enough so
that Uncle Bart can definitely hear it, so that I can hear it over on
third base, so that my cousin Loreen can hear it from centerfield, so
that everyone can hear it. Since it is my mother, though, since she is
a Kerry only by marriage and is stuck in a wheelchair, everyone—
including my uncle Bart—pretends that they have not heard my
mother say what she has said. The game goes on and my uncle
keeps his promises to himself.

Why do I mention this ugly moment in our family reunion? Because my mother has said the meanest, most truthful thing possible
and has gotten away with it. Because just hours earlier my mother
fell out of her wheelchair, and I thought she was dead, and she is
not dead yet but she is dying, there is no way around it, and somehow she is *still* not a victim. It is quite an accomplishment. I am
proud of her. I forget all about our little tiff from before and find my
anger replaced by a great, deep feeling of admiration for my
mother, a feeling that is indistinguishable from love itself.

I come up to my mother after the game. I haven't spoken to her
since our run-in earlier in the day.

"Mother."

"Son.

"Do you want anything?" I ask her. I hold up my vodka tonic cup and shake it, rattling the ice inside.

"I want your uncle Bart to get sued and lose his job," she says. "He's getting on my nerves."

"Mother," I say, "if I grow up, I want to be just like you."

I put my hand on my mother's shoulder, and she reaches back and puts her hand on mine. It is a fine, emotional moment. Stalin and Roosevelt reconcile and start making plans to carve up Berlin.

AFTER THE softball game, the reunion gets diffuse, people wandering off to corners of the yard to smoke cigarettes and have their private conversations free from the sentimental group dynamic. I find myself, as drunks are bound to do, knocking around my parents' house looking for something and forgetting what it is. During my search, I pass by my parents' bedroom and see my father standing there in the half darkness. My father, who is an enthusiastic softball player, slid into second base during the game, and so he has gone upstairs to change out of his dirty shorts and T-shirt, into a clean pair of pants and polo shirt. As I begin to walk past the room, I see that my father has donned the polo shirt, but has not yet put on the trousers. He is standing there in his jockey shorts, staring out the window into the backyard.

"Dad," I say, stopping in the doorway, "you forgot your pants."

"I miss my brothers," he says, not turning around. His voice hasn't quite cracked yet, but it isn't entirely steady or strong, either.

"What did you say?"

He says it again.

"You do?"

"Of course I do, Lamar."

Of course he does. Why have I never thought of this? What is wrong with me? My father was a stoic during Uncle Eli's trial and sentencing, didn't show any emotion at Uncle Lee's funeral, either. This, of course, was odd in my mind, especially since my father can be such a willing weeper. But aren't true adults always strange to us nonadults? My father had never, until now, even commented on the repercussions of his losses, as if both—the death and the imprisonment—were leaves that inevitably fall off the family tree. This was odd as well and was therefore properly adultlike to my child's mind. Being a child, I have neglected to consider how important my family's fallen and vanished leaves must be.

Of course.

"Do you know why I don't go up to see Eli anymore?" my father asks me, still staring out the window. I know that he hasn't been up to see his brother in over a year.

"Because you have nothing else to say to him?"

"No," my father says. "Eli tells me that I have too much to say to him. That's why I don't go up to see your uncle anymore. He doesn't want me to."

"He said that?"

"'Don't come up to see me anymore, Lamar.' That's a direct quote."

"I see."

"He says I make him angry."

"Because you think you're better than him?"

"What did you just say?" my father asks. There is a definite rise of anger in his question.

"I'm just guessing," I say. "That's what Uncle Eli thinks you think. That you're better than him."

"Something like that."

We fall into silent tableau, father staring out the window, son staring at father. Unfortunately, once you learn certain important truths about your old man, it is too late to do anything but stand there and be a patient, empathetic witness to his grief. The son's ability to make his father feel better is limited; this is what I'm discovering. Sometimes there is nothing more a son can do but stand there and wait for his father to exhaust his sadness and put on his pants and rejoin the family reunion, where a part of the family that really matters is absent.

This I do.

MY FATHER'S confession does something funny to me. I say this because before the end of our family reunion, I wind up having sex with my cousin, Loreen.

Why do I do so? I do so because my father's confession has made me very sad and lonely myself. When you are sad and lonely, then you go and find the person you love. If that person isn't speaking to you, if you are fearful that she will never speak to you again, then you must grab someone else. So I do. Everyone is outside, waiting out the last, sighing moments of the reunion, except for my cousin Loreen, whom I find flipping through my parents' record collection in the living room. Loreen is looking very lonely herself. I grab her with no sort of preface or apology and, miracle of miracles, she grabs me back, and we stagger up the stairs, groping and stripping as we go, and have sex in my parents' room. When Loreen and I are done, we look at each other, not speaking, and do it again. It is an absolute feast in there, a carnal Last Supper. We are both starving in our loneliness; if there were other willing cousins, we would have sex with them, too.

I have no idea how long we are in the bedroom. It could be five minutes, could be an hour. It is dark outside when Loreen and I enter the bedroom, dark when we leave. All I can say is, I feel better, immeasurably better. It is the kind of moment where you should say, It will never happen again. But I don't say this, and neither does Loreen. We finally break our clinch, dress, and then part, saying nothing.

But what does this say about me? Am I the kind of guy who, missing his real love, finds a substitute in kin? Am I the kind of guy who, in the face of family tragedy, flirts with greater family tragedy? Am I the kind of guy who has sex with his cousin in his parents' bedroom while his and her parents are outside, eating the last remains of the German potato salad and apple pandowdy?

Best to admit none of this. Best just to say, I had sex with my cousin, and it wasn't bad.

CHAPTER 7

THE ADULTS are tired. I notice this after our family reunion. Me, I feel
very youthful in the immediate wake of my incest. In comparison, all
the real adults seem exhausted.

My mother, of course, is always tired, especially when she is
trying not to appear tired. My uncle, in his obesity and his breathless incompetence, always appears tired as well. But it is my father's fatigue that attracts my attention. On the Tuesday after the
reunion, I come into work at ten in the morning and find my father
sitting at his desk, his white cotton shirt slightly pulled out of his
pants, his tie already loose, his face unshaven. Most people would
mistake my father's appearance for the newspaperman's conven-
tional sloppiness; but my father has always been neat for a newspaper editor.

"You all right, Dad?"

"Fine."

"You look tired."

"I'm fine."

"OK." I quit examining my father's fatigue, sit down at my desk, and turn on my computer. "What am I doing today?" I ask him. "Am I an obit writer? Am I a photographer? Am I a plagiarist?"

"You are a local media contact."

"What's that?"

My father explains that early this morning, before he came into work, he received a call at home from a reporter in New York City who wants to do a story on the Mark Ramirez case. The reporter said that he would be in Little Falls around noon; was there anyone from the paper he could talk to? he wanted to know.

"I'm going out to lunch," my father says. "You'll have to be the contact."

"Fine," I say. "What should I tell him?"

"Whatever you want," my father says wearily. He gets up out of his chair and goes to leave the office.

"Where are you going?"

"I told you. I'm going to lunch," he says and then walks out the door. It is five minutes after ten.

Sis is out covering a city planner's meeting, and so I am by myself when the downstate newspaper reporter comes into the office, around noon, as promised. He is about my age and height and social class. In fact, the downstate reporter looks like someone I might have gone to college with: blond hair parted to the side, jeans shirt, and broad striped tie. I find out that the reporter doesn't actually work for a city paper at all; instead, he works for the White Plains *Union,* a suburban daily. Our visitor's absurdly professional demeanor tells me he has certain illusions that this story might get him a better job at a bigger paper.

"Michael Barnes," he says, shaking my hand.

I tell him my name and that I am pleased to meet him.

Michael Barnes ("*Michael,*" he says, after I have made the mistake of abbreviating his name. "Only my mother calls me Mike.") is the only nonlocal journalist who has come to town for the purpose of covering the Mark Ramirez story. This does not seem strange to me: over the last six months, there have been more concrete, more easily solvable hate crimes to attend to—the black man murdered in Texas, a gay man robbed, mutilated, and left to die in Wyoming. But once Michael Barnes starts asking me questions, it becomes clear that he is the source of my father's fatigue and his extremely early lunch. Michael Barnes makes me feel tired, too, even though I am in the rejuvenation of my cousin-love.

"What can you tell me about Mark Ramirez?"

I tell him everything I know. It is not an impressive narrative, nor is it a particularly long one. Michael Barnes is obviously dismayed, even though he attempts to veil his dismay with his professionalism.

"What can you tell me about his murder, then?" Michael Barnes asks, tapping his ballpoint pen against his spiral-bound notebook.

"What do you want to know?"

"Are there any leads?"

"None to speak of."

"What's the reaction around town?"

"Apathy."

"Are there any relatives of the victim I could speak to?"

I mention Jodi Ramirez, their kids, and Mark's father. I tell him about the police chief's (I don't mention that the police chief is my uncle) and my recent visit to Mark's father's trailer, and how fruitless it turned out to be.

"What's his name?"

"Whose name?"

"Mark Ramirez's father."

"I don't know," I admit.

"You don't *know*?" Michael Barnes asks. This question—its incredulity, its attendant accusation—is why my father was so tired, and why I am now partner to his weariness. Michael Barnes's questions feel like reprimands: reporters have a responsibility to their subjects, he suggests through his incredulity. What we are supposed to be responsible for is unclear, but obviously, Michael Barnes believes that through our incompetence, through our inability to find out anything tangible about Mark Ramirez's murder, my father and I have abdicated our responsibilities.

This implied accusation is no small outrage. I would beat Michael Barnes over the head with his own spiral-bound notebook if I weren't so fucking *tired*.

"Who else might I talk to?" he asks me, efficiently snapping his notebook closed.

"You should talk to the chief of police himself," I say. "Chief Bart Kerry."

I again do not mention our relation, and Michael Barnes doesn't notice our shared last name. A minor victory. Our visiting reporter is not that much better than me after all.

Michael Barnes goes to find my uncle Bart.

I put my feet up on my desk and take a small nap.

Three hours later, I get a call from Michael Barnes. He is calling from a pay phone outside of the Shopper's Square, and he sounds considerably less professional than he was earlier.

"I just thought you should know," Michael Barnes says. "I didn't find out *anything*."

"Sorry to hear that."

"The chief of police doesn't know *shit*."

"No, he doesn't."

"I thought maybe he would know something," Michael Barnes says, his voice cracking and breaking like an old, swollen wood door being slammed shut. "I thought he would know something and just not want to tell it to me. I expected him to at least be *evil*."

"Evil," I repeat.

"But he's not evil. He's just incompetent."

"Can incompetence not be evil?" I ask. It feels very good,

throwing Michael Barnes this philosophical curveball. But Michael Barnes isn't even at the plate, doesn't even have a bat. He doesn't appear to be listening to me at all.

"And you were right," he says. "I asked around town. No one seems to give a damn about the murder. They seem totally apathetic."

"Can apathy not be evil either?" I ask.

"There's no *story* here," Michael Barnes says. Then he hangs up.

The dial tone is satisfying for a moment, extremely satisfying, until I consider my own unanswered questions: Is incompetence evil? Is apathy? Is ordinariness?

CHAPTER 8

UNFORTUNATELY, ONCE satisfaction dissolves, guilt sets in. And once guilt sets in, one cannot simply sleep off its consequences. Michael Barnes's interrogation doesn't just make me feel tired; it makes me feel older than I did. Feeling older, I am increasingly dismayed by the implications of my youthful, irresponsible behavior. In particular, I begin to fixate on my incest. During the week after Michael Barnes's visit I gradually begin to feel more and more guilty about my fling with Loreen, and nothing I do—work, exercise, crossword puzzles—makes me feel any better. I am plagued with self-doubt. Will someone find out? Will Glori find out? What will she do if she does? Can I find happiness without Glori? Have I killed any and all chances at reconciliation? What is going to *happen* to me?

Friday afternoon arrives. I am sitting in front of my computer at work, far removed from the immediate pleasures of my satiation, and I am feeling bad, real bad. I decide that something must be done if I am to be rescued from the shipwreck of my incest.

So I call Glori at the end of the workday, about three in the afternoon. It has been more than three weeks since we last spoke.

"Monroe Street Elementary School." It is her voice.

"I am calling you from work."

"Good for you."

"I've learned some things," I tell her.

"For instance."

"For instance, I've learned that innocence is meaningless."

"When were you ever innocent?"

"That, too."

"And?"

"And I've learned that I'm sorry. I'm calling you to tell you I am
sorry."

"For what?"

"For everything. I am sorry for leaving, and I am sorry for not
apologizing when I returned. I'm sorry for abandoning you when
you needed me. And I'm sorry if I made you unhappy."

"You should be," Glori says. "Is that it?"

"That's some of it," I say.

She hangs up. Three hours later, I am knocking on her apartment door. I do not use the key she gave me way back when. Because this is not something a person of substance would do.

"What's the rest of it?" she asks, not opening the door. It is a
heavy wood door. When Glori speaks, it sounds like she is talking
through a wet mattress.

"The rest of it," I say, "is that I am very, very sorry. The sum of
my regret is great. That is all I can say."

And I stand there, waiting outside the door that does not seem
inclined to swing open. I don't care. I still stand there. "Sorry" is all
I can say and having said it, I can think of nothing else to do but
wait, even though apologizing and waiting is not likely to be
enough. The racial-remediation instructor is inclined to agree. As I
stand in front of Glori's apartment, waiting, the racial-remediation

instructor is having a cigarette outside the school with the romantic-remediation instructor, and the former is telling the latter, "Believe me, you've got your hands full. I have his uncle in class and get this: He's *sorry*, too."

But there is remedial education and there is another kind of education, not remedial and not advanced, either, and I am about to receive it: it is an education in luck. If you need luck and if you wait long enough, then luck might possibly find you.

Luck finds me after two minutes, standing outside Glori's door, waiting.

"Get in here, Lamar," Glori says, swinging the door wide open. Her voice is very grave.

I am still myopic with fear, but I am more afraid not to look. And so I look into Glori's face, and I see that she is much more than beautiful. She is so beautiful she is underneath beauty. Glori is underneath beauty because she has done something that no one who is perfectly beautiful would have done: she's settled for someone like me, someone who after weeks of exile and penance and soul-searching can only apologize and then wait for luck to find him.

"Lamar, get *in* here," Glori says again. I am still standing there on the welcome mat (there really is one). "Happy birthday," she says.

And it is my birthday. I am twenty-eight years old today. Glori remembers this because she is a person of substance, and because she is a person of substance, the *Happy Birthday* means something. It means we are back together, although how far back is still a mystery. Me, I am obviously not a person of substance yet, because I chose to prove I was one on the dramatic carpet of my birthday. I did not have to pull the carpet out from under Glori, but I would have if all else substantial had failed. I would have, but did not have to. I have received an education in luck and I am happy, not thinking of drama, not thinking at all.

CHAPTER 9

THE ONE thing you want to do in this life is find the few truths you must resign yourself to, and then do so as painlessly and efficiently as possible. It has taken me five years, but I have finally resigned myself to this: my mother is not going to get better. I have also resigned myself to the fact that I am in love with Glori, and yet I don't really know what love is, don't really know what happiness is either.

Soon after our reconciliation, I ask Glori these questions.

"Are you in love with me?"

"Yes," she says. "Absolutely."

"Why?"

"*Why?*"

"Forget it," I say. "Are you happy at least? Do you know what happiness looks like now?"

"Jesus, Lamar," she says. "I don't know about any of this stuff. Ask me the first question again."

"Do you love me?"

"*Yes*," she says.

So maybe this is love, the not knowing. Or maybe you only truly know what love is when you fall out of it. Either way, I know that I love Glori and that I *need* her. Need might not be the whole of love, but it cannot be too far from it. To this, I am happily resigned.

As for my cousin Loreen, I do not tell Glori about our little tryst. I will keep it a secret. The truth will emerge at some future moment, and I will struggle to explain it and I will fail, and there will be consequences that might be serious, might be comic. But for now, I will do the easy thing and keep it a secret. To this, I am also resigned.

That settled, I move into Glori's apartment and we make plans to be married. We are to be married on March 21, the first day of spring. This is Glori's idea.

"I've always wanted to get married on the first day of spring," Glori tells me.

"You have?"

"I have," she says. "You didn't know that about me, did you?"

I admit that I did not.

"What else don't I know about you?" I ask.

"It's impossible to tell."

"Fine by me," I say, and before we go any deeper into the well of what I don't know, I kiss Glori. A taste of tobacco, mint chewing gum, and then something vague: perhaps saltine cracker, perhaps sweat, perhaps something else entirely. It is impossible to tell.

MY PARENTS are *giddy* about our engagement; they are so pleased.

"We had resigned ourselves to you two never getting married," my father tells Glori and me. The four of us are eating dinner at Ponzo's, to celebrate our engagement.

"Me, too," Glori says.

"Me, too," I say.

"We're so happy for you," my mother says. We are all drinking red wine, even my mother. My mother is not supposed to drink alcohol of any kind. Her doctor told her so. But she is drinking a little red wine, and I am not going to tell her to stop. My mother raises her newly filled wineglass and I clink it with my own. I will visit her tomorrow while she is in bed, recovering.

"I want to make a toast," my father says.

"No," I say. My father is a little drunk already. I fear a reprise of him telling us that he was never as good a father as his father was.

"That would be nice," Glori says.

"To your happiness," my father says. And that is it. It is a nice, vague, hopeful toast. More clinking of glasses.

To further celebrate our engagement, Glori and I go to the Renaissance after dinner. I have been so busy proving myself to be a man of substance that I haven't been in the Renaissance since I returned to Little Falls from my exile. Glori has not been back, either, she tells me. She also tells me that her friend Sheila quit work, quit my old friend Andrew Marchetti, quit Little Falls itself immediately after Andrew left to take the job at the prison.

As for Andrew, I have told Glori, of course, that I went north with him, but I have not told her that Andrew never did go to work at the prison, and I have not told her that the last time I saw Andrew he was alone in a motel room. I promised Andrew that I would not tell anyone where he is or what he is doing, and even though I've broken promises to almost every person I've cared about, for some reason I have kept my promise to Andrew.

But nothing has changed at the Renaissance. Surprisingly, even our old friend Andrew is behind the bar, working.

"What the hell are you doing here?" Glori asks. "I thought you were working at the prison."

"I was," he says, giving us two bottles of Utica Club. He looks at me, and his eyes are wet and soft and old and grateful. With his eyes he is saying, "Thank you for not telling anyone." And this is why, I suppose, I have kept Andrew's secret: because he needed me to. Because he needed me to witness him at his saddest and keep his secrets and still be his friend. And I am. I will not be the same lifelong fuckup friend I was before our trip, but both Andrew and I left home, and we both failed in our leaving and then came home again, and if shared failure isn't true friendship, it is close enough.

"I quit the job at the prison," he says.

"You resigned!" I say.

"Whichever," he says, his eyes a little less soft and grateful.

"Why?" Glori asks.

Andrew will not go into details, obviously, since he never worked at the prison in the first place. All Andrew will say is that he has resigned from his position at the prison, and in doing so, he has resigned himself to working at the family bar for the rest of his life.

"Guess what?" I say to Andrew, hoping to brighten his mood with our good news. "We're engaged!"

"It doesn't surprise me one bit," he says, bringing us two more beers, on the house. "Congratulations."

"Thank you," Glori says.

"Thank you," I say, holding her hand underneath the bar. Glori looks very brave, sitting here on the far lip of engagement, looking out onto the big, scary world to which we have just resigned ourselves. And if Glori looks brave, then Andrew and I must look brave as well. Yes, I am truly proud of the three of us. Who would have thought we would be so courageous in our resignation?

Of course, we may not know exactly how brave we are or how brave we may yet need to be, but then again, the brave never really do know how brave they are until the need for courage has passed. Do they?

CHAPTER 10

AFTER YOU'VE resigned yourself to being brave, there is very little else that you will want to resign yourself to. After Glori and I are engaged, I find only one thing worthy of my additional resignation. In December, my father sends me down to take a tour of Corrigan's Paper Company. A year ago the mill was placed on the EPA's list of most prolific polluters. Now, a year later, all the local media have been invited to take a tour of the facilities to see how seriously the mill has taken the terms of its probation. We are all given a press release entitled, "Corrigan's: Cleaning Up Its Act." The press release promises that the company will lead the paper industry "into the 21st century." All of this is bogus, of course. We are shown the large front room on the factory's main floor, which is spotless and beautiful: newly cleaned brick walls and high arcing ceiling and brilliant faceted glass. The room is also empty of actual workers. We are not shown the incinerator or the actual working conditions or the river itself, which is still dark brown from all the pulp and chemicals the mill pumps into it. Nothing has changed except the mill's *attitude*. Attitude, the mill would have us believe, is everything. Twenty-first century, indeed.

But the mill's continuing pollution is not the thing to which I am resigned. That comes after the tour, after I have left the building itself. As I said, it is December, one of the first wild days of true winter, and it has just finished snowing, about twelve inches or so over the span of six hours. The snow is piled up on cars, on the roads, is hanging from power lines and trees, and the sun has just come out and it is blinding. After my eyes have adjusted to the light and the gleaming snow, I see two men sitting on the bumper of a pickup truck. The two men have either just gotten out of work or are taking a break. They are covered with a kind of brown film that could be pulp, could be almost anything. They stand out in remarkable dirty relief against the backdrop of the new, clean snow. I don't recognize either of the two men, although it's possible, even likely, that we went to school together. One of the men is smoking a cigarette.

"Enjoy your tour?" one of them asks.

"I enjoyed it."

"Did you really enjoy it?" the other man, the one with the cigarette, asks.

"Not so much."

"We would have enjoyed the tour."

"You work here?"

"We've never even been in that room you were in."

"Is that right?"

"I've worked for ten years," the cigarette smoker says. "Never seen that room."

"Nothing much to see," I tell him. "It's like a hotel lobby, an empty hotel lobby with brick walls."

"Like a hotel lobby." It is clear from the cigarette smoker's deadpan voice that he's never seen a hotel lobby, either.

"Or something like that," I say. "You're not missing much. Nothing much to see."

"We know that," the noncigarette smoker says.

"There is too much to see in the rest of the plant," the cigarette smoker says. "You walk through the back door and it's all there: the pulp, the machines, the burning in the back of your throat, all of it. We see it all the fucking time. That's why we'd like to take the tour."

"I understand," I say.

"We want to see that lobby."

"I understand."

"You don't understand one goddamn thing," the cigarette smoker tells me.

"You're probably right," I say, and then take my leave of these two men before our conversation and its emotional pitch and its sociopolitical meaning gets away from me entirely.

But I do understand, sort of. I understand three things, all of which are part and parcel of that to which I am resigned. One thing I understand is that I am a middle-class Kerry who lives in a working-class town and who has just taken a tour of the world of the working class, minus the working or the class, neither of which I have much in common with. The second thing I understand is that the life of a middle-class Kerry is easy, while the life of the working-class mill worker is hard. This is why the middle-class Kerry has so much time to breast-beat about his ordinariness, and the mill worker does not, which is why we have nothing much to say to each other. And I am fine with it, fine finally with being an ordinary white boy estranged from other ordinary white boys. The House of Ordinary, after all, has many rooms. And since the House of Ordinary is so spacious, I am fine, also, with the knowledge that ordinariness can be evil, is often evil, but not always, and not absolutely. I have reached a détente with ordinariness; perhaps, when I get back to the office, I will give my father the proper truce agreement papers and we will both sign them. It will be an awkward, vague truce that finally ends our Cold War of ordinary whiteness. But it will still be a truce, nonetheless.

The third thing that I understand is that the working class itself has been buried so deep in its work that its members need a tour of their own world, or at least what is supposed to pass for their own world. There are many tours needed here, is what I understand. Epcot Center should take note.

CHAPTER 11

AND WHAT of Mark Ramirez and his killer? What of the second act of our local production of Small Town Hate Crimes? Will anyone be joining and then replacing my uncle Eli on the racial merry-go-round of our penal system? Will the audience walk away happy? How will Jodi Ramirez and her daughters feel about the drama's conclusion? Will the second act be a disappointment?

The second act *is* something of a disappointment. And yet maybe it is not. I am not at all sure. The theatergoers aren't sure either. After the second act, the theatergoers remain in their seats in the high school auditorium. They are utterly confused. Was that *it*? they want to know. Did we miss something? Last year, the theatergoers complain, the high school drama club did a production of *To Kill a Mockingbird*. It was so beautiful. Everyone in the audience was bawling. And let me tell you: This was no *To Kill a Mockingbird*.

The theatergoers are correct. This is no *To Kill a Mockingbird*, and there is no righteous, shining Atticus Finch and no dim-witted, good-hearted Boo Radley. The falsely accused black man is not exonerated. He's not even black. He isn't even accused of anything. He is Puerto Rican and he is murdered and, months later, it appears that those two things have nothing to do with each other. It is a strange development. No one in the audience is bawling at the end of the second act, no one is even reaching for their tissues except maybe for the bereaved family of the victim. Everyone else in the auditorium is scratching their head and looking at the program. The audience doesn't care about the bereaved family or their grief. All they care about is getting the grief to make sense and then *go away*. In order for it to make sense and then go away, there must be another act. So the audience decides to take a stand: we are not leaving, they say, until we see another act, until we get the proper conclusion. The pitch of moral outrage is high. *To Kill a Mockingbird*, indeed.

Four months after my birthday, one month after my tour of Corrigan's, the police in Burlington, Vermont, arrest a jewel and antiquities thief. The thief is from Watertown, New York, up near the Canadian border. Two years earlier, he'd been granted parole for a felony larceny conviction. Anyway, four months after my birthday, the thief breaks his parole by leaving the state for Vermont. He leaves the state for the purposes of relieving a Burlington rare book dealer of his collection of John Audubon's private letters. After being apprehended midtheft by the Burlington police, the thief is then returned to Watertown where, apropos of nothing except the normal police lockup and interrogation, he confesses to a series of murders, all involving coin dealers, booksellers, and small-time jewelers. The thief is white, as were all his other four victims, except for Mark Ramirez.

Once my father hears the news, he heads up to Watertown with other local reporters and television people—and with Uncle Bart and his deputies—to find out what he can about Mark Ramirez's killer. I stay in Little Falls, with Sis, to crank out today's edition of the paper.

My father gets back to the office at about five o'clock. I am slowly typing up the farm report for tomorrow's paper, killing time, just waiting for my father to return and to tell me what he's found out.

"Well?"

"Well, he's definitely the one." Then my father tells me everything I have just told you. "He confessed to everything," my father says, falling back into his chair. He doesn't even bother taking off his snow-covered parka. "In writing."

"He was only a jewel thief?"

"A little disappointing, isn't it."

"He didn't even know Mark Ramirez?"

"He didn't even know Mark Ramirez," my father says. "He didn't know anything about anything, really. He had never even been to Little Falls before. Apparently he had heard that there was a coin and jewelry shop in town, on Albany Street, and that the owner left at five every night."

"But Mark Ramirez did not leave at five that night."

"He did not. And so the guy knocked Mark out with the butt of his gun. He waited in the shop until it was dark, and then dragged Mark out to Paine's Hollow, where he shot Mark and then left his body."

"What about Mark's shoes?" I ask. "What the hell happened to his shoes?"

"Mark wasn't wearing them in the shop when the thief busted in. The thief said he didn't want to leave them behind, and so he took Mark's shoes with him. He threw them out of his car window after he killed Mark."

"Out the car window?"

"Somewhere between Syracuse and Watertown. The police are looking for them right now."

"Christ," I say. "It was only a robbery? Mark was killed in a robbery? Are you sure?"

"I'm sure."

"But the murderer didn't even take any coins." I remember this detail from the original police report. "No jewels, either. Did he?"

"The guy said he got flustered," my father says. "He said the same thing happened with the other murders. He got flustered." Like Atticus Finch, my father has his gray hair and his wire-rimmed glasses. But unlike Atticus Finch, he looks dumb, like a man who has lost complete hold of his own intelligence. His eyes are wide like a young child's and his mouth hangs open a little bit.

"I would've been flustered, too, I suppose," I say.

"The guy said his conscience was killing him."

"I don't blame him one bit."

But the truth is, I do blame him, the man who murdered Mark Ramirez, except not because he was Puerto Rican, not because he was a Puerto Rican man married to a white woman in a white town, but for being a jeweler who stayed after hours when he shouldn't have. If the only Puerto Rican in a town of five thousand Uncle Elis can be killed for reasons other than race hate and miscegenation, does this really mean our world has changed? Is this progress? Is this a happy ending? Does this mean that we are no longer Uncle Elis, not even Uncle Eli himself? And if so, who exactly are we?

"What's his name?" I ask as an afterthought.

"Morgan," my father says. "Brian Morgan."

"He doesn't sound especially like a murderer. He doesn't sound especially like *anything*."

"No, he doesn't."

"What did Uncle Bart have to say about all this?"

"My cousin, the chief of police, was beside himself for not solving the murder," my father says, chuckling a little, more a cough than a real laugh. "I mean, he was really upset. He's got himself convinced that he's going to lose this lawsuit. Bart was thinking that by solving Mark's case, he might be able to save his job."

"He said this to you?"

"On the way up to Watertown. He confessed that he doesn't know what he'll be once he's not police chief. Your uncle is worried about being just like everybody else."

"Tell him not to worry. The House of Ordinary has many rooms."

"What?"

"Nothing."

"And Bart was doubly furious that he was so wrong about the motive being racial. He wouldn't talk to me all the way home."

"Uncle Bart wasn't the only one," I say. "Mark Ramirez's father had the same theory. So did I."

"So did I."

"A jewel thief was obviously not what Uncle Bart had in mind."

"A jewel thief," my father says, "was what nobody had in mind."

"What we had in mind," I say, "was Boo Radley. Maybe Atticus Finch, too."

My father laughs again, hesitantly, guiltily, the way people do when they feel good about something they shouldn't. It is a most ordinary gesture: the gesture of someone who doesn't expect big accomplishments from his son, who doesn't believe he is morally obliged to lecture a wayward, violent, racist brother. No, my father's little laugh is the gesture of someone who, after finishing a long, grinding day of work, is going to go home to his wife and watch television and be dumb and *like* it.

"I don't know about you," he says, heaving himself out of his chair, "but I am going to go home and relax."

"I bet you're going to watch a little TV when you get home."

"I am going to watch *a lot* of TV."

"I'll see you tomorrow," I say.

My father laughs once more before he leaves the office, and this time the laugh is not guilty or hesitant. No, this laugh is full of fine paternal feelings and high relief: my father has resigned himself to

THE ORDINARY WHITE BOY   255

my ordinariness and in doing so, finds it easy to resign himself to seeing me tomorrow, and the next day, and so on.

SO THAT, after everything that has happened, is that. I will finish typing up the farm report down at the office. Once I am done, I will return to Glori's and my apartment. We will sit on the couch together and have our go at ordinary domestic life. She will put her stockinged feet in my lap, and I will rub them and tell her that the case is solved, hallelujah.

"Is the case really solved?" Glori will not be smoking because she is quitting as part of our trip to domesticity; I will not be drinking because I am doing the same. As long as the trip lasts, I will be supportive and hide her rolling papers and her tobacco, and she will distract me from alcohol and my nagging desire for it.

"The case is solved," I will tell her. "It truly is. Mark's murderer is captured and has confessed. We are not so obviously racists after all, and the color-blind murdering jewel thief has told us so."

"You're wrong," Glori will say. "The case might be solved, but we're not any different than we were. We are racists-in-waiting is all."

"Probably," I will say. "But someone else is going to have to do the waiting. Let someone else wait for the return of the racist."

"You'll wait."

"I will not wait. You do it. You wait with the audience. You stick it out through the second intermission, then into the third act. I am going to watch a little television and then I'm going to bed. When I wake up in the morning, I will go to work and write about the Newport Grange meeting. I will be rested and my article will be meticulous. Informative, too. I will let you tell me what happens in the morning. You will tell me all about how the audience loved the third act."

"Will the audience love the third act?" Glori will ask. "Will they even come back for the third act?"

"They *always* come back for the third act, especially if they've seen the play before, which they have. They only like a couple of plays, and this is one of them. And the third act is their *favorite*."

"What is going to happen in the third act?" Glori will ask me. "Tell."

But I will not tell. Nothing will really happen in the third act anyway; or rather, plenty will happen, but none of it will be particularly surprising, no thrills or spills. In the third act, the audience will find out that the second act was a ruse, just as they suspected: they will discover that the murder is somehow racially motivated after all, that evil is always identified and punished, and that justice is always done. But I will not tell Glori this. She is smart enough to know all about the third act anyway. Besides, I want to be done with this racial set piece. Let the theatergoers watch their third act and weep and purge themselves with fine social feeling. Let them come up to Jodi Ramirez in the parking lot afterward and say, "I'm so sorry, so very sorry, but at least justice is done. At least you have *that*." I am going to sit on the couch and spare myself the weeping. When I get off the couch, I will run into Jodi Ramirez downstreet and I will say, "So, what do we do *now*?" and she will say, "I have no idea." Then, we will part and our parting will tell me this: the Mark Ramirez case has reached closure, and I am going to let it be closed, even if it is really not. True, the solving of Mark's murder opens as many questions as the murder itself; true, the racial-remediation teacher is staying up all night, revising her lesson plans. But let her plan, for I am a racial theorist no longer, was never really much of one to begin with. This is why so many theorists forsake theory: they take themselves out of the theory game once they find out that their lives are easier that way. I am taking myself out of the theory game.

But if I am no longer a racial theorist, what am I? What I am now, I suppose, is a faithful lover and future husband one step removed from theory, one step closer to my own private reality. This is my choice. Do I make the choice because it is more noble to be a faithful lover than a racial theorist? No. The truth is, I make the choice because I am afraid, flat-out terrified at the prospect of being a racial theorist in a laboratory where the theories already on the books have been called into question. The truth is, I know less about how the world works than I ever did, and I am scared. And so what am I going to do? I am going to pretend that I'm not scared at all. I am going to watch TV with my fiancée and pretend that I am perfectly at home in the world. After all, this is what us ordinary white boys are supposed to do. Is it not?